Of Ash

And

Angels

KC DECKER

Cover Design by Grady Earls

Cover Model: Marco Sartore

Photographer: Alessandro Guerriero

Copyright © 2019 By KC DECKER

ISBN: 1-7329645-0-5

ISBN-13: 978-1-7329645-0-1

Chaos, leave me never.

Keep me wild

and keep me free,

so that my brokenness will be,

the only beauty

the world will see.

--r.m. drake

Chapter 1

JUSTIN

Father Vincent's voice sounds like slivers of glass in my ears, and I grow to hate him for it. The fluctuations in pitch and fervid incantations make the hair on my arms prickle and then lay down as though singed. I think it's an effort to stave off the rough baritone that's bouncing around the small space. It's not natural, the deep resounding noise coming from his throat. He's too lanky of a man for that voice. If you saw him, you'd agree that he must have to run around in the shower just to get wet.

He's thin at best and spindly at worst. Tall too. So tall, I had initially worried about his safety regarding the ceiling fan spinning shockingly close to his molted head. Each blade of the fan repeatedly buzzing past with reckless abandon. But after about ten minutes or so, I had stopped watching the whirl of the fan. By then, I was fairly convinced Father Vincent wouldn't be scalped by the ceiling fan while presiding over my mother's funeral.

After a few tense minutes of silence, Father Vincent clears his throat. The gruff sound rouses me from my thoughts regarding the shine of his shoes and my near certainty that he uses them for up-skirting unsuspecting women.

"Excuse me?" I ask, purely out of a need to fill the heavy silence.

"I asked if you have anything you would like to add," he states, loosening some of the tightness in his ribs with each delivered sound. He annunciates each word as though it stands alone, heavily punctuated.

"Like what?" I cock my head at him and knit my eyebrows in question. What would I possibly need to add after his overzealous delivery of whatever he's been going on about for the last hour? Is he interested in my thoughts about my mother? It's just the three of us in here, and my mother stopped listening to me on Tuesday, so I don't feel a particular duty to speak simply for Father Vincent's sake.

"Or any questions in general? The afterlife is a glorious wonder, but people often misunderstand it. Frequently, those left behind by the loss of a loved one have a lot of questions." He rocks forward on the balls of his feet, and I hold my breath, waiting for the strike of the ceiling fan.

When nothing catastrophic happens, I say, "Ok then, I guess I do have a question." I take a deep breath and then slowly let it out. "If the Cincinnati Reds were the first Major League baseball team, who did they play against?"

Father Vincent looks disappointed. He can't hide his feelings either because he looks at me as though I just stumbled in drunk, with my pants around my ankles.

"That's what you are thinking about at a time of immeasurable loss such as this?" He is stunned that I'm unable to glean some comfort from his yammerings. Did he even know my mother that well? Father Vincent sighs and continues with the unyielding patience normally bestowed upon children.

"Mr. Abernathy, the death of a loved one is quite difficult, and I certainly understand why you would wish to deflect such a painful truth. However, I'd like to assure you that your mother now rests comfortably in the arms of our Lord, Jesus Christ."

"What a relief. Because she was a spitfire, my mother—and things could have gone wildly in the other direction. If you know what I mean," I give Father Vincent a conspiratorial wink and a nudge with my elbow. What I *really* want to say to him is, *get the hell out of my house. You've tracked the world in on the soles of your shoes, and now I'm done humoring you and this farce of a funeral.*

"The finality can be quite hard to grasp," he continues as he takes my hand, choosing to ignore my callous sentiment. I'm distracted from the unwanted contact by the fact that his grip is delicate, evocative almost.

"I will be praying for you, as well as for your sweet mother's soul," he says, with a final squeeze of my hand that I feel like I have to wipe off on my slacks.

"Mr. Wallace from the funeral home will be in shortly to see to your mother. Good day, Mr. Abernathy."

After I close the door behind Father Vincent, I walk to my mother's casket, where heaviness settles around me like falling volcanic ash. The display doesn't even look like Clara Abernathy. Her hair is combed straight back instead of the vintage finger waves she toiled over when she was alive, and the slack curling of her lips belies the joyful heart she carried with her everywhere she went. In truth, if she were alive, she would have sat up and slapped away the hand that

3

applied the ridiculous red lipstick that now runs up the small vertical creases in her upper lip.

In life, she looked youthful and pretty. Death had only contributed an added expression of peacefulness across her still face. Now that the funeral director has left his irreversible mark on her, she appears aged and wanton. As I look at her Rosary wound hands, I find myself angry they didn't tend to her chipped nail polish. Clara Abernathy would defy God Himself to come back and fix her nail polish before her big reveal at the pearly gates.

Overall, my mother would be horrified by her funeral appearance. To know that society women would see her in such disarray would upset what little peace she took with her. The fact alone that she isn't being laid to rest in her pearls would torment her beyond measure. Truthfully, I kept her pearls. She will wear the earrings for eternity, but I couldn't bear to part with the necklace that was so paramount to her look.

I may have kept her pearl necklace, but I gave her mine in return. The silver chain and crucifix that protected me at work are now hers. The betrayal I feel toward the necklace doesn't transfer to its new owner, only the fact that it has been a part of me since I was a teenager. The disillusioned promise of safety and protection traded for the same strand of pearls I clutched as an infant.

"I'm sorry I couldn't come to your real funeral, Mom. You deserve better than me." I mark my words with a tentative reach toward her face. I don't know if I want to wipe off the red lipstick or feel if she really is gone, but I stop short of making contact. I'm afraid to touch the cold marble of her skin. My own mother, the one who dropped everything to come take care of me when I needed her.

A knock on the door snaps me momentarily from my self-loathing. It's the guy from the funeral home, the one whose name I immediately forgot because he is of no consequence to me.

I watch him rigidly tuck in the decorative satin cascading from the sides of the coffin. Then, with no further fanfare, he closes the casket and wheels my mother away from me forever.

Now, I am well and truly alone. Trapped in my house. Even the priestly stain left by Father Vincent's presence is gone.

Chapter 2

Norah

As I sit across the desk from Principal Weinstein, all I can focus on is the way his nostrils flare with each stumbling pause in his less than smooth delivery. Socially inept is a good place to start if I had to describe him in a couple of words. Really, his ineptitude is legendary. How this man leads the school is well beyond my understanding because he can't even seem to lead himself to a snack.

For seven years now, I have had to sit through his bumbling attempts to inspire greatness at each kindergarten graduation, not to mention his awkward attempts to introduce both the yearly talent show and the "Cultural Awareness Celebrations" that have taken the place of the classroom holiday parties.

Yep, no more holiday parties in elementary school. Now, we have a celebration to honor the many different cultures of the world, which is amazing, in theory. In reality, there is next to no diversity in this entire pretentious school district. So, the cultural celebrations usually consist of the two Indian families bringing little balls of Gulab Jamun to share and the Lithuanian kid tying a sash around his waist.

"Are you listening to me, Miss. Carpenter?" Principal Weinstein asks, as his eyes struggle to meet mine and he continues to wring his hands above the simple desk calendar.

"Of course," I answer, and if it weren't for the flaring of his nostrils, my statement would be true.

"As I was saying, the district has a zero-tolerance policy when it comes to such things."

"I understand, Principal Weinstein, but the part I'm hung up on," I pause and try to clear the accumulated dryness from my throat, "Is the fact that we had been seeing each other for three years. Those photos were never meant for the public, at least not by me. I sent them to him in good faith as his girlfriend and *intimate companion*. If Daniel—if Mr. Stoddard chose to violate my trust and plaster my very personal images on his social media networks, I fail to see how I am the villain."

He tries to cough, and even *that* is awkward for him. "As a representative of the school, you should have used better judgment, Miss. Carpenter."

"On that account, you are certainly right. Mr. Stoddard is a vile human being." I finish with a mumbled statement about how I should have trusted my instinct regarding Daniel's controlling nature and the delicate look of his hands.

"Excuse me?" he asks while his own dainty hands begin to fidget even more and at a tremendously anxious pace.

"What?" I panic at my horrific lack of an inner monologue and have no choice but to play dumb. "I'm sorry, hmm? What was that?"

Principal Weinstein nervously wipes the sweat from his brow with his palm before stepping up to go to bat for my douche-y ex-boyfriend. Although, it *would* sound more convincing if his voice didn't crack.

"Mr. Stoddard is an exemplary member of the faculty, and I'll remind you that it is not lascivious photos of his breasts that have brought us here this afternoon." His face turns beet red at the mention of breasts, and I almost feel sorry for him. He must be a real joy in the sack.

"Exemplary member of the faculty?" I scoff, "No, Mr. Stoddard is a gym teacher, a distributor of pornographic material, and a deceitful, lecherous stain on society." Just when I thought I couldn't hate Daniel any more than I already do, I lose my job, and my disdain ratchets even higher.

"You understand we hold our community of consummate professionals to a higher standard. Our pupils deserve the very best," he says, this time taking his self-righteous piety too far, which causes me to launch myself into a standing position. How dare he imply that I am not a consummate professional?

"My students love me, and I am quite certain my tits have not flashed across their five-year-old social media feeds!" I shout before realizing I should have kept my brazen, insolent mouth shut. Now that I've burned that bridge, I'm going down with it in a fiery blaze of glory.

"That is quite enough. Trudy has already cleaned out your desk for you. Good luck, Miss. Carpenter."

***

Once home, I throw my keys toward the basket that holds our keys and mail. When they miss the basket entirely, skittering across the counter and falling to the ground in a jumbled heap, I can hardly muster the energy to care. The rage I feel toward Daniel has drained me into an apathetic puddle.

When Sophia walks through the door about thirty minutes later, I still see red through my pent-up fury. However, now that I'm a full bottle of Prosecco in, I have finally swallowed the fact that I am, in fact, jobless.

Sophia sees my commitment to getting drunk in the empty wine bottle lying beside me on the couch. "Rough day?" she asks, with her eyebrows raised.

"You could say that. Principal Weinstein saw my boobs," I manage, through my thick tongue and discourteous lips.

"Aaaand, now you are worried he'll be thinking of you when he takes care of himself?" she asks as she scoots my feet off the couch so she can sit down next to me.

"Ewww, no! Well, yeah," I concede as I stop and give the idea some thought. "But that's not even the shittiest thing that happened today," I say with unnecessary drunken emphasis and a choppy delivery.

"He asked you for a blowie?" she questions with a huge grin, as she slaps my thigh to emphasize her deconstruction of the matter. Her pin-straight blonde hair is pulled into a high ponytail, giving her a look of sweet, tender innocence. Laughable, that image.

"No. Plus, that man has probably never had a hard-on in his life, and I can't very well tend to a doughy…flaccid…Wait, what?" I ask while looking at her through a haze of something resembling confusion.

"The principal of your school," she prompts, "What did he do?" Now she is tilting the wine bottle and squinting at it, as though she needs to verify there is none left for her.

"Oh. Yeah. He fired me," I say while slow blinking. Her mouth drops open, probably aghast at my downward spiral.

"It's because of Daniel's erotic pics of you, isn't it?"

"Yep."

"What are you going to do?" she asks while she flicks her shoes off the edge of each heel and then tucks her feet underneath her on the couch.

"I'm going to get drunk. I thought that was obvious?"

Chapter 3

JUSTIN

For the first couple of weeks after my mom's funeral, I couldn't even go in her room, much less pack up her stuff. But for some reason, today, I'm anxious to sort out my new normal. I figure I can't move on with my life if I'm hanging on to the ghost of my mother. It's bad enough the essence of her is everywhere. The constant reminders of her continue to deliver one gut check after another.

It's going to be raw and intensely difficult for me to clean out her room. But if I can knock it out today, then it won't hang over my head like the rusty guillotine it has become.

My buddy, Davis, is coming over tonight with wings, beer, and an unwaveringly strong conviction in his steely agenda. That should at least be a moderate distraction for me after having to erase one of the best parts of my life all day. Davis is a friend from the firehouse and perhaps the only one to truly understand me, so I'll go ahead and humor him as he tries to bend me to his will.

He'll be here at seven. That gives me eleven hours to pack up the childhood innocence linked to my mom and void yet another room in my home.

***

Lying on the floor of my mom's room is not going to get me where I need to be, but after seeing her unmade bed, I felt the need to fix it. That's as far as I got with the room clean-out, though. Clara Abernathy never left the bed unmade. Not once in her life. She would have tidied her room and arranged all seven thousand deco pillows during an air raid siren. So, the fact that I had thrown off the covers and attempted to resuscitate her long-dead body was obviously out of the realm of normalcy. Everything in her room was exactly how I left it that day after what remained of my world crumbled.

As soon as I opened her bedroom door and got a whiff of her scented lotion, I could almost hear her, *Justin, Darling, hand me those pillow shams. What on earth happened in here?* Anyway, the smell of her caught me off guard and hit me like a roundhouse kick to the temple.

At any rate, I made the bed for her. Now, I'm sprawled out on the floor like a snow angel and staring at the ceiling, wondering if a nap is in order. Some people are lucky in life. Those people are not me. No, I am decidedly unlucky. And now, with the death of my amazing mom, I no longer have two shits to give.

I'm still on the floor in a horizontal position when Davis starts kicking the front door. His hands must be full because he knows good and well the door is unlocked. I don't move from the floor. Who knows where the day has gone? I'd say I was productive, but that would be a lie. Unless by productive, I mean fully self-destructing, losing my shit, and then deciding to do metallic epoxy floors in my garage.

Getting up is a chore, and after so much time flat on my back, I feel like I have been allotted my own batch of rigor and pooling lividity. I shake out my stiff arms and roll my head around to ease the soreness that has nestled so lovingly against my neck.

When I swing the front door open, Davis charges past me, leaving the stinging aroma of spicy chicken wings swirling in my nostrils. He is already unloading a case of beer in the fridge before I get around to closing the front door and turning toward the kitchen.

"Sup, Buddy? I thought you could use some sustenance," Davis says as he puts both hands on his hips. Davis is built like a brick shit-house, and his presence fills the kitchen. However, his huge personality entirely dwarfs his stature.

"Now a case of beer is considered sustenance?" I ask, wishing he would have brought a case of Jack Daniels instead. Though I have talked to him multiple times, this is the first time I've seen him since my mom died.

"Nah, that's why I brought the wings."

"Well, what the hell are you waiting for then?" I ask with a half-assed shrug.

He drops his hands from his hips, takes three long strides, and accosts me with a man hug. While slapping two succinct blows against my back, he says, "Dude, I'm so sorry about your mom."

"Thanks," is all I can say, but it doesn't properly project my gratitude toward him. Davis has been with me through my darkest tours of hell, and without him, I'm not even sure I would be standing right now.

I met him in the fire academy and knew instantly we would be friends because he showed up with red silk panties inside the sleeve of his bunker gear on our first day. Purely by accident, of course, but he still gets shit about it. In his defense, he *did* marry the owner of the panties. At least for a little while.

The other reason I knew we would be friends is that he doesn't let any sort of adversity get in his way. Not even the prosthetic leg, courtesy of his tour in Iraq. He started the academy with every intention of flying that highly engineered piece of carbon fiber pylon under the radar of the Chief, but in the end, he was too much of a smartass for it to go unnoticed.

First, there was the leg-trapped-under-the-fire-truck bit. Which would have got him shit-canned from the academy if the Battalion Chief didn't like him so much. Also in his favor was the fact that the truck was being serviced, so it was already out of commission. Being the asshole that Davis is, though, he locked the doors to the fire truck and had every set of keys to the rig tucked away in his pocket. He screamed and carried on for nearly thirty minutes while everyone tried in vain to help the bastard. The next day, I shit you not, he sat in the Station 18 dayroom with his leg propped up and an above the knee 'prosthesis' made entirely of Legos.

Anyway, Davis is great. He goes through women a little quickly these days, but he is a good guy. Once, when West Metro Fire partnered with The Children's Hospital for a charity event, they put together a calendar. Davis, that fucker, made it on the cover. Everyone said it was because of his bionic leg, but because his legs were both inside his turn-out pants, I suspect it was because of his tattoos, of which there are many. Davis himself claimed he made the cover because he has the strength and agility of a wombat.

"I'm going to miss her cinnamon rolls, man," Davis says as he slowly shakes his head with both sincerity and longing.

16

"Me too," is all I can get past the lump in my throat, so I cough and then add, "Let's eat some wings." I pull two beers from the fridge and grab a roll of paper towels, then follow him into the living room.

We eat in silence for about three and a half seconds before he starts in. "Man, don't you miss it?" he leans back as though I am going to give him a different answer than the one I always give.

I've heard this same line of questioning so many times I hardly let the bite of chicken hit my gut before taking down half my beer in one swig. "Yeah, Davis, I miss a lot of things."

"Maybe, with your mom gone, it would be a good time to get back out there, you know?" He speaks as though he's my designated Oracle and has all the right answers. I also think he knows when I'm vulnerable and purposely chooses such times to tighten the screws. My mom just died, for fuck's sake.

"Sure. Maybe tomorrow," I say, the answer sounding canned and dismissive.

"Dude, you used to have pussy flying at you like frisbees," it's a statement he lets hang there for a minute before I sit forward, my hackles up.

"Is this about getting laid? I get ass whenever I want it." I wave him off. I hope he takes the hint because I have spent the entire day looking at my mother's ceiling. I don't need any more redundancy in my life, especially with this tired line of conversation.

"The women you have on standby are not what I'm talking about. I'm talking about life, about real connections, about doing something that matters again—like coming back to work. If you can get back in the headspace of helping people, maybe you won't wallow so helplessly in your own—"

"My own what?" I challenge. I can feel my jaw squaring off, and I can vividly picture myself punching him in the face hard enough to make his head snap back.

"Buddy, I know," his voice softens, almost to a whisper. "I'm here for you, no matter what. I just want you to be happy."

"What the fuck *is* happy? Eating cinnamon rolls? Having your dick sucked? Davis, being happy is an illusion. Don't you get it? I mean, nobody posts Instagram pictures of low bank accounts and failing marriages. Happiness is pretend. It's something everyone strives for, but it's always just out of reach. No one is ever happy. They're only working toward the elusive happiness of *someday*. We live in a world of school shootings and epidemic rates of suicide. Kids die—"

"I know. You're right. The world is full of sadness and crushing disappointments. But it's also full of beauty and triumph. I don't want you to forget there is still good out there in the world. You used to get such a rush out of coming to work. Every day, you knew you could make a difference in people's lives. You had a purpose. You had a gift."

"And where did that gift get me in my quest for happiness?" I challenge before plopping my Styrofoam container of wings down on the coffee table and reaching for the remote.

"You were happy, Justin. Life was good. Until it wasn't."

Chapter 4

Norah

My do-gooder roommate, Sophia, wrangled me into this. I don't know what I was thinking. I'm really awkward around the elderly, and I loathe running my own errands, let alone someone else's. The fact I will need to make conversation with the old-timers is laughable and the very reason I worked with kindergartners. Sophia said I should do it to supplement my income while I transition into a real job, but what she really meant was, I'm too much of an adult to be jobless and broke.

Unemployment has been a process for me. It started with the best of intentions, and I'd like to say I hit the ground running, but so far, not so much. I had delusions of going to the gym every day, staying on top of the laundry and cleaning, and reading book after book while sending out resumes here and there. However, the reality of my existence is far bleaker and involves a lot more Netflix and swiping left.

A few months ago, I shaved off a hundred-and-eighty-five-pound parasite, but once I got rid of him, I wondered why I didn't stick it out. The dating world is treacherous these days, and I figured the douchebag you know is better than the douchebag you don't. I didn't take Daniel back, though, more out of apathy than anything, really. That was before he plastered my private photos all over social media. There was no denying it was me either because I have a heart-shaped mole right where my collarbones come together. Well, actually, it's two moles, but they are really close together, so they look like a heart. Not to mention, no one has hair like me.

I did learn one thing from dating Daniel, though. Narcissists are toxic, and I will never date another one. Thanks to Daniel's immersive training program, I can spot them from a continent away now. It's crazy because, in three years with him, I didn't recognize what was happening, only that I didn't know myself anymore. The longer we were apart, the easier it was for me to get some actual perspective and see things for what they were, destructive.

Daniel was manipulative in an emotionally needy way, so much so that I became trapped trying to fill a bottomless pit. He would take and take from me and always leave me feeling drained. But what I initially thought was needy, turned out to be *entitled*. It never would have mattered how much I gave to him, it wouldn't have been enough. He always wanted more, and he was absolutely under the impression that his needs were my sole responsibility. If given the chance, he would have drained everything from me, leaving me parched and, no doubt, to blame for my own situation.

The thing is, you don't dare leave a narcissist until they finish using you up because they will turn on you like a pit viper. Once Daniel could no longer control me, he tried to control how everyone else saw me. Enter the titty pics all over the social media feeds of my coworkers and his ridiculous slander about me being a slut, and God knows what else. So, you see, I've learned the hard way to pay close attention if someone gets prickly when I try to establish boundaries because it demonstrates precisely where their respect for me ends.

I can't say I'm eager to jump back into the dating game, scarred and depleted as I am, but I do have an awful lot of free time on my hands. My first date after falling off the Daniel horse was a complete nightmare, and it set me back at least a few more months. Don't get me wrong, the guy was hot, he was just a shit show, pure and simple. He had a couple of kids, which I have come to expect here and there in the post-college dating world, but that wasn't even the problem. The problem was his fetish. He had a pegging fetish—and I don't mean a cute little collection of colorful pegs. He asked me right out of the gate if I would be willing to wear a strap-on. I blocked his profile and number and even showered after our date. I mean, he should have at least let me finish my coffee before asking me right there in the café to ass fuck him, right? Or are my standards too high?

My navigation system directs me to a house on the left, and then I sit in the car long enough to start worrying about the state of the milk and eggs I'm supposed to deliver. This is only a temp job, but the fact alone that the agency was ready to put me to work immediately, with no more credentials than a pulse and a driver's license, tells me all I need to know. I need to spend sixty to ninety minutes with each client, and to be honest, I'm kinda wondering how many of those minutes I can spend in my car.

When I finally knock on the door after shifting my feet on the front porch for a solid five minutes, the thought of how uncomfortable this will be consumes me. I haven't the foggiest idea what we will talk about for sixty to ninety minutes. I don't even talk to Sophia for that long, and she's my best friend.

The door eases open, and a medicinal smell that stings my nose greets me. I wonder if the smell is the result of my imagination and blatant stereotyping or if I can actually smell it.

"Mrs. Cobb? My name is Norah. I'm from the Hand to Heart program."

"What is that on your head?" she asks, eyeballing me up close. She certainly is a direct little thing, isn't she? Nervously, I shift both grocery bags to one hand and reach up to feel my head. I'm sure she is referring to my less than conservative look, but I check my head anyway.

"That's my hair, Mrs. Cobb. I have some small braids and feathers underneath, see?" I pull a braid forward and settle it in front of my shoulder. I can see why she might be a little surprised by my appearance, so I'll give her some room on the generation gap, but she should at least close her mouth.

"Why is it so bright, dear? I've never seen such a red." She speaks and openly gapes as if the bluish tint to her hair were altogether natural.

"Can I come in? I have some groceries for you. Then I'm going to strap you down and dye your hair bright red too," I smile, just to take the edge off my threat. I'm just saying, a brain-to-mouth filter wouldn't kill her.

"Oh, you!" she smiles and playfully slaps my arm. At least she can take a joke. Anyway, about my hair, the color is cherry cola red, and it's very popular on Pinterest. It is bright and vibrant on top, but the bottom couple of layers are dark brown, so it softens the intensity of the red where it shows through. With the beads, feathers, and braids underneath, my look is kind of stuck somewhere between a glam pirate and a rocker chick. Or, you could say, the exact opposite of sweet, direct Mrs. Cobb.

"Kids these days! Well, come on in. I'll put the kettle on."

Chapter 5

JUSTIN

After swimming laps at a punishing pace for the last hour, I still don't feel any better about getting talked into using a service. I don't think it's a good idea. In fact, I'm cursing Davis for even forcing it on me. He wore me down, though, and I agreed more to shut him up than anything else. Now, the fateful decision is like having cinder blocks around my ankles. I'm considering letting them pull me to the bottom of the pool so I can drown myself instead of using the service.

I go back under and push off the side. Maybe another hour of laps in the pool will change the course of my life. Fucking Davis.

***

I've strained my muscles so far past the point of fatigue that I really am in danger of drowning if I don't get out of the water. On limp noodle arms, I push myself up from the edge of the pool and then flop down on my back, panting like I just finished the Ironman. The sun feels good on my skin, so I drape my arm over my eyes and settle in. I have probably thirty emails to return, twelve or so of them urgent, but I can't deal with work right now. And I certainly can't deal with grief counselors.

I have never had a therapist I didn't want to murder where they sat. Every one of them, spilling over with wild attempts at empathy and seriously misplaced encouragement. As a collective group, they all say there is no way around grief, only through it. What they don't realize is some grief you can't get through. Some grief is so consuming that there is no way around *or* through it.

Sometimes grief becomes who you are, and the idea of shedding it is as ludicrous as stepping out of your own skin. Grief changes people, so expecting them to somehow work it all out and then resume where they left off before the world swallowed them is an absurd notion.

The fact is, some things can break you. I mean, shatter your soul and cast it into the wind in a billion tiny pieces. To think, with a little grief counseling, you might be able to find all those infinite pieces of yourself, patch everything back together, and move on with life—well, I don't even need to dignify that with a response.

I can tell you one thing, not one of those sunshine blowing therapists has ever lost a child. If they had, they would realize the futility of their mission and stay home instead. Church leaders are just as bad, they want you to jump on their rainbow of trusting in God's plan and allowing Him to strengthen and heal your heart if you'll only just have faith. I'll tell you what, I *had* faith. Right up until God betrayed me.

I hear the security system chime from inside the house, indicating a door or window has just opened, and my system floods with adrenaline. I'd like to see someone try to steal from me. They will learn quickly that I have nothing left to lose before I hospitalize them. I jump up and charge toward the back door, just looking for a reason to lay someone out. My dick is already stiffening with the anticipation of it.

I slip in quietly through the back door, my stealthy approach aided by my bare feet and lack of any substantial clothing. Then I hear the intruder call out, it's a woman. I sigh, almost disappointed.

"Hello? Is anyone home?" she asks with trepidation from the living room. She sounds like she expects to encounter Jack the Ripper, so I lean up against the kitchen counter, cross my arms over my chest, and wait.

Chapter 6

Norah

Please don't let me find a dead guy, please don't let me find a dead guy. It's a chant from inside my head, but it's no less a plea. When my next client didn't answer the door after ten minutes of me pounding, I called the agency. The manager assured me that Mr. Abernathy lives alone, homebound due to his ailing health, and that I should try the doors and windows in case he fell and broke a hip....or *passed away*.

I can tell you this was *not* in my job description. In fact, screw this job. I have a master's in childhood education. I'll have a job before school starts back up in the fall. I don't need to be an errand girl, and I sure as hell don't need to conduct periodic welfare checks. I've never seen a dead person before. If that streak ends today, I want hazard pay or—

"HOLY SHIT!" I yell. While looking down at the floor for a dead guy, I find a not-dead guy. Not even an old guy. He is leaning on the kitchen counter with his arms crossed, looking at me with something of a smug or maybe an amused look on his face.

"Jesus Christ! You scared the shit out of me! Where is Mr. Abernathy?" My heart is pounding, but it's doing it from inside my throat, so it's hard for me to swallow.

"Depends on who's asking," he says through a tight, ridiculous smirk. He's hot. And wet. And almost naked. His hair is short on the sides but longer on the top, so it hangs wetly in his face before he swipes his fingers through it, pushing it back for a few seconds before it flops back down again.

"Who are you, the pool boy? I don't have to tell you who *I* am," I say, not very convincingly, though. I try to adopt an aloof stance to match his, but I'm not sure how it reads. Jittery, maybe, from the adrenalin surge.

"Did you just call me *pool boy?*" he asks incredulously, with his eyes cut down to slits. Then he seems to change his mind, "Never mind that. At least tell me why you are here." He uncrosses his arms and instead holds the edge of the countertop by each hip where he's leaning back against it. His swim trunks hang pretty low on his hips, so it takes a Herculean amount of self-control to keep looking him in the eyes.

He is pretty. He knows it, too. Not pretty in a feminine way, though, because he has the muscular body of a man, but his features are somehow delicate, in a sexy, aristocratic, perfect nose kind of way. His eyes are light, even more so up against his tan skin and dark hair, but they still brood.

There's a rebellion behind those eyes that almost distracts from his body. He looks on one hand like he has an ax to grind, and on the other, like he finds all of this amusing.

"You want to know why *I'm* here? Well, I… I've come…to see to Mr. Abernathy's needs," I blurt out, as though those stupid words will add credibility to my presence. My palms are sweaty, but I can't give him the satisfaction of knowing he unnerves me by wiping them on my shorts.

"You're here to see to his needs? In that case, he's waiting upstairs…for his sponge bath." His eyes twinkle at that, but the rest of his face still holds its position of polite superiority.

"No. I mean I, I'm subbing at the agency—"

"Oh! Why didn't you say so? Mr. Abernathy likes for his subs to wait for him in the dungeon. Don't forget to crawl submissively once you get down there, though. You know how he is with the paddle." He says this with a straight face, almost conspiratorially, so I don't know how to gauge his seriousness.

I'm horrified, and it must read plainly on my face. "I mean, temping. At the Hand to Heart agency. Sorry, I'm a teacher, so sub just popped out, I don't mean…" I'm babbling like an idiot. So much for not letting him know his near naked effect on me.

"Ri-ght. Hand to Heart," he looks like the clouds are finally starting to part. "So, here's the thing with that. Mr. Abernathy got coerced into signing up for the service by his pimply faced, impotent, micro-penised friend, and he really doesn't think he needs an errand service in the first place. Because, you know, Amazon Prime and all."

"Ok, but…it's not just an errand service. Sometimes, the elderly need help with light cleaning or cooking. And sometimes they are just lonely," I explain. I'm not too sure why I feel the need to defend my temporary position with the elderly, but there it is. He crumples his brows together as if contemplating something while staring off into space.

"Wait. Did you say cleaning?"

Chapter 7

JUSTIN

This whole Hand to Heart thing may not be such a bad idea, especially with that feisty looking piece of tail they sent over. She looks wild and untamed, which immediately catches my interest and jumps her to the forefront of my imagination during my alone time. She's obviously the type of woman who wants to stand out, but I suspect, also the type that once she has your attention, she doesn't quite know what to do with it.

I booked her once a week, on Thursdays, for the decrepit Mr. Abernathy, and I look forward to exploring just how feisty she really is. I figure she can't look like that without backing it up with some degree of intensity. Shit, I bet she's a box of lit firecrackers in bed. I want to grab a handful of whatever she has going on underneath her hair, all those beads and feathers and shit, and introduce her mouth to the less polite parts of my body.

I have women that I see here and there who are mostly comfortable with my situation, but without fail, each one has eventually tried to change me. They all think they have the magic formula to modify that which can't be changed. I don't know why women do that. They set their sights on someone without seeing him for who he is. Instead, they see him for who they think they can mold him into. I don't get it. A wife-beater is a wife-beater. An addict is an addict. A cheater is a cheater. An introvert is a fucking introvert.

Why should we wear masks that defy our true nature to convince someone we are what they want? Who I am was created by fire, and that's not campy firefighter humor, either. Life has molded me with the strength of ten thousand eternities. It has carved and honed me with the precision of the universe. Why would anyone stand a fleeting chance at reforming me into something different than I am at my core? What's more is, why would they want to, only to have me deny my inherent being and fight every natural instinct I have?

I wasn't lying to Davis. I can get laid whenever I want to, all the dating apps see to that. The problem arises when the women try to change me. They get tired of my lifestyle, and when beating the dead horse becomes exhausting and redundant for them, they inevitably tire of it. I can't say they move on immediately because something about me pulls them in. Somehow, they deny their gut and continue to swim upstream. They *should* trust their instincts about me, though, because they have no real future with a guy like me.

The fact is, I'm broken. The only person who could make me whole again is lost to the ether. So, now I accept life for what it is, endless moments ticking by on the metronome of my existence.

Chapter 8

Norah

I have spent a few weeks now at my new job, and thanks to being thrown to the lions, I have realized there are two extremes for my client list. On one end of the spectrum are the sweet, lonely ones who are nothing but grateful for my time. These include those who only want to chat and feed me shortbread cookies and the ones with arthritic hands who merely need help with folding laundry, changing light bulbs, and peeling potatoes. As well as the handful who I shop for and then assist with preparing meals for the coming week. This group is my favorite, and I find that ninety minutes flash by in a snap of the fingers.

I have learned to knit, prepare chicken fried steak from scratch, and slow-motion Polka dance with these gentle souls. I have cried from their stories of loss and sat completely enraptured in the retelling of Mr. Kocinski's account of his formative years spent in a forced labor camp. I have also set rollers, painted fingernails, and dusted the hard to reach spots. I have honestly enjoyed my time with *most* of the Hand to Heart clients. Some of the ones from the other group, not so much.

On the other end of the client spectrum are the crusty, cantankerous few whose independence I threaten with my presence. For these, I tend to drop off groceries, prescriptions, and their accumulated mail and then sit quietly with them while watching the Game Show Network or doing crossword puzzles. Mostly, their frustration simmers with a quiet acquiescence, sometimes not. I have had doors slammed in my face, newspapers thrown at me, and in what has to be an unprecedented occurrence, Mr. Hatsenbuler, after running out of magazines to toss my way, tried to yank off his own penis just to throw it at me.

These particular people are herded from my roster of clients and assigned to a more experienced member of our crew. Probably one who is paid better or doesn't mind having penises chucked at them.

Even though this is now my second week with the newly acquired Mr. Abernathy, I still have not met him. I sit parked in front of his house with his chart open on my lap. He is new, so there are no ongoing notes from other employees, no shopping lists, no pharmacy or medications listed. He is a mystery. I know nothing about him except that he is homebound and has a smokin' hot guy taking care of his pool.

The other strange thing about the mysterious Mr. Abernathy is his house. In my time with Hand to Heart, I have seen copious amounts of linoleum floors, Formica countertops, wood paneling, and enough doilies and framed cross-stitch ingenuity to sink a ship. Most of my clients have lived in their homes for fifty years. The houses are closed up, quiet, and stuffy, with mostly dim lighting. Mr. Abernathy's house is different. It's in a hip, urban development. There are boutiques, galleries, and cafes splattered everywhere. His home is bright, with an open floor plan and a contemporary design style. His furniture even looks new and current.

Now that I have a little experience under my belt working with the elderly, I'm starting to smell a rat. I wonder if the man I ran into last time has assumed Mr. Abernathy's identity in order to clean out his bank accounts and collect his social security payments. Maybe the real Mr. Abernathy is dead, and that scam artist is riding that sweet old man's coattails.

This is the second time at this house in as many weeks that I have thought I needed hazard pay to be here. Something is definitely not right. I shove the chart back into my messenger bag and take a deep breath. I guess I have sixty to ninety minutes to flush out this fraud. I do, however, question if I would be so willing to personally get to the bottom of this matter if the impostor wasn't so good-looking.

***

This time, when I knock on the door, it only takes a minute for it to swing wide open. The young "Mr. Abernathy" is standing there with a sexy grin on his face that lets me know he thinks I'm too dumb to realize what he is doing. Last week, that smile would have disarmed me, but knowing what a low-life this guy is makes him less attractive. Last time, I wanted to sit on his face; now, he is just a deceitful con man. Even with his looks, a swindler like this would be a step down from Daniel, and that says a lot because I didn't think there was a step down from that asshole.

"Hi, welcome back," he says, all charming and hustler-ish. He steps aside for me to come in and then watches me as I do.

"Hey," I say. "Will I be meeting the elusive Mr. Abernathy this time?" my voice sounds almost venomous, and my unnatural smile bounces right off of him.

"Without a doubt," he says with a stern confidence that further pumps up his chest and wry half-smile. I can tell this man has gotten everything he has ever wanted in life. People don't say no to guys like him. Panties drop at his feet, velvet ropes swing wide open, he snaps his fingers, and his minions come running. What a dick.

"I'll just wait here until he is ready to come out of hiding," I say as I slip the messenger bag strap over my head and then plop down on the couch. The expensive leather feels soft and exotic against the backs of my legs, and the puff of air resulting from my drop to the couch smells enchanting and masculine. Were it not for my stony demeanor, I'd like to bury my face in the leather and inhale the pure sexiness of it. The scent would fill my lungs like some sort of inhaled, manly life force.

"Sounds good. Should I get back to work then?" he asks with a nod to his laptop. He speaks as though I'm not receiving a paycheck to be here, like my presence is optional and of no real significance to him one way or another.

"Oh, you work?" I scoff. "What is it that you do?" I ask in a challenging tone, as if he will actually say, *swindle old people out of their money.*

"I'm a digital marketing strategist," he says before narrowing his eyes a bit. If he suspects I know about his little scam, he isn't letting on. He just looks puzzled by my tone. Or maybe the fire behind my eyes.

"Is that what they call it?" I ask, as patronizing as possible. His looks have not unraveled me so far that I don't roll my eyes after his throaty reply.

"Last time I checked," he says before placing the laptop on his lap and promptly dismissing me. I think he is intrigued by me but also probably annoyed, so his chilly indifference continues to stonewall.

Minutes go by before I bubble over, "So, how do you do it? Huh? This 'job' of yours." I do air quotes at the mention of his *job*, making his chest rumble with a stifled laugh. He clears his throat before answering because the fucker actually has to dislodge his smug laugh from the confines of his throat.

"Well, I use web technologies to help companies achieve business growth and create opportunities to increase their brand awareness," he finishes his explanation but has already turned back to his laptop.

"Listen, *pool guy*, I don't know where Mr. Abernathy is, but you fleecing him of his money and squatting in his home is wildly inappropriate. You should be ashamed of yourself! Taking advantage of a sweet old man like that. You are disgusting, and I'll be turning you in to the agency and making a full police rep—"

"Did you just call me... *pool guy* again?"

"Yeah, I did. Because I don't know your name, but I know what you are doing!" I'm panting now, and having jumped to my feet during my tirade, I'm now talking down to him.

"Then perhaps I should introduce myself," he says as he stands up and extends his parasitic hand.

"My name is Justin Abernathy."

Chapter 9

JUSTIN

The look on her face is priceless. My dick was getting warm just watching her get all ramped up, and now that she looks contrite, I want to bend her over the back of the couch while she screams, "*Fuck me harder, Mr. Abernathy!*"

She peels her hand away from her mouth and says, "I'm so sorry! So, you are related to Mr. Abernathy?"

"No. I *am* Mr. Abernathy," I'm trying so hard not to bust out laughing right now. She roared in here all piss and vinegar, feisty like her hair, and now she looks like she wants to dissolve into the floorboards. She stands there, slowly shaking her head half a dozen times before she comes to an internal resolution and then confidently meets my eyes.

"Just making sure. My name is Norah." She steps forward and boldly extends her hand to shake mine. I like that she doesn't remain embarrassed, in fact, the whole thing seems to slide off of her. It's like she didn't like the feel of that emotion, so she just changed out of it like a sweaty old shirt. Then she continues, "But before I apologize further for my assumption, why don't you explain why you have a service like Hand to Heart coming to your house?" and that sets the hook for me. She just expertly shifted the blame for her outburst and wild accusations succinctly back to me. I can already tell this chick is not used to defending her actions, and she's as slippery as a bag of warm eels. I think I like it. Perhaps, in the same way, a cutter likes to open their flesh, but still, she'll be a challenge for me.

"I don't get out much, and I just lost my mother, so my friends thought the service would be helpful," I explain, but the sound of it makes me want to punch Davis in the throat. Voicing the whole thing makes me sound like a pussy. Or a helpless mama's boy.

"So, are you looking for company? Or more tangible stuff like meal preparation and basic house cleaning?" she asks. I want to suck on her bottom lip and tell her those aren't the kinds of things I want from her at all, but I can't because I still want her to come back next week.

"Any of that is fine, or you could swim, or sit and read," *or you could ride my dick.* "I don't need the service. I just want to appease my friends and give it a try." I still sound like a pussy, but thankfully, less of a mama's boy.

"So, your friends want someone to come over here and do nothing for ninety minutes once a week?" she asks this with her eyes squinted and head cocked to the side as if she is calling bullshit simply with the air around her.

"I don't care what you do. Or if you come at all. I was just giving you some options besides cooking meals and cleaning the hou—"

"Easy, hotshot. I'm just trying to figure out your angle, that's all." Her voice and demeanor would be soothing, except for the fact she just called me *hotshot*. "I don't mind doing nothing. I just don't want to take advantage of a *poor, sick, housebound* client," she points her glance and purses her lips. I can't tell if she swallowed a bug or if she's trying not to crack a smile. I'm not used to women putting up such a fight about being around me. Part of me wants to show her the door, and the other part wants to grab on tight and ride the eight seconds to glory.

"Don't worry so much about my circumstances. You couldn't understand them if you tried. So, why don't you just sit over there and scratch your ass for the next," I look down at my watch, "Seventy-six minutes. That way, when you leave, you'll feel like you accomplished something while you were here." I don't wait for her indignant response. I turn around and head back to my laptop. I'll ignore her while she simmers and see if she comes back next week.

She surprises me by dragging her messenger bag next to her retreating feet and sitting down heavily in the chair. Ahhhhh, not so quick to get away from me after all. I'll interpret that as me regaining the upper hand.

I promptly ignore her, and it's not five minutes before the first heavy sigh. I ignore that, too, even though I can't focus on work anyway and might as well be playing Solitaire. As far as she knows, I'm chest deep in analytics and SEO algorithms.

She deposits her feet on the coffee table before crossing her ankles and settling in like she owns the place. Both of these actions accompany her next heavy sigh. When I don't respond or even glance up, she starts to whistle. *Whistle*. This is her counter-strike for being ignored. Damn, if she is not a worthy opponent.

"Do you have something to say?" I politely inquire without looking up.

"What me? No," she answers before resuming her whistling, perhaps even louder this time.

At least twenty minutes of nails on the chalkboard whistling go by while I bang out an email to Davis. The message is mostly full of expletives cursing him out for his very existence, but I do close with a promise. *I will fuck this chick before the summer bleeds out and the leaves fall.*

Chapter 10

Norah

I have had it with men who think the sun rises and sets just to show them their own shadow. My ex, Daniel, trained me in the ways of the arrogant, so I know I should circumvent this motherfucker like he has the Plague. But apparently, I'm a flawed, unrestrained glutton for punishment and remain in some sort of steep nosedive. Justin Abernathy is clearly not a frail old man in need of a few special services, and the idea that he is homebound is beyond absurd because he didn't get that body by avoiding the gym. I just haven't figured him out yet. He is an enigma, and here I come, like a moth to a really sexy flame.

I don't acknowledge to myself that I spent extra time getting ready this morning or that my heart pounds outside of my chest when I think about knocking on his door again today. In fact, I'm trying very hard to be unaffected by that asshole, but damn it, here I sit, almost too nervous to approach the house.

I brought a book this time so I can pretend not to stare at him while he works, but eventually, he will have to talk to me. He said his friend thought hiring me was a good idea, but I still don't know how that translates. His house is clean, he appears well fed, he is perfectly capable of fetching his own groceries and dry cleaning, and guys that look like him are never lonely, so what does that mean for me?

I guess it's not important as long as he is paying for my time because there is no way I'm backing down from him. I'll read a hundred books, I will dominate Candy Crush, hell, I'll even sit there and teach myself to crochet if it takes him that long to come clean about his motives.

While I check my lipstick in the rear-view mirror and make sure I don't have food in my teeth, some giggly movement catches my eye. I look over to see him standing on the front porch with a woman. She is holding her shoes behind his back as they kiss passionately. The woman is beautiful from what I can tell, so I already hate her. Justin is shirtless, and his tumbled hair gives him away. Now, I have to walk in and smell their sex and dodge his pheromones for the next hour and a half. *Awesome.*

I'm only fifteen minutes early because Mrs. Cobb had an eye appointment that her daughter showed up to take her to, but I would have been grateful for those minutes not to have to witness this. The fact I have to go inside and face him, all sexed up and cocksure knocks me down a few more insecurity pegs.

I watch them suck face for far longer than I should be exposed to before I observe him close the door, and then I watch her walk all springy-stepped to her car. The smile on her face must be visible to the NASA Space Station, and her flowy hair makes me want to spit my gum in it. As if I couldn't hate her enough already, she chirps the locks on her yellow convertible and then slides into her stupid little car. I should be thankful for her ridiculous vehicle, though, because it prevented me from parking right in front of Justin's house. This way, at least, he couldn't see the sour look that seeped out through my pores.

I recline my seat all the way back and text Sophia. Me: *Young Mr. Abernathy just screwed the stereotypical perfect woman, and I had to witness the aftermath.* I drop my phone in my lap and cover my face with my hands. I have ten minutes until I'm late, so I'll wait twenty. It will probably take that long to stop visualizing him having sex anyway. I can vividly picture him above me, his tousled hair hanging forward while his arrogant face tightens in ecstasy, bringing me closer and closer—

My phone hums in my lap with an incoming text. Sophia: *It's worse than I thought. If he's screwing unattainable stereotypes, then he really IS in need of a service. He must have lined up the wrong one, though…I bet he meant Dick to Mouth…not Hand to Heart. Honest mistake.*

I groan. Sophia's text should be funny, but her humor doesn't penetrate the thick haze of jealousy coating me. I take stock of my dowdy outfit and realize I need to up my game. That woman plays in the Big Leagues while I sell peanuts in the parking lot. I'm wearing forgettable jeans, Vans, and a simple black t-shirt. While surrounded by her banana-yellow car, she wears a short, trendy skirt and a tank top that showcases her perfect body. And inside—Justin wears their sex.

I fire back: *I don't suck D for seventeen dollars an hour. And he doesn't appear to need a cut-rate hooker service.*

When I finally exit my car, I do so with a new resolve. I plan to show him my value; I need to earn my place in his friend's master plan. And next week? Next week, I'm trading in my flaccid-penis-inspiring outfit. It's time to turn this up a notch. It's time to garner his attention.

***

"Stop putzing around and cut to the chase, Norah. Did you earn your keep or not?" Sophia asks over the bad music and crowd noise in the bar. Something you should know about Sophia is that she has a look of pure, tender innocence about her, and she drips with Southern charm. Still, I'm not exaggerating when I say she would line five guys up at the bar we are standing at and give each one of them a hummer, one right after the other. She is the one who would seduce her college professors to encourage better grades or open a few extra buttons on her shirt before the cop made it to her car window. Over time, though, I have come to realize it's not sex that compels her; it's having a certain level of control over men that prods her forward like a hot poker.

I know her family well, and if I were to psychoanalyze them, which apparently I am, I would say her authoritative, demanding father and her meek, spineless mother had four solid hands in the molding of their children. Her brother, Christian, is cut from the same cloth as Sophia. Sweet as pie on the surface, for appearance's sake. But in an affront to their southern honor, they are just as rebellious and wayward as Amish runaways. Sure, they will cap the end of every sentence with a well placed "*Sir*" or "*Ma'am*" when even mildly appropriate, but get to know them on a deeper level, and you will see they are both as spicy as a ghost pepper on YouTube.

"If by *earn my keep,* you mean coated myself in his semen, then no," I smile and tip back my bottle of pretentious microbrew.

"Did you figure out why he needs the service?" she presses. I agonized over that very question and am still no closer to an answer. The bartender winks at me and then points to my overly hoppy craft beer. I give him a thumbs up because it's not worth telling him it tastes too skunky, and he should have given me the Corona I ordered in the first place.

"The only thing I can decipher is that he is a huge introvert. He has friends that he talks about, and *lest we forget,* the perfect female specimen he has sex with but obviously doesn't live with. Clearly, he has a social life and isn't lonely. He referenced that he orders what he needs online, so he doesn't like to shop, but that's nothing remarkable," I say while thinking out loud.

"Did you get anywhere? At all?" she asks before thanking the bartender for our next round and then damn near waving him off.

"He got fairly prickly when I offered to help pack up his mom's stuff. I guess she lived with him before she died. But otherwise, no. He is still a mystery." I finally tire of the guy behind me who keeps trying to get my attention because now it's escalated to the point that he is toying with a feather from underneath my hair. I spin around to face him.

"What?"

"Hi," he says with a mischievous grin. He's attractive, but not enough to be this annoying.

"Hi," I say before turning back around to Sophia. She is leaning forward enough to tease the bartender with the wide neckline of her drooping shirt and ordering shots. When he slides them over to us, the guy behind me hands him cash to pay for them. I close my eyes long enough to put my defensive attitude in check and then turn around to thank him.

"You're welcome," he replies. Then, after a short pause, he says, "I just figured it out."

"Figured what out?" I ask. I can't believe I'm letting him draw me into a conversation, but I staple a smile to my face anyway. It feels fake and maybe even a little rusty.

"Who you look like," he says, and I wait for the standard, *a sexy, Captain Jack Sparrow* comment, but it doesn't come. Instead, he surprises me with his next statement.

"You look *exactly* like my next girlfriend." *Oh, Jesus.* I can't respond right away, which is good because Sophia jumps in with her wing-woman reply.

"Sorry, babe. She doesn't like dick..." This is the go-to response used to repel guys we aren't interested in. Even in my adventurous phase, I never passed first base with a woman, and even then, kissing a chick was only to turn on a dude. Plus, if I had to be intimate with a woman, I'd need a round of antibiotics before I got with Sophia.

Once we fulfill the requisite amount of small talk after having drinks bought for us, we turn away from the crowd. Personally, I'd rather buy my own shots and retain the fifteen minutes I'll never get back, but whatever.

Sophia leans closer to me so I can hear her over the live band's soundcheck. "What were we talking about before we got interrupted by your charming but unsuitable admirer? Oh, yeah—the sexy hermit, Justin Abernathy. So, you were saying you're going to help him pack his mom's stuff before you press his face between your thighs?"

Chapter 11

JUSTIN

I'm trying like hell not to let Norah get under my skin. I hate that Thursdays are any different than every other day of the week, but now the anticipation sits on my shoulders, oppressive in its diligence. I don't know if it's because Norah acts like I'm a wad of gum stuck to the bottom of her shoe, persisting though she has already tried to scrape it off, or if I am simply captivated by her looks. She is unquestionably striking, but her apparent disdain for me is what has made the most significant impact. Her commitment to resisting me is downright prolific.

What started as her belief in me as a con artist trying to swindle poor Mr. Abernathy out of his fortune has waned only slightly. She is unruffled by my efforts at charm, and I've got to be honest, I'm not at all used to women taking such an agnostic approach to me. The logical side of my brain points to her spurring my attraction simply because she poses a challenge and asserts that her scant interest in me is what stokes the fire, but my whole life defies logic, so it can't be that.

Someone else might argue that her unique beauty is what has such a tight grip on my balls, but beautiful women are a dime a dozen, and there is no shortage of them to fill my time. No, it's not the challenge or her beauty. It's nothing so typical or specific, but I'll tell you what, something provocative has taken root.

If I had to guess about her staunch indifference, I'd say she has been so often *or* so ruthlessly burned by men in the past that she leads with her musket drawn. Which is fine for now because Norah, with her hackles up, makes my dick stiff. Maybe her feisty attitude can smooth the corroded edges of my misery—or at least create a worthy diversion.

She'll be here in about thirty minutes. So, in preparation for her arrival day, I jerked off before my feet hit the floor this morning, I swam like a manic aqua-beast for over an hour, I drank a pot of coffee, tugged on my dick again, and then sat unproductively at my desk next to a hardly touched turkey sandwich for the next five hours. The whole day is one giant, spinning ball of irony, though, because the reality I have wasted this much time thinking about her defies the fact that I have two massive projects that go live on Monday.

When she gets here, if she plays the aloof card again, I will dutifully work on my deadlines and let her suck on the quiet for a bit. The last thing I will do is plead for her attention, no matter what runs through my mind while she's here. I won't beg for someone's recognition, period—my right hand works just fine.

When she arrives, she drops down in the leather chair, fishes out her book, and then sits back, looking at me with expectant eyes. I've moved from the desk in my bedroom to the couch and have toted my laptop down with me to uphold the pretense of working.

"What's on the agenda today, Sunshine? Heavy sighs and derisive eye rolls?" I ask. She responds by tilting her head to the side and narrowing her eyes at me—disappointed, I think. Maybe annoyed.

"I just need a heads up, so I can work myself up to the appropriate level of stoicism," I say, with a defensive hand position. I'm trying to be playful, not snarky, but she has already decided I am a certain way, so she is taking everything all wrong. Consequently, I realize how fun it is to get under her skin.

She takes a few seconds to size me up before opening the book on her lap, dismissing me as if I were a pesky gnat. *This is nothing, Sweetheart. I've got swarms of gnats in my arsenal.*

"Listen, Justin, my familiarity with guys like you is a little high for me to let you bait me like that. I don't owe you anything, and you certainly are not *entitled* to my kindness or virtue," she delivers her words like a voodoo priestess—unnerving and arrogantly spat out.

"You still have your *virtue*? No wonder you are so uptight. As for your familiarity with guys like me, you know nothing about me. That doesn't exactly bode well for your profusion of knowledge, now, does it?"

"I know everything I need to. Cocky. Self-righteous. Narcissi—" she starts, as she ticks the reasons off her fingers. It looks like she is only ramping up, so I boil over.

"Just as I thought, you know nothing about me," I interrupt, even if I do have a sort of grim ownership of her assessment. I happen to be self-actualized enough to admit internally that at least some of her slander has hit the mark.

"Maybe I'll swim today after all," she announces as if tired of breathing the same air as me. "Got a suit I could borrow?" The visual crystalizes of her topless in my swim trunks just before she adds, "You have a revolving door of women, right? Have any of them ever left a suit?"

The sheer emphasis she uses when she tosses out *revolving door of women* is enough to piss me off, but then I have an idea—and it's all I can do not to howl with laughter.

"Yes, I do. A whole stockpile of them. Droves, really. Hold on, I'll be right back." I dart up the stairs, trying to swallow the snicker resting on the edge of my mouth. Giving her one of my mother's swimsuits is nothing short of genius. Clara Abernathy's one-piece water aerobics, older lady bathing suit should be perfect. I'd like to see how Norah gets out of this one. *Fucking revolving door of women.*

When I returned downstairs, I'd already anticipated her refusing it, so I beat her to the punch, "Here you go, freshly washed and everything." I give her a hearty smile, and even *I* can sense the twinkle in my eye. She snatches the suit from my hand without even looking at it and walks to the bathroom to change.

She is in the bathroom for a while, which allows me to answer a few emails, but my focus is definitely on the ridiculous swimsuit Norah must be wrestling with right now. It's so perfect, the thick straps that support the busty top and the modest, almost straight across leg holes. *Come on, Norah, let's see how your know-it-all, smart mouth handles this one.*

I hear the door open, wait a few seconds, and then look up.

Gulp

Holy Shit.

Chapter 12

Norah

Fuckin' Justin. He gave me a granny bathing suit. Which, as I hold it up, gives me absolutely nothing to work with. When I first mentioned swimming, I had planned to swim in my bra and panties, but on further reflection, I realized that I hadn't bothered with laundry lately. So, I am wearing ugly panties that I normally reserve for my period and a basic cotton bra. After the announcement had left my mouth, there was no backing up. Who would have guessed this is what he would come up with?

I decide to put it on to see if I can tie up the straps or something. It's way too big—the chest, the middle. Sadly, the butt fits pretty well. That is, if you like a Pollyanna fit, that could serve as a chastity belt as well.

I try the only reasonable thing, and that is to tie a knot in the abdomen of the suit, which is harder than it sounds. It's big, but it's not giant, so I have to stretch it to get enough fabric to tie off in the first place. While struggling to complete this asinine task, the thick straps tug down, exposing more of my chest.

With a smile, I work the suit into an even bigger knot. Now, the modest brief cut at the legs pulls up into a more flattering style. As for the thick straps that tie around my neck, they now stretch to the point where they hardly cover my areolas, leaving the rest of my breasts mostly visible. It's not a perfect situation, but I caught most of the ugliness of the suit inside the knot, and at least now, there is little question I have curves. I wouldn't go out in public like this, but it will serve as a nice little checkmate to arrogant Mr. Abernathy.

When I step out of the bathroom after shoving my ugly bra and panties in between the rest of my folded clothes, Justin is too distracted with his work to look at me right away. I feel half sexy and half ridiculous, and the chest exposure alone is making me want to swallow my heart back down where it belongs. *What if he starts laughing at me? What the hell am I doing?*

He looks up from his laptop, and the look on his face says I both plague and excite him at the same time. By the time his jaw swings shut, I'm feeling more confident because the look on his face is the loudest thing in the room.

"Where are the towels?" I ask, with a grin that acknowledges I've won this round, and we both know it.

He recovers quickly, or so he thinks he does. "There is a cabinet outside with towels. Just leave it on one of the lawn chairs when you're done, I'll wash it later."

If I had more nerve, I'd ask him, *how's this for an agenda, Sunshine?* But the huge, stretchy swallow that slowly drags down his throat is enough for me right now.

***

Justin's counter-punch lands when I come inside after floating on a raft in the sun for forty-five minutes. He is doing pull-ups from a tension bar in the arched doorway of the dining room. Unfortunately, the French doors to the patio are right off the dining room, and the archway he hangs from is in my direct path.

He's shirtless, has a weight belt hanging from his waist, and a heavy, round weight dangling between his bent knees. The extra load causes his back and arms to ripple with muscles. I bet he's been at it for a while because he is covered in sweat and grunting with each chin up. It looks as though he is punishing himself or blowing off weeks of steam.

"You done staring yet?" he asks, which snaps me out of the illusion that he didn't know I was standing here.

"Just wondering how I'm going to get by. All your sweat and b-o are in my way." Ok, so he doesn't stink. In fact, he smells like the perfect man—warm, with like, two-day-old cologne. He smells faint yet alluring.

I'm picturing what his back would feel like underneath my fingernails when he finally drops down. "I thought you had ninety minutes?" he says as he turns around, veins popping from his biceps. A trickle of sweat takes the path down his abs that I want to take with my tongue before it soaks into the waistline of his athletic shorts. I am dizzy with this guy's seductive existence. Too bad he's a self-righteous asshole.

"Yeah, but it will take thirty minutes to get this knot out," I say, hoping I've held my blush at bay. Suddenly, I'm shy under his scrutiny—well, his scrutiny and the fact that my nipples are hard as pebbles underneath these stupid straps. He notices them, too; they make his eyes prickle in an uncivilized manner. Testosterone looks good on him—in a supremely alpha way. He is all sweat and muscles, and the swaying weight plate hanging between his legs requires me to consider the length of his penis. Gah! I'm in so much trouble now that I'm thinking about his dick.

By the time I've gotten dressed and completed my silent pep-talk about resisting the now primal desire I feel for him, Justin is wet from the shower and back at his laptop.

"You showered already?" Pity, I wasn't done inhaling his provocative maleness yet.

"Yeah, but don't worry, I'll wait until you leave to masturbate," he says, not even taking his eyes off the computer screen when he says such a thing. Now, it's impossible not to picture him jerking off. He probably knows I'm thinking about it right now, and I'm sure it offers him some sick satisfaction.

Justin is like quicksand. The more I fight it, the more I get sucked in. I glance at my watch nervously because the image is still there, *stroke, stroke, stroke, his bottom lip trapped between his teeth, his head lolled back, and his neck veins straining against their captivity. Stroke, stroke, stroke.*

"That's quite a mole you've got there," he says. I don't even need to ask. I know exactly which one he is talking about—the one that outed me as the owner of Daniel's social media tit-blitz. "Is it a heart? It looks like it."

"You tell me," is all I can come up with in response. It does look like a heart, but like I said before, it's really just two moles close together. They are dark and flat but usually always visible because of where they are. They are front and center, just about two inches below the hollow of my throat.

"I'd need to get a closer look," he says offhand. The thought of Justin taking a closer look at any part of my body creates a loud surging in my ears. Then he adds, "I have a mole too." His statement hovers in the air for what feels like an eternity before I bite.

"Should I take a closer look?" I ask. Now, he meets *my* eyes. I don't think he was ready to hear his own words served back to him.

"Do you think you can handle it?" he asks skeptically.

"Depends on how impressive it is."

"Ok then, come get your closer look," he says, placing his laptop on the coffee table and standing up. I take a few steps toward him but stop when he starts to unbutton his jeans. As he scoots one unfastened side of his fly over and stretches it forward, he says, "I'll let you be the judge of how impressive it is." The innuendo burns in my ears because he is basically holding the front of his jeans out for me to look down them.

I take a tentative look down his jeans. *Oh, Jesus*, he's not wearing underwear, and he trims his pubic hair. He is pointing to a tiny freckle near the crease of his leg. I laugh without meaning to, "That's not even a mole!"

He laughs, too, and his smile spreads through me, warm, like a shot of whiskey. "Sure it is!" he insists. The playfulness in his eyes makes me wonder why I didn't see it before. "What? Are you saying it's not impressive?"

"No, it's not impressive at all," I say.

"Well, perhaps you should see it in action then."

"What? Your freckle?"

"Oh, are we talking about freckles? My bad."

Then he reaches out and places his fingertip on my heart mole, an actual mole—the peer group of moles that form a heart. "This one *is* impressive, though," he says. I feel the warm touch of his finger as it flutters in my chest. Impressive indeed.

Chapter 13

JUSTIN

The email notice from Hand to Heart about the schedule change pisses me off. They didn't even ask if it was ok to switch my days. Apparently, they don't much care if I baked an apple crisp to show off for Norah yesterday. They also don't give a damn that tonight is poker night with my buddies. Their excuse was that another client needs her longer in the afternoons due to their failing mobility. I'm kind of angry about that failing mobility. You know what else shares a lack of mobility? Poker night. That's right, we've been doing it for so long on the first Friday of every month that the mere hint that we might need to change days heats my temper to a rolling boil. That, and Norah will think I bought the apple crisp because you can't even smell cinnamon and brown sugar in the house anymore.

Her new schedule with me is Fridays from 4:30 to 6:00. How am I supposed to work with that? The guys start getting here at five.

Not to mention, her being here will be like a lone Gazelle on the African savannah, surrounded by a pride of hungry lions.

I tried to cancel this week by claiming I was sick, but it only reinforced to Hand to Heart that I needed their help. So, now I have to get everything ready and prepare all the food *before* Norah arrives. A street taco bar sounded good until I realized I had to complete a massive project for work before prepping it. Oh yeah, and all of that before the clock strikes 4:30.

When she gets here, I'll tell her I have a migraine and need to lie down. Hopefully, thirty minutes is enough time to convince her of my splitting headache and shoo her away. I don't usually lie, not because I'm such a morally upstanding citizen, but because I'm crap at it. I've never been able to do it. I don't know if it's my facial expressions or the blazing sign above my head, flashing *Liar, Liar,* but off hand, I can't think of one time I've ever gotten away with a lie.

It turns out today is not that day, either. When I open the door for Norah, all thoughts of trying to get rid of her leave the stratosphere. She looks especially alluring in her plum-colored sundress because her golden brown eyes absorb some of the color from her dress and take on an almost purple hue. Her hair is missing the usual feathers clipped underneath, but the pirate beads and braids are still there.

You'd think that big of a contrast in someone's hair would be too wild. It's extreme, the red and the brown, with the top as vibrant as it can get and underneath, tame and dark. But the whole look does not seem wild at all anymore. It's exotic and suits her perfectly. She also has more makeup on than usual—it's like her *on the prowl, Friday night look,* and it makes me jealous for no good reason whatsoever.

"You look nice, hot date later?" I ask, despite not wanting to and certainly not wanting to hear her say yes.

"No, I'm hoping my roommate, Sophia can meet me out for a drink later." She steps past me while I watch the swish of her dress a little too closely. "I need one bad."

"Rough day?" I ask, peeling my eyes off her body and meeting her intensely golden eyes.

"You could say that. One of my clients had a stroke, so his family moved him to a nursing facility." She sees my eyes go wide with horror, then adds, "He didn't have the stroke while I was there. He is just a really sweet man, and I will miss him. I know all about his life and his family, and he always tells me jokes and beats me at Wheel of Fortune." Her eyes mist a little, which has a two-fold effect on me. One, it endears me to her sensitive heart, and two, it makes me want to plug up her open emotion. I can't avail myself to another person's pain—I don't even have a clear handle on my own.

"I have beer here. They are nice and cold. Do you want one of those? Or should you not drink on the job?" I ask, hoping I didn't just blurt that out as fast as I think I did. Wow, my empathy for others is truly staggering. I didn't exactly shrug and walk away, but I didn't address her sadness either. I think, to demonstrate the poles of my versatility, I smile at her.

"Yeah, I'll take a beer. If I get fired for drinking…or swimming, it will be because someone ratted me out," she squints her eyes and gives me a tame scowl, "Are you going to rat me out, Justin?"

"I wouldn't dare." At least not until we get all this pretense of her *job* out of the way, and she's here of her own volition—to anoint my dick and warm my bed.

"Good, but this is only a temporary job anyway. Now, how about that beer?" she says, dissolving any hint of sadness and overlooking my awkwardness to her show of emotion.

She follows me into the kitchen, and because I'm still so starstruck by her, I entirely forget about the five-guys-drinking-all-night state of my fridge. That is, until she starts laughing unabashedly.

"No! You do *not* have a fridge chock full of nothing but beer and condiments." Her laugh is clean and free of smudges—it sounds buoyant and free. Have I ever laughed so effortlessly?

Whoops. I forgot about that little detail. Poker night. Right. I don't have a solid comeback, so I say, "Hey! There is steak and taco stuff in there, too."

The heartiness of her laugh has died down, but it continues to rumble beneath the surface, still an admirable register on the Richter scale. "Are you having a party?" she asks in a teasing tone. "Or do you live off beer and tacos?" She delivers the last question on a giggle that sprinkles the words out with extra spacing, one at a time. Her playful disposition reminds me that, although suffering has been my sole triumph for three years, I may have an itch around my heart that I would like her help scratching.

"That's enough out of you. Hand me that steak and help me get ready for this party." The concession to have her help me get ready for poker night is only fractionally because I want her help. Mostly, I think it's because right now, I would rather have her company than the next hundred poker nights.

I think she is impressed with all the different salsas I made, and she has fun displaying them—worthy of a Pinterest or Instagram post—on the table with the other toppings. The guys are going to know there was a women's touch involved because she labeled everything and presented it as if for royalty instead of a bunch of obnoxious, beer guzzling, ass scratching dudes.

By the time I finish chopping up the steak and scraping it all into the frying pan, she is sitting on the counter next to me and sipping her beer. Street tacos are kind of my specialty, but she has no idea she is in the presence of greatness. She'll learn, though, I'll see to that.

She looks contemplative and then says, "I guess there is only one question left." *Shit!* She is fishing for an invitation. I want her to stay. I do, but the guys will eat her alive, and I can promise not one of them will filter a goddamn thing before it rolls out of their stupid mouths. I hesitate, waiting for her incendiary question, and I'm still not sure how I will answer it.

"Corn or flour tortillas?" she asks and then guzzles the rest of her beer before hopping down from the counter. "You should get them warming in the oven."

My body remains frozen with indecision. *Ask her to stay, do it.* Then, a sharp knock on the door precedes my buddy, Alex, and his armful of potato chips. He enters the house and murders all the fluttering butterflies in my stomach with one statement.

"Looks like co-ed, naked poker tonight! I like it!" Fucking Alex. See? This is exactly what I was talking about. Not a goddamn filter for miles, and it's too late to muzzle him.

"Alex, this is Norah. Would you mind shutting your pie-hole until she heads out?" I ask. Even though I'm dead serious, they both laugh and shake hands.

"Don't worry, I want no part of your sausage fest, Alex. Plus, I don't think you brought enough potato chips," Norah says as she wide-eyeballs the two giant bags of chips Alex holds under his arm. I swallow my snort, but secretly, I like her response to this jughead.

"What do you mean you want no part of poker night?" Otto asks after walking in at the same time as Hambone and Wally. The three of them enter the space like they are storming a castle, loudmouthed and unrefined.

"Uh, swordfights aren't really my thing," she says. I love her smart mouth, and she hasn't even cringed once. I see her locate her purse with her eyes, and then I hurry to her side. My decision may not be a smart one, but I'm too impulsive to be intelligent as well.

"Norah, will you stay for poker?" I ask. "I promise I will throat punch the next guy to say something out of line." She starts to decline, but Wally hands her another beer, and both Otto and Alex encourage her to stay while promising to be on their best behavior. Otto even holds up the three-finger salute, and while pinching a laugh with his face, he says *Scout's honor*. I guarantee you, Otto didn't spend five minutes as a Scout. He may have been the one selling weed to the Boy Scouts in the school bathroom, but that's about as close as he got to a Scout's honor.

"Uh….I don't think—"

"Stay for a few hands and eat a taco," I encourage her. I'm surprised by how much I do want her to stay. It feels kind of crisp and fresh to want something again.

"Did Justin say he wants to eat Norah's taco?" Wally asks the guys, making my lungs deflate and my head drop in disappointment.

"Wally, right?" Norah asks. "Wally, it sounds like you have no personal experience with women's tacos. I'm sorry that your mouth works as such an effective cock block, but I'm sure the guys would be happy to diagram the process for you in the event you ever come into contact with one," she smiles brightly at him while the rest of the guys roar with laughter.

"Yep, she's staying," Hambone says, and I have to agree.

***

If I'm honest, I'd say Norah was holding her own, both in poker and against the onslaught of testosterone-infused loudmouths. I'd also say that seeing her buzzed and laughing with all my friends makes my dick feel warm and a little twitchy. The guys have no idea about Hand to Heart, mainly because Davis got called in for overtime tonight, so his flapping gums are at work instead of sitting here with us.

The main issue with them not knowing I am a client of Norah's is that they assume I'm sleeping with her. Therefore, they have plundered normal boundaries, as well as dissolving any courteous level of outsider respect for her. They already see her as one of us, which will present with its own list of complications soon enough.

I'm too guarded to relax, and being the token sober guy amongst the tuned-up masses is an undesirable position to be in presently. While she is here, I fully intend to keep my wits about me for her sake, but I hate the feeling of being on high alert. I know Norah wanted to have a drink with her roommate after work and that she has had a rough week, but seeing her let loose like this makes me want to kick my buddies out and introduce her to the rebound capabilities of my mattress.

My instinct to remain sober was a gentlemanly one, but it wasn't for nothing. I knew it would only be a matter of time before some dickhead proposed a change to the normal run of things, and, as predicted, it happened.

"How about we switch things up a bit?" Wally suggests. I know he has been plotting something ever since Norah put him in his place a couple of hours ago. "Losing hand has to answer a truth or take a dare."

"No fucking wa—" I start before Norah interrupts me.

"Yes! The losing hand does the truth or dare, and you can't change your mind after hearing what it is." Norah announces this as if she's not the only female at the table. She is either too drunk to be sensible, or she is completely underestimating my friends. Either way, I'm on guard.

Surprisingly, we have fewer folds than I thought, and after an ambitious round, Otto comes out on top. "Wally, truth or dare?" he asks, with his trademark insidious grin. I know Otto is about to stick it to Wally, and I can't wait to watch him squirm after suggesting this nonsense.

"Dare." A surprising choice, but go big, Wally.

"Ok. I dare you to unlock your phone and pass it to Alex so he can read off your search history." Otto winks at Norah and then tips back his beer. The wink wasn't him flirting, it was one of solidarity because everyone at this table knows Wally will get the brunt of his stupid rule change.

"Bunch of assholes," Wally mumbles as he fishes out his phone and presses his thumbprint to the home button. I'm not sure why he is surprised unless he expected his dare to be something dumb like we did back in middle school in his parent's basement, like drinking a beer through a straw or swallowing a spoonful of cinnamon.

"Here we go," Alex says as he cracks his knuckles dramatically and then picks up the cell phone to start scrolling. "We've got some Amazon sign-ins, how to roast a whole pig, blah, blah, blah… bunch of shit about drones. Oh, wait, here we go—y'all, there are pages, and I mean *pages* of searches for *sharking*. You sick bastard!"

"What is sharking?" Norah asks, bleeding innocence.

"It's when someone runs up behind a chick and pulls her top down in public, so dudes hiding with cameras can take video and pictures of her tits and then post them online," Hambone explains with a shake of his head, almost disappointed in Wally but not quite.

"Not just tops either, sometimes entire strapless dresses," Alex adds.

"Well, all of you have a disturbing amount of knowledge about this sharking phenomenon, now don't you?" Norah says. "I'll have to remember that if I ever brave a tube top again."

"Wait! Wait, there's more," Alex snickers, "Spanking porn and lots of it. Especially wheelbarrow spanking!" Wally snatches the phone away, effectively shutting Alex up except for his laughing, which is only marginally hidden by the side of his own fist.

"That's enough, you bastards," Wally says as he shoves the phone back into his pocket. I have all kinds of friends. Really, their personalities run the gamut. I just hope Norah doesn't judge me based on this sea of idiots.

Norah smartly folds the next few hands, and we are forced to watch Alex shotgun three beers and then set the timer on his phone for an hour, during which time he can't go to the bathroom. Then we have to listen to Otto tell us what he thinks about when he masturbates— which is tits bouncing above him while a chick rides him cowgirl, or ass fucking some porn star that I've never heard of.

"Are your ears bleeding yet, Norah?" I ask her as I tip my head toward her ear and get a whiff of something that smells like fresh sheets and makes me think of her cotton panties. Who even knows if she wears cotton underwear, but the thought of her in white cotton panties is almost enough to make me nut right here, under the table. She giggles in response.

When Norah goes all in, I make sure I do, too. It will cost me dearly, but I can only hope I have a worse hand than she does. Personally, I only have a pair of threes, and I hope it's enough to lose the hand. I seriously don't want her to take a dare from these yahoos.

A truth would intrigue me, but I still want to protect her from telling us about when she lost her virginity or something equally ridiculous.

Shit.

She was bluffing.

She's got nothing.

Wally wins the hand, and fuck me sideways, Norah chooses a dare.

"Ok, doll, get up on your man and let him spank you…" he pauses for effect, with a lascivious grin, "Wheelbarrow style."

"Wait! No, I'm not her ma—" I try to come to her rescue. I fucking TRY, but she stands up and winks at me. "Guys, she is wearing a short dress, don't b—"

"Don't be such a prude, honey. Just tell me what wheelbarrow style is *so you can spank me.*" She squeezes between me and the table, so I have to back up my chair. She has no idea what she is about to do to me.

Fuck!

I'm going to pop the biggest boner. This might be worse for me than it is for her. Not to mention, it's going to give me masturbation material for decades.

"You need to sit forward on his lap, with your legs on either side of him, and then lean forward, putting your hands on the floor and bringing your knees up by his hips," Wally explains.

If there is anything positive about her accepting this dare, it's that I will be the only one she exposes herself to. However, if there is anything negative about it—it's the same goddamned thing! She will be leaning over in front of me with her legs spread open. I have to somehow continue to look her in the eye after this, as her *client,* not some slavering, walking hard-on.

Who knows if she would ever do this sober? And I'd like to say out of respect, I will not even glance at her panty-clad, open-legged secrets, but I also know that would be a big, fat, disgusting lie, especially after she sits on my lap and shimmies her ass against my dick before leaning forward and bringing her legs up.

I have to widen my knees to make room for her torso so her palms can rest against the floor. Our position brings my cock within a song of her lacy core, so my imagination goes wild, with no hope of reeling it back in. I can feel my heartbeat in the pounding throb of my brain. Damn, it's hot in here.

She is in a light sundress, so it comes as no surprise, especially reaching forward to touch the ground like she is, that the bottom of her dress pulls up. Now, it's hardly even covering her ass. Here's the other thing, her panties are *not* practical and cotton. They are sheer, white lace, and while not quite a g-string, they are nothing substantial either. The entire lower part of her ass cheeks is visible to me, and *her legs are spread wide open.* Oh my God! I want to fuck her just like this. This exact position. Ten thousand times.

"Anytime, Justin," Otto says.

Oh, crap, I'm supposed to spank her, not just sit and gawk at her barely covered crotch. Now it's getting *really* hot in here. I'm sweating like a whore in church, and my shirt starts to adhere to my back.

All these guys think this is chartered territory for me and that it's at least relatively familiar, but they couldn't be further from the truth. My imagination has also not prepared me for the reality of this moment. Although, now I'm quite sure she *is* bare down there. Christ, I will never get this image out of my head.

It would take almost nothing to slide the lace of her panties over. The curl of my finger is all that would be necessary. She'd be open to me. In my fantasy mind, she begs me to touch her. So, first, I would graze her silky skin with my thumb, back and forth, spreading her arousal. Then, I would slide my fingers under her so I could rub her favorite erogenous zone while I ease a finger in. OhMyGod.

She shimmies her hips a little, rocking against my lap and raising the hem of her dress even more. The motion works like a clap in front of my face, forcing me to close my eyes and attempt to gain some composure. "All the blood is rushing to my head, Justin," she says as she looks back over her shoulder at me with a teasing smile.

Before I can even open my mouth, Alex says, right on cue, "All the blood is rushing to Justin's head, too." Of course, everyone laughs and encourages me to finish the dare. I still need to spank her. What I want to do is grab two handfuls and squeeze this perfect ass while I spread her open for my voyeuristic viewing pleasure.

I'm conflicted about the whole thing because I know she owes this behavior entirely to the fact she has had too much to drink. Conflicted, that is, until she whines, *"Do it, Daddy. Spank me,"* and waves her ass at me again.

Alright then.

Smack

Smack

Smack

I don't spank her that hard, but her cheek pinkens right up. She gasped after the first spank, bit her bottom lip while looking back at me for the second, and groaned for the last one. She *groaned.* It was the sexiest, most erotic sound I think I have ever heard.

My dick is trying in vain to salute the fact that sexual sounds rumble out of her. She is also getting wet from this, which is driving me mad with lust. I feel like a rabid animal, and it could *not* be more inappropriate.

"All right, you two will have to get a room if you keep this up. Who's in?" Alex asks, moving right along.

I help her up, but before she sits back down and smooths out her dress, she risks a quick look into my eyes before she sheepishly turns away.

I can't help but wonder if tonight will be one giant sexual harassment lawsuit. I *knew* her staying for poker night was a bad idea.

"I'm in," I say.

"I'm in…I mean, *obviously*," Norah scoffs as she looks around at the guys. Maybe it's my imagination, but was there some double meaning in her words? I'll have to give that some thought later on tonight when I spout like a three-day-long volcanic eruption. Damp, white lace. Fuck it. I'm gone.

Chapter 14

Norah

Sophia picked me up from Justin's last night because I was too tipsy to drive. At least, I rationally knew I was too impaired to get myself home. Never mind that I became instantly sober when Justin spanked me. Until then, everything was all in good fun. His friends were great; the street tacos were outstanding, and the drinks were cold and entirely too welcome. Then it happened. I spread my legs for him like a two-bit whore. Virility and lust had loitered in the background while the crack of his hand served as a sharp warning for my waning sobriety.

Now, and a thousand times since last night, all I can think about is how he must think I'm a slutty, hot mess. I was holding my own against his strong personality and galactic sized ego until I drunkenly threw myself at him. No shame either, I tell you. *Hi Justin, here is my ass in your face, like it or not. Here is the trampy introduction from Hand to Heart you were probably hoping to avoid. Ack!* Don't even get me started on what my ass must have looked like jiggling under his smack. I'm beyond horrified and feel like a cheap, polyester suit that no one wears anymore because it *has no class*.

My hangover serves me right. I deserve every last throb in my temples, every dry heave in the dirty toilet, and every lurch of my self-respect and dissolving pride. One week! One week until I need to face him again. He, no doubt, will be able to read the blistering shame across my face, and he will go in for the kill.

"will I have to increase my payments to Hand to Heart now?" Or, *"Next time you flash me, at least give me a heads up."* Or maybe, *"You're underselling yourself, Norah. Or do you work for tips now?"*

I pull the blanket up over my head. I didn't sleep well last night. You would think I could at least do that without over-analyzing my behavior, but no, you would be wrong.

I free my head once the self-loathing becomes too thick to breathe under the covers. Just in time for Sophia to toss my phone on the bed in front of me.

"Wake-e, wake-e. It's almost noon. Plus, I think your client, the sex demigod, is texting you. That is if you have him in your phone as *poor, decrepit Mr. Abernathy* because that's the name that comes up."

"Ugh."

"You are not even close to being off the hook either, Missy. Just because you passed out last night and didn't share the goods doesn't mean I won't withhold coffee until you do," Sophia says. She is way too cheerful to be in my room—she is sucking all the oxygen right out of it.

"Gimmie my phone," I say, muffled into the pillow. I suppose it's better to see what he has to say before I eat something and have food to puke back up.

"It's like, two inches from your hand. I think you can manage." Then she is gone, like a phantom mist. Now, I'm all by myself, to face my demons alone. Even the sexy demons that I'm considering quitting my job to avoid. I peel my eyes open and bring my phone to my face.

Justin: *I don't know if I should start with, I'm sorry. Or, please don't judge me because of my friends.*

Wait. What? I read it again, just to make sure I read exactly what he texted and not what my blurry mind wanted the words to say. He is sorry? He's worried that *I'm* going to judge *him*? Well, Halleluiah!

Me: *Let's never speak of it again.*

I know it's level-one avoidance, but I'm ok with brushing it under the rug. It will be hard enough to look him in the eyes after burying this. There is no way I want to re-hash it now. With any luck, he will forget about it. Or his afflicted brain will repress it entirely.

Justin: *Please come back next week. Maybe we can tackle my mom's room or something equally torturous for me.*

Me: *Ok*

Me: *Full disclosure…I puked in the shower.*

Justin: *Full disclosure…I will never think about white lace the same ever again.*

Chapter 15

JUSTIN

I've decided I will never pack up my mom's stuff if I have to do it on my own, and back when I showed Norah around the house, there was no getting around it. She didn't ask any questions when she saw Jax's empty room; she probably figured the previous owners painted it like that, and I was too clueless of a bachelor to change it. But when she saw my mom's room, as though she never left and would come waltzing back in at any minute, she knew I was stuck. I think she could tell how lost I was about what to do with everything. I remember how her eyes softened toward me and how she had suggested we do it together. Davis offered to help me a hundred times already, but until now, I didn't want anyone's help. I wasn't ready.

It was the same for Jax's room. I left it exactly how it was for more than a year. I wasn't ready to move anything for a very long time, plus I still needed his room to cry in. I cried gallons of tears in that room, oceans even. Then, one day, I was ready. I didn't get rid of a solitary thing, though, not a single pacifier. Everything from the still-full baby wipes warmer to the baggie of hair from his first haircut is packed nicely in my basement. Davis helped me that day. Maybe because he was also completely destroyed when Jax was killed, or maybe because he loved my son like he was his own, I let him help me.

Anyway, I guess I need a little push to clear out my mom's room. Or maybe support is a better word. Norah suggested she help once before, and I also mentioned it in my tail-between-my-legs text to her, so I guess I'm that much closer to getting it done. It will be nice to move my home office out of my bedroom, but no part of me is looking forward to emptying out my mom's room.

I'm not sure how to proceed with the fact that I see Norah's open legs and lacy panties on the backs of my eyelids every time I blink or try to go to sleep. I have no clue how to dial everything back to me simply being a client of hers—no clue how to make small talk and pretend I don't masturbate thinking about her.

She didn't want to talk about it—you know, the part where I spanked her bare ass and stared hungrily at the lace between her thighs, but I'm hoping she at least knows I'm sorry. I truly wanted to protect her from all that nonsense, but instead, I ended up taking advantage of the situation—and I'm not that guy. I am not at all proud of my behavior, and if she even gives me the time of day, I will conduct myself like the gentleman my mother raised.

She shows up right on time, of course, and when I open the door, it takes me a bit to finally move out of the way to let her in. She is wearing a tiny sundress and sandals that I highly doubt are on her work-approved list of attire, considering how Viagra has probably worked its way through the ranks of her elderly clients.

"I brought some flattened boxes. They're in my trunk. Want to give me a hand with them?" she asks with a smile. My heart rate picks up, but I can't honestly say if it's because of the way she cocks her head and points over her shoulder with her thumb, making her body twist in an inadvertently sexy way—or if it's because she wants me to brave the outdoors.

"Uh, yeah, sure," is my delayed response, but she is already headed back to her—what is that, an Audi maybe? Yeah, she drives a silver A4. I pictured her in a Jeep, so the Audi is a little disappointing, but whatever. I glance nervously around and then hustle after her to help bring in the boxes.

Inside, when she leans forward and drops a stack of large, flattened cardboard on my mom's bed, it creates a breeze that lifts her dress enough for me to see the backs of her thighs and a tiny hint of what I think are black panties. I have to bite the inside of my cheek to redirect my attention from the heat trying to race south to the taste of blood in my mouth. She has no idea what she does to me.

"Ok. Where should we start?" she asks, and it's an innocent enough question, but I feel like a fox in a hen house. Apparently, poker night wasn't enough of a hand slap to quiet the devil on my shoulder. Some incredibly raunchy answers to that question roll through my head, but I can only deliver the tamest one.

"How about we start with you bending over again with another batch of boxes?" It's like I'm a Great White shark, and there are smoky tendrils of blood in the water *everywhere*. I feel like a feral beast having to deny its truest, most basic instinct. Can she *see* how my nostrils are flaring and how blown my pupils are?

She doesn't skip a beat before she volleys back, "I would, but I don't want to show off. Let's start with the closet." She is perfect. She knows exactly what is going on, yet she is still playing it coy. This whole shy resistance or oblivious routine of hers makes me wonder if I make her nervous. Does she touch herself thinking about me and then have a hard time looking me in the eyes? Does she watch my mouth when I talk and wonder what it would be like to kiss me?

"Ok," the grin on my face is downright predatory, and I know she recognizes it for what it is, but I don't mind having to work a little harder for it. For her. Work harder for her. Damn, I'll tell you what, never mind poker night, there is enough sexual tension in this room to crackle like static-y sheets.

"I think you should choose a couple of items of clothing that are special to you, and we'll put them in the "sentimental" box. That will make it easier to part with the rest," she plops down on the bed, widens her eyes and nods for me to get started.

Ok, it looks like Norah is going to ignore the fact that I must look like a sputtering bull, stamping its hoof and getting ready to charge. She steers us right back on track. The diligent professional—who I want to introduce to my 600 thread count sheets. Little does she know, I've already claimed the most sentimental thing of all. Clara Abernathy's pearls.

***

Once ninety minutes are up, which happens in a heartbeat, she finishes taping the box shut and looks at me appraisingly. I've had a massive lump in my throat the entire time, and it's been difficult for me to decipher what is sentimental and what isn't. She was my mother—every single thing is sentimental.

Norah gets up from behind the box and approaches me carefully, like I might detonate. Only then do I realize my hands protectively clutch the baby blanket my mom knitted for Jax against my chest. Even though it feels like sixty air-conditioned degrees in here, I have beads of sweat across my brow, and I want the floor to open like a trap door and suck me into it. Bonus points if there's a noose around my neck.

Norah brushes her fingers against my cheek, which breaks the spell I'm under and says, "I think we will hang on to this one," as she reverently places her hand on the baby blanket. It's pearly white and perfect. We baptized Jaxson while wrapped in it. As I stand here, I can still remember the smell of the scented oil the priest swiped on his infant forehead, making the sign of the cross. The scent was strong but somehow not aggressive, in the way that something smells warm and welcoming. Jax had sucked on his fist the whole time, even when held over the baptismal font, while the water ran down his head and into his eyes. He didn't even cry. He was such a happy baby. At his baptism, we took a picture of his little hand grabbing the crucifix I used to wear around my neck—the one I traded for my mother's pearls. Now, I don't have Jax or the cross necklace, only the image of the photo burned into my gray matter. I can only nod in response to Norah's voice because my mouth is so dry that words can't begin to form.

"Justin?" she says, brushing some of my hair back so it's out of my face. "That's enough for today. We can finish up next week."

I absently nod, but I don't know what I agree to. I'm in a tunnel, and it's closing on me fast.

***

It was late when I finished packing up my mom's things, but I had to keep up with the momentum Norah created. I appreciate that she approached the whole thing as though it wasn't all crap headed to a homeless shelter or local thrift shop. She dove in, knowing I wanted to keep parts of my mother's story while helping me whittle away at the rest. Deciding which of Mom's possessions were worthy of keeping and which ones I should cast off was a raw and bitter experience, but coming across Jax's baby blanket hit me like a thousand-pound, medieval war hammer.

It's safe to say the loss of my son was equivalent to the loss of my soul. The little reminders here and there that prove I'm still living as an empty shell are enough to spin me on my axis. The blanket was one such reminder. In the beginning, I was spinning so hard and so constantly that I couldn't hardly draw breath. The fact that my heart continued to circulate blood to a necrotic body was evidenced only by the searing pain that gripped me in its talons. My heart still beat, yes, but I didn't breathe again for years.

When Vivian left me and moved across the country, it hardly registered as a blip on my radar. I didn't miss her then, and I don't miss her now. I loved her, I think, sure, but her loss was a gentle wave, whereas Jax's was a raging tsunami times infinity.

Anyway, my takeaway from this whole miserable day, besides the reminder that I'm eternally and prodigiously empty, is that I'm going to have to pull it together. I will need all my faculties to rein in the feisty streak that is Norah. It's becoming abundantly clear that I may have to work harder for her attention than I have ever had to work for another woman's.

As I lie in bed, I close my eyes and can almost feel the touch of her hand on my cheek. Is it weird that *that* is what I'm fantasizing about instead of the glimpse of her panties and naked thighs provided by the cardboard breeze? At the time, all I could picture was pushing her down on my mother's bed and spreading her legs apart, but now? Now, all I can think about is the feel of her hand on my *face*.

Chapter 16

Norah

The intoxicating smell of Saturday morning freshly brewed coffee wafts through my apartment, and though it calls to me like an angel song, it's still not enough to get me out of bed. Part of the problem is that I need to fire off a bunch of resumes today. I need to update and polish the thing first, though, which doesn't exactly draw me out of my comfortable dormancy. But the other factor keeping me anchored to my bed are swirling thoughts of Justin.

It's beyond clear to me that he has been traumatized by the loss of his mother. The trance he fell into while cleaning out her dresser drawers marked him as clearly as if he'd sent up a rescue flare. I wonder if she fell horribly ill, or suffered an agonizing death, or maybe she was disabled—but *something* about her left a wretched scar across her son.

Justin doesn't know it yet, but I kept one of her flannel nightgowns. I'm going to make it into a set of pillows for him. Not that he has to keep them on his bed or anything, but maybe it's better than exiling the tangible memory of her to a box in the basement. He was caught in such a fierce, almost catatonic spell that he didn't notice me take the nightgown with me. Hell, I could have wheeled his mom's bed right out of the room, and he wouldn't have noticed. He didn't look sad or like he was going to cry. He looked more like he was about to turn to ash and crumble into a pile of dust at my feet.

I think about him more than I'd like to admit, and I'd be lying if I said his suggestive comment about me bending over didn't tingle between my legs a little bit. I'm just worried that if he says something like that again, I'll fall right onto his penis. He is the kind of guy that sticks with you, like a bad haircut—no matter how much you try to deny it, and pretend it's not there, it's always on your mind. He's no bad haircut, though. In fact, I would wear him around like the Crown Jewels.

After glancing at my laptop and immediately dismissing the fleeting ambition to open it and get on with my day, I grab my phone instead. I have a text from a number I don't immediately recognize.

Unknown: *Come over for a BBQ. Bring your swimsuit. Or not.* The last part gives away who the text is from—that, and Justin is the only one I know with a pool.

I reply: *I don't skinny dip with strangers. Who is this?*

Justin: *Just a poor, infirmed, housebound man, texting from his work phone because he forgot to charge his regular one.*

Me: *I wouldn't want to further complicate your frail condition. I better wear my swim tent, it's nice and frumpy for pool parties such as yours.*

Justin: *Good, that should prevent my pacemaker from misfiring. Plan on 4:00-ish.*

The new gallop in my heartbeat *does* get me out of bed, directly, and with the force of a reverse bear trap. I run to the kitchen, where Sophia is burning toast if the smell is any indication.

"We are going to a pool party today!" I shout as I round the corner to the kitchen at a double-time clip and crash right into Sophia. "At Justin Abernathy's!"

"Does that mean I have to shave my legs?" she asks, without mention of me almost plowing through her.

"Of course not. I mean, maybe braid it so it stays out of the pool filter, but let's not get crazy."

"Mmmmmm, I bet his friends are yummy. Ok, I'm in," she says, as if there were any doubt. I've been talking about him constantly, and I would drag her ass kicking and screaming even if she said no. Obviously, that won't be necessary because her curiosity level regarding Justin Abernathy is a forty-five on a ten scale. Especially after my re-telling of the poker night antics. Once she finally found the crank that wound her gaping jaw shut, she had been proud of me for my sluttiness. But remember, Sophia casts a pretty wide net around what whorish behaviors are perfectly acceptable.

"Get your purse. I need a new swimsuit, mine isn't skanky enough," I say as I pour a mug of coffee for myself, and Sophia chokes on hers behind me.

***

Ok, so if I'm being honest, my ass is bigger than the last time I bought a bathing suit. There, I said it. And if you are wondering if that bit of knowledge factored into my new bikini purchase, the answer is, no. Though maybe it should have. Now that we are walking up to Justin's front door, me with a giant bowl of cut up watermelon and

Sophia with a six-pack of beer, and feeling the suit work its way between my ass cheeks, I wish I would have respected the extra lbs.

I'm nervous, so when I smile, my upper lip begins to twitch disconcertedly. Now, when Justin's hot friend opens the door, he catches me with my mouth pinched together before I can give him a lukewarm attempt at a not-awkward-at-all smile.

"Hi, I'm Sophia, and this is—"

"Norah," he finishes for her. Holy shit, he knows who I am. "I'm Davis. Let me take that for you," he says, relieving us of our respective burdens. "Come on in, everyone's out back." When he turns and walks toward the kitchen, I peel my eyes off his tattoos and naked torso. Only then do I notice he has an artificial leg.

Sophia licks her lips and whispers, "He's mine." That didn't take long at all, did it? Must be his broad, tattooed shoulders. Or his stunning good looks. Or his greedy smile. Anyway, Sophia's done for, and it only took two point five seconds.

We head out back, where music plays, and twenty or so people disperse in and around the pool. There are rafts and pool noodles floating aimlessly in the water, jostled only when someone, who I think is Otto, does a cannonball into the pool. The sheer recklessness of the cannonball makes me think of frat parties and idiot-drunk, handsy guys. This is no frat party, though. For one thing, there is too much food. And for another, no one is doing keg-stands or drinking from a beer bong.

I can't help but notice every last one of Justin's female friends is disgustingly beautiful, and I suddenly feel insecure. Well, not suddenly. I should say I feel *even more* insecure. It's tricky standing out as much as I do in a new crowd. I like being different from everyone else, but in a closed environment like this, where everyone fits a mold, I feel as prominent as a turd in the punch bowl.

"Can I get you guys a margarita?" Davis asks, while the rest of the crowd dutifully ignores us. I scan quickly for the woman with the yellow car, but I don't recognize her or anyone else. Except maybe Alex, and of course, the cannonballing Otto. I assumed I would see her today, which is what prompted the new bathing suit purchase. The same bathing suit that is still getting acquainted with my ass crack.

"Yeah, sure," I say through my acute nervousness and then silently chastise myself for not saying thank you before he left to get them. Ugh, this is very uncomfortable for me and nowhere near my element. Sophia, however, has already taken full stock of the men here and is just getting started. She would feel comfortable in a leper colony, though, because not much rattles her. She has a very, *love me or fuck off* attitude that I admire a great deal, but emulate not one single bit.

"I would shag every one of these guys, Norah," Sophia says, which makes me laugh in spite of my awkward tension. "Maybe even some of these women. Which one of these guys is your pheromone dripping client, anyway?"

"Sophia, I'm going to need you to turn on your brain to mouth filter, ok?" I say. "Besides, he's not out here. You'll know when I see him, though, because you will hear my thighs slap together to squeeze my special spot."

In what has to be the worst timing ever, after mentioning something as crass as squeezing my legs together, I feel a cold drink pressed against my shoulder. My flimsy tank top is much too insignificant to temper the cold against my skin, so I sharply suck in my breath before turning around.

Davis and Justin stand there, both shirtless and disturbingly sexy. Each holding their own margarita in one hand and offering the other to Sophia and me. It's hard to tell what Justin is thinking, but he is definitely up to no good. His smile is brazen, and I can see my own reflected back at me from his brown aviator sunglasses. Although, this time, the smile sits naturally on my lips, surprisingly enough. Is he taller than normal? Or am I just closer to him than usual? I thank him for the margarita, complete with a salted rim and lime wheel garnish. Yep, not a frat party because Justin serves drinks in specialty glasses or beer bottles instead of red Solo cups and aluminum cans of cheap beer.

"Justin, this is Sophia," Davis makes quick introductions while the two of them shake hands. "And now I understand why you're suddenly so on board with Hand to Heart. I'd question your sudden willingness if I didn't see why for myself."

"Yes, ok, that's enough," Justin jumps in before Davis can embarrass him any further. It's clear that both Davis and Sophia are sitting on a goldmine of insider information, but Davis's loyalties aren't as steadfast as Sophia's. She would submit to waterboarding before she'd let on that I had so much as mentioned Justin's name to her.

"Come inside, I want to show you something," Justin says as he places his free hand against my lower back. His touch resonates through my body like the ring of an ancient church bell. We head toward the back door, neither of us giving a backward glance to Sophia and Davis, who I'm sure will be just fine in our absence.

"Should I worry about Sophia?" I ask as he casually drops his hand from my back, opens the French door, and waits for me to enter the house first. His manners feel natural, like they're completely ingrained and well established. There is also no hint of his wily arrogance. Maybe the last few weeks have chipped away at his emotional fortress. Perhaps he has only lowered the drawbridge, but I like what I see. I like it a lot.

"I'm more worried about Davis right now," he grins, "There's a woman here that he has been casually dating for a few weeks," he says, as my eyes widen and I come to a dead stop at the base of the stairs. "I'm actually looking forward to seeing him squirm," he adds over his shoulder.

"But, Sophia—" I start.

"Is a big girl. You can rush to her aid in a minute. I want you to see this first," he titters with a playful energy that instantly puts me at ease. I'm seeing more and more of these glimpses into the sweet, fun side of his personality, and the more I get to know him, the more I think I may have been wrong to compare him to Daniel. Justin comes off as arrogant, but I think it might just be stone cold confidence, with no real sense of entitlement at all.

He stops outside his mother's room and sweeps his arm in a dramatic flourish as if to say, *Ta Da!* When I look in, I see he has finished clearing out his mother's things and set the room up as his home office. There's no trace of the room's previous inhabitant whatsoever.

"Wow, new paint and everything. It looks amazing, Justin." My words are slightly less than completely sincere, only because I wanted to help him finish it. "What will we do next time I come?"

He swipes a hand through his hair and covers his grin with a sip of margarita as I realize just how suggestive my comment sounded. I scramble to say something else to fill the sexually charged space, "What do your tattoos say?"

I've seen him shirtless before, but I didn't pay attention to the line of bold letters along the tops of his shoulders and trapezius muscles until today. It's easy to miss the words on top of his shoulders when you get caught up on his abs, and the way his swim trunks hang, drawing all kinds of sexy attention to his hip-shelves, and that mesmerizing V that leads—

"This one says, *Non Sibi*," he points to the top of his right shoulder, "And this side says, *Sed Omnibus*, which translates to, *Not for self, but for all.*"

"Huh," is my stupid response while I try to deconstruct even the translated saying and still can't figure it out.

"Don't hurt yourself, Norah, it's a firefighter motto," his grin is infectious, and even though he is teasing me, I beam right back at him like a love-struck fool. *A firefighter motto?*

"So, let's see this swim-tent," he says as he takes a step forward, making my insides clench into a hot, tight ball. He is close now, close enough to reach out and drag the backs of his fingers up the side of my ribs. I can feel his touch through my burnout tank top, and it stops my breath. This is the first time he has ever willingly touched me outside of being gentlemanly or polite, and his knuckles scorch a path across my skin that screams, *this is more than just polite or friendly.*

"Hey, **BOOT**?" someone yells from downstairs. The voice charges in and ignites the moment like the spark that brought down the Hindenburg. I'm surprised when Justin responds to it. He exhales heavily and then walks out into the hallway.

"What?" he calls downstairs.

"**Where are the karaoke mics**?" the cockblocker asks as if their location were a matter of national security. Justin was just about to make a sexy move. You know that moment that hangs in the air right before someone kisses you for the first time—we were having that moment! The anticipation of his kiss grows on me like a vine, and my skin still tingles from where he touched me with his knuckles.

He looks back at me with a cloudy acquiescence across his face, his lips still moistened and deliciously kissable, then holds out his hand to me, "Come on, let's go save your girl."

Five seconds, that's all we needed. Five more seconds and his lips would have been on mine. Does that cockblocker even know how long I've waited for that very moment? The disappointment lies shattered at my feet, but I step over it and take a deep breath. It's still early.

"Did that guy call you *Boot?*" I ask as I take his proffered hand and follow him downstairs. Once down, he doesn't let go. The whole hand holding thing is so smooth and natural it belies the giddy-up tempo of my current pulse rate.

His repeated contact has not gone unnoticed by me. In fact, it feels territorial, almost like he's claiming me. I am definitely not here in a working capacity, and the knowledge of that raises my temperature and tingles in my new bathing suit.

"Yeah, he did. But that's nothing; we call one of the guys Wolf Bagger," he looks over and meets my eyes, "You're going to have to look that one up; I'm too much of a gentleman to elaborate." His rangy smile tilts enough to pique my curiosity and make me take mental note of the term.

Once outside, we see Sophia and Davis right away, but this time, a statuesque supermodel type with wavy black hair and marauding gray eyes joins them. The sight of the three of them together makes Justin chuckle, so I can only assume the woman is the one Davis is seeing. Feeling protective of Sophia, I let go of Justin's hand and start to walk toward them.

"Careful, that field is sown with Agent Orange," Justin says, this time openly laughing. "I'll be right over. I need to grab the microphones first." Then he steps forward and leans into me, his body touching mine at more than a few electric contact points. His bare chest is warm as it fuses against my burnout shirt. Bringing his lips to my ticklish ear and faintly grazing the shell of it, he whispers, "Try to stay out of the fray, *my little warrior*, I'd like to keep you in one piece." His rumbly voice and term of endearment make every single hair on the back of my neck stand up.

Every milli-second that ticks by makes me more and more keenly aware that if I were to turn my head, even slightly, his mouth would be on mine in an instant. His presence today is not at all broken or docile like when we worked together packing up his mother's room. Nope, today he wears a commanding presence, today he is a King among peasants.

Feeling the pull of my loyalty along with a whole bundle of crackling nerves, I step back, breaking the enchantment. I need to make sure I didn't leave Sophia vulnerable to the circling wolves. Justin's wicked little smile as I disengage doesn't read as rejection, though, it reads as something else, challenge maybe?

As I approach the three of them like the Bermuda Triangle, I see Sophia laughing, and it disarms me. Maybe there isn't any tension between them after all. Once I breach their conversation circle, I see things differently.

"Awwww, bless your heart," Sophia says, with a look of sweet concern that cuts like a machete. I know the level of volatility here based on those three words alone. *Bless your heart.* Now, a Southern woman will use that simple phrase in a variety of ways, each one highly nuanced and distinct. First—there is the completely sincere sentiment, as in, 'You just finished a chemo treatment? Well*, bless your heart.'* Next, there's—pity. For example, someone whose roots have gone a touch too long without a salon visit, bless your heart, which reads as, 'You poor thing, you're a mess.' Then you have, as is with this case—condescension. As in, 'you silly girl, you think you have a shot while I'm here? Aww, *bless your heart.'*

I step right into their airspace and extend my hand to the woman, choosing to ignore the apparent bloodsport for the moment. "Hi, I'm Norah," I say, forcing a peace treaty for the immediate future.

She meets my eyes, but I'm sad to report my friendliness has no effect on her. In her case, she wears a sneer masquerading as a smile.

"I'm Anna." She shakes my hand, but only so she doesn't look like a petty bitch. "So, you're seeing Justin? I hope you like to lay low," she says. I can't decide if she is sneering or if she can't smile quite right through all her lip filler.

Even though I'm not exactly *seeing* Justin, I secretly love that she assumes I am. It must be the hand holding. I do, however, get the distinct impression that people know who I am—like he has talked about me. Just the thought of that makes me feel like I swallowed a handful of Adderall.

"What do you mean, *lay low*?" I ask, ignoring the rest and letting her assume whatever she wants to about Justin and me. Actually, I hope she thinks we are having tons of dirty, hot sex—sex you can feel deep down in your joints. Sex that rattles you to the core. I'm fine if her imagination runs with that.

"Never mind. I'm thirsty. Have fun, Davis."

"Thirsty is right," Sophia comments behind her back, then refocuses her attention on Davis while Anna stalks off.

I shift gears, too, and ask Davis, "So, how do you and Justin know each other?" I'm trying really hard not to acknowledge or dignify what just went down with any kind of a response. Davis may be a manwhore, but Sophia is nobody's fool, and she can take care of herself. As far as the Davis hierarchy goes for her, number one, he's hot. Number two, he has an impressive amount of sexy tattoos. Number three, he's a womanizer. For Sophia, hot and tattooed still trumps everything else.

"We used to work together. Right, buddy?" Davis says just as Justin strolls up to us, cocky grin fully intact.

"Yes, we did," then he turns to me, already bored with the conversation. "Want to float on some rafts while we drink our margaritas?" His skin looks soft and as smooth as oiled glass, even though it's pulled tight over well-defined muscles. His bare upper body begs for my hands, my lips—I want to rub up against him, naked, sweaty, and gasping for breath. I'm sure my eyes have glazed over with my industrious thoughts, but I muster up an answer to his question anyway.

"Sure." And just like that, Davis and Sophia are dismissed, along with any bubbling catfight drama that I want no part of anyway. I have much better places to direct my attention now. Especially because Justin's hair keeps slipping forward to skim over his brow, and his ashy blue eyes look like they are scheming up something indecent. Something loud but unspoken tells me he no longer thinks of me as a Hand to Heart employee. No, now he is a predator, and he is beginning to circle his prey.

Chapter 17

JUSTIN

"I pretend to be valiant while I hold Norah's raft still so she can get on it, but the truth is, when she stripped off her tank top and stepped out of her ragged cutoffs, all my blood made a discourteous and rapid descent straight to my dick. I felt like a fifteen-year-old kid trying to hide his boner from the class. I hadn't thought far enough ahead to wonder how I would get on my own raft from inside the pool with any semblance of grace, but whatever, at least I won't pitch a public tent. Let's face it, the number of times I have entertained erotic thoughts of this woman was bound to be a hundred percent evident in the visceral response of my obedient penis.

"Don't laugh," she says, now perfectly stable on the raft. She hands her drink back to me, "I'm going to flip over, and I can promise you it won't be stealthy." Her comment makes me laugh out loud. Shit, the less stealthy she does it, the better.

"I will do my best," I say without a solid commitment. I'm surprised at how struck I am by this woman. I can't quite put my finger on what has drawn me so completely to her. She is beautiful for sure and as unique as a four-dollar bill—and her body in that bikini will prevent me from ever stepping out of this pool. It's more than that, though, something intrinsic. I want to *own* her body, but I also want to find out all about her. I want to know her. Usually, my attraction to women is pretty single-minded, and the affection stops there. But Norah? This one I may decide to let in.

She flips over without too much fanfare, and I mask the severity of my disappointment behind a bright smile. Then she settles her chin on her crossed forearms. Her knees are bent with her ankles crossed as they hover above her perfect ass. It takes supreme restraint to keep myself from untying the side of her bikini bottom, so instead, I guide her raft closer to my standing figure. I know the attraction is mutual because it's crackled around us for weeks, but also because of how she watches my lips when I talk. It's like she put in the required amount of resistance, and now she wants to know my mouth—intimately.

"You are sexy as hell. You know that?" I say before taking a tentative sip of my margarita.

"And you, Justin. You are dangerous," her words are severe, but her grin is mischievous, and it tickles at the base of my spine.

"Why do I have to be dangerous? Why can't I be intoxicating? Or tempting? Or devilishly handsome?" My words are pouty, but I can't get my laughing face to close around the corners of my smile, so it reduces the pouty-ness quite a bit.

"You are all of those things, Justin. That's what makes you dangerous." She takes a sip of her drink, eying me over the rim. She masks the twinkle in her eye behind her sunglasses, but I feel it like a flutter of happiness somehow assigned to me.

"Then, I hope you like danger because I have all sorts of dangerous things on my mind," I tell her, and maybe it's too much honesty right out of the gate, but I don't want to hide my intentions. With her, I feel a crack of nervous energy split my stomach, and it's unfamiliar because the last time I felt it must have been when I was a kid on the playground watching Courtney Sorensen twirl around so her dress lifted up.

Norah slides her sunglasses on top of her head and looks at me with one eye squinting against the sunlight. She appraises my words, then licks her lips. The way she stares at my mouth lets me know she wants me to kiss her, but I don't. Not yet.

When I don't react to her flirty glance and supple lips, she changes tact, "Why do your friends call you Boot?" she asks, putting the get-to-know-you train back on track while derailing the one headed to my bed. Usually, I don't open up a whole lot to women because everything I say leads to more questions. With Norah, I want to spill everything. I want to bare my soul—but I don't want to chase her away yet. I will be cautious with this one, but for once, I'm not going to hold anything back.

"I used to be a firefighter. With most of these fools, in fact," I indicate to everyone around us, though we are only two out of five people in the pool right now. "Every year, we did a fundraiser for work. We would stand near busy intersections holding one of our turnout boots, and people would put money in them." I stop there, hoping to spare myself the embarrassment of the rest, but she doesn't let it go.

"And?"

"And, *pretty boy* here was always the first one to fill up his boot," says a guy from my station named Eddie, who happens to be floating on a giant Pink Flamingo. "And he always collected the most money. We called it his seduction boot." Norah laughs at the implication, which makes me suddenly feel shy around her. I'm not the playboy Davis is. I'm too much of a headcase on my own to even think about juggling women.

"That's some big talk coming from someone called Hefty. Go on, Hef, tell Norah how you landed your nickname," I encourage, with a slap on Eddie's solid thigh.

"Ahhh, perhaps a story for another time," he says with a jovial laugh, right before a football hits him square in the chest.

Come on, Hefty. Eyes on the ball, you numb-nut," shouts the dude who threw the football. I don't remember his name because he came to the station right before I left. He's a nice kid, though; he kind of reminds me of myself back then.

As Hefty paddles away from us with the football tucked under one arm, I lean closer to Norah's face. I'm dying to nibble on that bottom lip. "Are you ready for a little more full disclosure?" I ask. My voice sounds cryptic, but the words are delivered through a playful smile, so her breath catches, and then she licks her lips.

"Of course. Is this when you finally tell me why you have Hand to Heart weekly services?" she smiles broadly in return. Her question makes me realize that she has given the whole thing some thought. Well, that and the fact I've been pretty elusive with my reasoning behind having the service. For right now, though, I'm going to have to continue to evade the question. I don't want to get into it here, not now. The well is too deep.

I ignore her question and resort back to my declaration of full disclosure. "I can't stop thinking about you," I murmur, then reach under her ponytail, cup her head, and float her raft closer to me. Then I kiss her. Just like that. With me standing chest deep in the pool and her flaunting her sexy body from on top of the raft. The kiss is fairly tame but hotter than I expect, so I can't help when my brain fast-forwards the night—straight to wild sex up against my bedroom wall.

By the time I break the kiss and pull back a bit, I feel dizzy from the dopamine surge charging through my neural pathways. Screw these margaritas, I think I'm drunk on her. I had nearly forgotten what endorphins felt like. *Welcome back, old friends.*

"Do it again," she whispers through a faint smile as her eyes flutter closed. So, I do. I'm still holding the back of her head with one hand and my drink with the other. We kiss well together, it's not at all hurried, not aggressive or needy, just slow and sensual. It's the kind of kissing that happens when you slowly enter someone you love. It's tender, yet hungry at the same time.

I want to leave her wanting more, so I pull back again. This time I suck her bottom lip as I disengage our mouths. I set our drinks on the side of the pool and hop up on the other raft. She closes the gap between us with a half-hearted attempt at paddling, using only one hand because the other arm still supports her chin.

My wet trunks cling tightly to my package. So much so, that even a peeping neighbor would be able to make out the head of my cock. The whole thing is somewhat awkward to remedy while on a bobbing raft, but it's hot that she is looking at my dick.

"See something you like?" I ask, calling her out on her lascivious stare.

"Yeah, I see a cheeseburger that just came off the grill," she says with a completely straight face and raised eyebrows. I like that I don't have her eating out of the palm of my hand. A lot of other women don't bother with such restraint.

"We can eat," I say just as stoically, then add, "first." Water droplets run in rivulets down my chest, and I think about how, if she got off the raft, the water would soak through her bikini top and make it cling to her body.

"Not just yet. First, I want to hear why you aren't a firefighter anymore. You said you're a digital marketing strategist or specialist—whatever. That has to be horrifically boring after being a superhero, right?"

"Not boring. Just different. I needed a change. A lot happened around that time," I realize I am babbling and not completing a single coherent thought.

"You wanted to lay low?" she asks. The words *lay low* feel weighted when they leave her lips. I can see her try to disentangle my statements like she is trying to solve a riddle or crack the DaVinci code, and it deflates me completely. This is when I lose her. When I'm honest about how fucked up I am. It will end before it even gets a chance to start.

"Yeah. I wanted to work from home," I hesitate to say more because I just want to enjoy this day. "Let's go get some food."

Chapter 18

Norah

Mindful of the fragments of coverage I call my bikini, I only eat half of my cheeseburger. However, instead of the other half, apparently, I'm having a pound of potato salad. I've also consumed enough salt from the margarita rims to retain water for a decade. With any luck, the impending fluid bags under my eyes tomorrow will deter me from falling on Justin's dick tonight and spending the night with him. Salt is more of an enemy to me than the tequila. The thirst alone has caused me to take in a metric ton of watermelon, and the evening is still young.

Sophia has spread her wings and chosen to divide her time among several guys. I'm not yet sure of her angle, but I'm sure part of her reasoning is to enlighten Davis of her womanly prowess with men. I imagine she would like to make sure he doesn't put too heavy of a checkmark by her name. She's not easy, but she's fun—as she is constantly reminding me. She won't sleep with any of these guys tonight, but she *will* leave several of them with a definite impression of the possibility. Perhaps, something for them to think about later. Especially Davis.

It's dark out now, except for the rows of white Edison bulbs above the patio and the bluish pool light that leaves the water looking radio-active. There has been a pretty steady drop in numbers over the last couple of hours. According to Justin, it's the responsible ones with kids at home and sitters to relieve that have thinned the crowd. There remains, however, a significant group who have taken rather loudly to the karaoke machine. They have replaced Justin's Spotify playlist with something that resembles music but is really just its ugly cousin.

When Justin and I head back to the pool, it's rowdy with two couples engaged in a chicken fight and a guy who has made a pool noodle into a water cannon. Between the water cannon and the dueling women's flailing arms, someone is bound to lose their bikini top, or at least some hair extensions. However, that may be the point at this juncture in the evening, especially with everyone's high saturation levels of tequila. I can't be sure about anyone else's motives, though, because all I want to do is wrap myself around Justin like a wily Kraken.

He has, over the course of the evening, gone straight for my jugular—and then backed off. In fact, he has me so worked up right now, I think my eyes are crossed. He is an expert at stoking the fire and has used every weapon in his arsenal. Sweet murmurs in my ticklish ear, hands grazing my back while telling innocuous stories, his casual yet possessive arm tucking me against his side when introducing me to new people, sexy glances that hint at pleasure and promise even more.

As we step in, submerging more of our legs with each advance down the stairs, there is a rambunctious splash containing four chicken fighters and a warrior's cry of victory. After this, the sputtering and laughing women decide to get out of the pool, followed shortly by the three men. How convenient. Now, it's just us and the otherworldly illumination of the water.

Justin has my hand as he leads me to the far edge of the pool, where it is dark and the water is almost chest deep. We are also somewhat hidden from the karaoke crew by a landscaping berm covered in decorative grass and brightly colored flowers. It's enchanting in here. The quiet in the pool almost echoes with its silence, making the movement of the water feel mystical. The artificial glow and shadows against Justin's angular face add to my sense of captivation. He looks imposing—and hungry.

When I decide to strike, he must have the same idea because we slap together like two opposing magnets. I push Justin against the wall with my hands threaded in his hair, kissing him with all the pent-up desire he spent the evening stoking. His hands slide down my back to my butt, and when they land there, he groans against my mouth.

"Fuuuuck. This ass," he says between kisses. When his hands move to the tied strings by my hips, first I panic, then I have an idea. It might abuse his predisposed nature, but I can see why having sexual power appeals so strongly to Sophia. I will give him a sliver of what he wants, but I'm going to get something in return.

"Justin," I whisper into the night. "I have four ties on my bikini, right?" He knows this because he is already slowly tugging the two by each hip. At his slow, almost savage nod, I continue, "I want to get to know you better, so I'm going to ask you some questions, and every time you give me a straight answer, I'll let you untie one knot. Ok?"

In answer, he slides one hand up to my bikini top and then drags his thumb roughly against my nipple. The movement of his thumb starts to ease the fabric triangle to the side, nearly exposing my breast.

"Silly girl. I don't need to untie anything," his near growl is playful, but he leaves out the *tisk, tisk, tisk*.

I back up before he can expose my nipple. "Just some questions, Justin. About your life, I'm not going to ask you to recite Pi or solve any quadratic equations or anything." The sizzle left from his hand on my breast prickles between my legs, and his erection is impossible to ignore. Seriously, it's impossible.

He rests his head back to ponder toward the night sky. It's as if he's weighing the feel of me intimately with whether to disclose a few things about himself. I'm not gonna lie, his hesitation drains away at my self-esteem a bit. Why is it so hard for him to reveal himself? What is he afraid I'll find out? Does he expect to hide the dark pieces of himself behind the ones that glow—and is that glow enough of a distraction to throw me off the scent? Wouldn't it be better to reveal yourself rather than hide?

Water droplets hang from a few wet strands of his hair before they drop one by one to caress their way down his chest. From this close vantage point, the dips above his collarbone, coupled with his tattoos—*Non Sibi, Sed Omnibus*—look so sexy that I can feel an ache in my throat. Why is he so guarded? What's up with this guy?

"Ok," he says finally. Resigned to his dreary fate, I suppose. "But I get to choose which tie, and just for the record, this is not simply to get your clothes off." He grins and then leans in to lick a tender line up the side of my neck. "That's just a perk."

I have so many questions to unpack I'm unsure where to start. I ease closer to him, pressing his need between us. I nibble his ear for a second while he slides his hands inside my bikini bottoms to grip my bare ass. His fingers are salaciously close to intimate skin, but for now, he keeps them on my rear. Whispering into his ear on an exhale, I ask, "Why aren't you a firefighter anymore?"

He captures my mouth with his, maybe to buy time to think about his answer or maybe to melt my bottoms off before needing to untie them at all. Either way, the effect on me is exhilarating. I didn't sleep with Daniel until our fifth date, but I'll tell you what, Justin *drips* sex appeal. It oozes out of him, and if he keeps this up, I will end up sleeping with him tonight. I won't have a single regret either, which will be a nice change for me.

He pauses our kissing but still holds me against the cannon between us. It's all I can do to *not* rock against it. "We had a particularly bad call. And after that, I didn't want anything to do with it," he says.

As suspected, his answer opens up even more questions for me. It's like puncturing a gut bag. That pause, or suspension of time for a hunter, before all the disgust surges out. There is much more to his story waiting just below the surface, pressure building. I guess it will take the right question to rupture the distended thing.

"A fire?" I ask before realizing I just carelessly burned through one of my questions.

"No. As first responders, Fire and Medics get called out at the same time. In fact, most of our calls were not fires at all." Then, his face widens into a devious grin as he tugs one string from each side of my swimsuit bottom. I can genuinely feel each strand of fabric as it finally gives up the fight against his slow, steady tug.

If I'm honest, I'd tell you I would have bet money on him undoing the ties on my top first. I'd also tell you that we are only recently alone in the pool, and the threat of company is ever present. And finally, I would tell you that in a blue-lit pool, the feeling of nakedness as my swimsuit bottom falls away is intensified by seven billion. The gentle movement of the water brushes against my bare skin, tickling at the raw parts and leaving me hyper-aware of the absence of cover.

I'm distracted from the predatory way he looks at me only by the slide of his hand between my legs. I gasp as his fingers make intimate contact. The touch is bold and salacious. He cradles my jaw with his other hand, looking me right in the eyes, and then pulls me into a kiss that swallows any further reaction to his explorative fingers.

"Spread your legs," he whispers into our kiss. When I do, he tickles a finger back and forth, not to penetrate, only to tease. Then he finds new territory and rubs little circles against it with his thumb.

I rest my forehead against his chin, and while openmouthed, I try to breathe, or gasp, or anything besides the suspended form of animation I'm currently caught in. Air is not coming or going from my lungs. It's like everything is on pause. All bodily systems held dormant. Everything except for the pressure that's steadily building against his fingers.

Then he does it. He slides a finger in. Even though it's just a finger, my warm resistance is evident, and I feel each tiny fraction of his advance. I wasn't expecting him to storm the castle right away, but I melt into the feel of him just the same. The thrill of the act, coupled with the stroking sensation against my g-spot is both anticipatory and wildly out of bounds. To my utter surprise, I moan into him. It's a quiet moan, but he hears it.

"Do you like that?" he asks, adding to the strum of his thumb against swollen nerve endings.

"Yes," is all I can manage, and it comes out hoarse at that.

"Do you want to come right here, on my fingers? Or would you rather do it on my tongue?" he asks. He is bold and assertive. I like his take-no-prisoners approach because, for him, there is no question about me getting off. The deliberation is only *where* I will do it.

The truth is, I don't want to come at all, not here when our aloneness is under constant threat. That little bit of self-awareness doesn't happen to slow my detonation point, though, and soon, I won't even need to answer him.

He withdraws his finger, and before I can make sense of what's happening, he lifts me out of the water and deposits me on the edge of the pool deck. He gently pushes me, directing me to lie back while he spreads my legs. He must feel me tense up because he says, "Don't worry, Norah, you're in the dark; only the inside of the pool is visible." I feel the breath of his reassurance against my exposed flesh, his words a soft breeze against wet skin. His intention runs down my neck and arms in the form of a billion little goosebumps. Then, his tongue is on me.

My thighs are on either side of his broad shoulders, with my feet dipping in the pool behind him. He has me spread open for his covetous mouth, and the chilly night air does nothing to cool the heat of his ownership. He flicks his tongue against me while he pushes my thighs further apart.

Somewhere in my brain, I'm aware that I'm acting like a restless whore, but I want this with a greed I can't describe. I've seen how he looks at me, and there is more heat behind Justin's eyes than all of my ex-boyfriends put together. I'm selfish. He is devastatingly sexy. So, I'm going to give in to this indiscretion.

He reverently groans as he directs a singular focus and blind talent toward my unguarded body. My spine arches, causing the backs of my shoulders to scrape across the pavement right before my climax shudders through me.

My jaw clenches tightly in an effort to keep quiet. While at the same time, I can feel myself pulsing against Justin's tongue.

He rests one palm on my stomach to hold me in place, it's unnecessary, though, because I couldn't move out of the way of an oncoming train right now. The droplets of water from his flattened hand curl around the skin of my waist and dollop somewhere beneath me. The tickling sensation caused by the rivulets of water helps to draw my focus away from the erratic, left-over spasms that remain from his talented tongue.

He speaks quietly as if to further bind me in place, "I'm not done yet," the words vibrating against my still-humming core. He lifts one of my thighs, placing my foot on the tiled edge of the pool. Then he changes his angle enough to lean forward and gently suck my *highly sensitized* flesh. At the same time, he glides two fingers inside to stroke my g-spot. It feels dirty and reckless. Dirty, reckless, and incredibly hot.

The combination of his fingers and mouth is so intense that my still-dangling leg tightens against his back, clamping him tightly against me. I think it's an effort to slow him down and ease the delirium brought on by his mouth. Part of me is trying to scoot away because it's too much at once, and the other part dissolves into the pool deck with shameless oblivion.

Within minutes, my orgasm hits like a wild clap of thunder. It comes on quickly and almost without warning, followed by the electrical rumblings of the lingering storm. I moan as my body tries to rock from side to side. I can't explain the need to rock, but it's a compulsion I can't fight.

Justin holds my thighs steady as though he's not yet fully ready for me to move. A heady groan rolls out of me without my permission. In fact, it comes out despite my explicit need not to draw any attention to the darkened shadows. He is relentless, though, coaxing every last shudder from my limp body.

Once I finally still, it's like he's drained the marrow from my bones—or effectively sucked the life force out of me. My back feels a little raw from the kiss of the pavement, but my attention is on how Justin just utterly claimed my body. Even though I'm splayed out in the shadows, potentially on full display, I can't close my legs—I can't even get control of my panting breaths yet.

Luckily, the crowd is behind me, and there are large boulders and pretty landscaping surrounding the pool because I don't completely trust the darkened shadows with my gratified and glistening self.

Soon, Justin eases me back into the pool, boneless and sated, where I wrap my arms and legs around him. Even the smallest movements create exquisite contact because of the indecent positioning of my body and its heightened perception. I'm glad his arms support me because I wouldn't be able to hold myself up on my own—not even to save me from drowning.

Entirely spent, I dissolve into our kiss, tasting the carnality of his performance on his lips. I'm acutely aware of feeling something akin to mania, and I will *never* be able to look at his mouth again without remembering this gold medal performance. The silky glide of his kiss is tender and poetic, even though it's the same tongue that just brought me to the edge of a cliff and then shoved me over. Twice.

"I feel alive again, Norah," he says in the space between the press of our lips. He shifts his position so he's holding me with one forearm wrapped around the small of my back while my legs circle his hips. With his free hand, he slides his fingers into the ponytailed back of my hair to cup my head. With the progression of his hand comes the yank of hair follicles as his fingers forge through unyielding, wet strands.

"There you are! I was starting to think you ditched me here," Sophia says from the other side of the pool. We both turn to look at her. Our lusty haze must damn near emblazon us with a corona of ethereal light, lighting us up like the Messiah. If she notices I'm half-naked and clinging to Justin like a tree frog, she doesn't mention it.

"The neighbors complained to the five-oh, so we had to shut down karaoke. Right in the middle of my perfect lyrical rendition of *Love is a Battlefield*."

"Ok," Justin and I both say in unison. I'm not sure if we mean, ok, no more karaoke, no more Pat Benatar, no more stealthy making out in the pool...

"There are just a few of us left, so I'll be up on the patio with them," she says over her shoulder as she walks away, completely unaffected by what she may or may not have witnessed. I'm sure she saw us kissing, but we may never know whether or not she knows the sopping wet mound of fabric sitting innocently on the edge of the pool is my swimsuit bottom. Justin's body shields me from any wayward glances, but I need to stop playing around and get dressed.

"And I was just getting to second base," he says with a handsome smile as he disengages his hand from the back of my hair and places it on my breast instead. He glides his thumb over the fabric in a way that, again, moves the bikini top to the side. With my nipple on the verge of popping out from under the fabric, he thumbs it back and forth, then says, "I understand if you need to get back to your friend, but you and I? We've only just begun."

The synapses firing from my nipple to the pleasure-seeking control center of my brain have already formed the words, *take me to your bedroom* on my lips, but what comes out is from the more pragmatic hemisphere, "Yeah, we should probably get back to our friends." The thought about us in his bedroom sprinkles to the ground like fine powder, having not made it past my lips at all.

I think we both realize our separate obligations, his as the party's host and mine as Sophia's friend, so we begrudgingly right ourselves. First, Justin hands me my swimsuit bottoms. Then he adjusts his ferocious hard-on. When he glances into my eyes again, a wolfish look takes the place of the previous unrequited one, making me blush in the darkness. He takes my hand and says, "Come on, Norah, the masses await."

Chapter 19

JUSTIN

Davis thought blazing up the fire pit was a good idea—God knows why. It still feels like eighty degrees out here. Six of us remain, four with marshmallows presently on skewers and the other two nursing beers. For me, the transition to beer was a natural one because I'm up to my eyeballs in salt and lime juice.

The other couple rounding out Norah, Sophia, Davis, and myself is my buddy Grouse, whose real name is Tyler, and his wife, Amanda. It's a fun group, even though Grouse keeps eyeballing Norah's nipples over the fire pit. It was bound to happen because she only had a tank top to put over her wet bathing suit. I offered her something more substantial, which she refused, apparently not realizing the effect nipples have on men.

The additional bit of knowledge shared between us, is that she didn't put her bikini bottoms back on before sliding her tattered cutoffs over her perfect ass. She said she didn't want to sit around with damp bikini bottoms on, though I suspect her motives may have been a bit more devious. The true motive probably was to hold my attention in a vice grip and hardly allow me to form coherent words.

My familiarity with her body, the crotch of which is hardly covered and probably visible from the leg of her shorts, is driving me toward lunacy. It's hard not to think about her soft skin without imagining myself buried deep inside, rooting like a feral hog.

"Jester, tell everyone how you calmed that kid down after he fractured his femur," Grouse says to Davis as he places a graham cracker on top of his heat-enlarged marshmallow and then hands the completed s'more to his wife.

Davis laughs, "It's an old parlor trick, really, but it never gets old." He takes a slug of his beer and continues, "I handed him my leg and asked him to hold it for me." Every one of us is a little tuned up from the free-flowing margaritas, so we all laugh uproariously at Davis' retelling of the story.

Amanda licks melted chocolate off her fingers and then asks, "Davis, when will you stop tormenting poor, unsuspecting kids with your fake leg?"

"The short answer to that is, never. But trust me, he wasn't tormented. He wanted to know every gory detail about how it happened. Then, he wanted to hear everything else about being a soldier. But I'll tell you what, he let me set and splint his leg, and fracture reduction of a compound femur break is no joke, even with pain meds on board. That kid was a beast."

While Davis continues the story about the little boy who was hit by a car while riding his bike, he predictably gives far more details than are strictly necessary. I take Norah's hand, sliding my fingers easily between hers. When she looks over at me, I wink and then ask if I can get her anything. She nods and then widens her eyes while glancing down at my lap.

I'm too much of a gentleman to throw her over my shoulder and run up the stairs to my bedroom, but I'm not saying I didn't think about it.

"I'll get you some water," I say instead, unable to hide the delight spreading across my face. After asking if anyone else wants anything from inside, I take my lustful feelings into the house to replenish the thirsty guests.

I stand in front of the open refrigerator for a solid two minutes before the blood starts to detour away from my half-hard dick. Then, after grabbing a variety of beers and bottles of water, I head back outside to face the crew who has made themselves so comfortable in my Adirondack chairs—only one of which I want to hang out with.

I place the cold water bottle right where Norah's thighs meet, and if it weren't for the cutoffs, the bottle's chill would be right against her bare skin. She gasps and clamps her legs shut at the same time while I hand out the rest of the beverages. The length of her shorts and the lack of any discernable inseam all but ensure that the glacial chill finds her warm skin and kisses it intimately.

***

After what started as begrudging acquiescence for me, hanging out with everyone has been enjoyable. The reluctance I had initially felt has gradually morphed into something else. The last couple of hours have been full of laughter, stolen glances, and mounting sobriety. Well, except for Davis. He is as drunk as a tavern rat. It's nothing to be concerned about, just par for the course. We both know he is crashing here, so the alarming rate at which his tongue thickens doesn't bother me too much. It has been a long time since I've seen him this drunk, so his slide back into his long-lost Australian accent is all the more hilarious.

"I'd like to draw everyone's attention to how happy this fucker finally is," Davis slaps me on the knee, and I inwardly cringe, wondering what his drunk ass is up to. "And, I'd also like to point out that I am responsible for the changing tides. No, no, hold your applause becau—"

"Shut up, Jester. Let's just be happy for him," Grouse says in a valiant effort to shut Davis's trap before he makes Norah uncomfortable.

"No, I want to hear this," Sophia says, opening the floodgate right back up. Davis certainly isn't holding anything back from her. Between the matter of Anna being here earlier and the fact that he is idiot drunk right now, he must be making an appalling impression on her.

"See, Soph wants to hear the story," Davis announces self-righteously before continuing. "You see, I'm the one who insisted the poor bastard get the service in the first place." Norah suddenly sits forward, tuning in. *Fuck.* I want to be the one to tell her this stuff, not this blistering asshole. Plus, Grouse and Amanda don't know about the service. I don't want them to think she is anything less than a girlfriend—certainly not a paid-for service.

"Yeah, I told her my pimply-faced, impotent friend forced me to set it up," I cut him off before he can spill any more of my secrets.

"No, you said it was your *micro-penised* friend," Norah corrects. Whether she is reading my cues or trying to be funny, I don't care because that shuts him up for a second. Everyone laughs, and if I could bottle up the tart look on Davis' face, I would market that shit worldwide.

"*Micro-penised?*" Davis asks, rolling the term around in his mouth before squaring his jaw, ready for battle. "I don't have a micro-penis, Bro. You know that as well as anyone else."

"Easy, Anaconda. We are just messing with you," I say, mollifying him for the moment. Thankfully, the comment derailed his train of thought. He turns to Sophia, probably to convince her of his bigger than average dick size. On that note, Grouse and Amanda stand in unison and begin gathering empty bottles and cast-off lids.

"We better get going; it's late," Amanda explains while Grouse busies himself, dumping an armload of beer bottles noisily into the recycle bin on the side of my house. This is a good time to wind everything down, before the wheels completely fall off.

I turn to Norah before bringing our clasped hands to my lips and kissing her knuckles gently, "Do you want to stay? Or do you need to go home with Sophia?" She hesitates a few beats while my inner monologue chants, *Stay! Stay! Stay!*

"I should go with her." She takes a long pause, long enough that I hope she's changed her mind. "I mean, I *want* to stay. But I better not."

"Ok, babe, that's fine," I say. *What the hell! I just called her babe.* It just popped out, and now I probably sound like some dip-shit that calls everyone that. On her part, she leans her head back against the Adirondack chair and smiles wistfully. "Want me to get you an Uber, or are you guys alright to drive?"

"We're good. I'll help clean up before we leave, though," she says as she stands up and stretches. Her bare stomach flashes for a second, calling my attention to the imminent fact that I'm going to have to jerk off multiple...multiple times tonight.

"No, don't worry about that. I'll get it tomorrow," I say before wrapping my arm around her shoulders and leading her inside, away from Davis and Sophia.

Once we get in the house, I envelop her in my arms and plant a lingering kiss on her juicy mouth. Then, perhaps to slacken my curiosity, perhaps because I can't keep my hands off of her, I slide my fingers up her inner thigh and then inside the crotch of her cutoffs. The back of my knuckles instantly grazes against her smooth skin. I was right, she *had* to have been visible from the leg of her shorts. At least she was concealed by the fire pit's height and the Adirondack chair's backward slope.

She moans an exhale as my fingers get acquainted, and the sound makes my balls throb. "Are you sure you shouldn't stay tonight?"

"You see? This is what I meant when I said you were dangerous," she says as she smiles against my lips, just before Davis and Sophia make their untimely appearance inside. I withdraw my hand, but only to be respectful of Norah. If it were up to me, I would get her off once or twice before sending her home.

When Davis and Sophia are distracted with their playful banter and cursory bottle collection, I bring my fingers to my mouth. She watches me with glassy eyes and gauzy covered lust. My feelings for her have long ago crossed the line of her employment. In fact, that line is so far behind us that it's not even visible in the distance. I hope she knows that she means more to me than any service could ever provide. And that she will never work for me again. I'm keeping the service, mind you, but she won't be here in a working capacity anymore.

It feels like I've known her for a long time, much longer than a handful of weeks. Even though tonight put us on the fast track in the space of a day, I have no intention of slowing down. I want to know everything there is to know about her. I want to devour her. Inhale her.

120

Bathe in her. I want to forget about everything. Everything except the two of us.

I only hope when she finally knows everything about me, she doesn't run for the hills without so much as a glance back at the scorched earth behind her.

Chapter 20

Norah

Good Lord, if that dude were any more skilled with a woman's body, he would have chicks following him around like the Pied fucking Piper. Every conversation or line of thought I have had for the last three days eventually makes its way right back to *him*. I'm a scattered mess. Things start out normal, like buttering toast or helping a client set rollers in her hair, and then my stream of consciousness inevitably goes to the feel of Justin's tongue along my jawline or the touch of his fingers. Just thinking about the brightness of his eyes and the flop of his hair when it's not combed back into its hip undercut style is enough to glaze my eyes over.

Luckily, Sophia is just as enamored with Davis. Even though her impression of him is clouded by the likelihood that he is a manwhore of the highest order, not to mention a potential drunk. But, at least she is going in with her eyes wide open. It's also possible that they are two peas in a pod. Two people who mirror each other as closely as the two of them have to be rare. I thought they broke the mold after making Sophia, but it appears I may have been wrong.

Last weekend answered a few niggling questions I had about Justin, but it also blew the doors off of something big. Something is up with him. Something massive. Something that all his friends know but no one will talk about—at least not openly. I knew I should have pressed Davis when he was all hammered and loose-lipped, but the change in Justin's demeanor had been so dramatic that it stopped me from wanting to hear it at all, at least from a drunk, gossiping, blabbermouth. Not to mention, that guy, Grouse, had practically thrown himself on the fire pit to change the subject.

When it's time, I want to hear whatever it is from Justin himself. The fact that his friends choose to tippy-toe around whatever it is that makes Justin clam up only adds fuel to the fire of my burning curiosity.

For now, however, his latest text has prevented me from working on my resume for the last three hours. And once I respond to it, the one after that will guarantee the dusty state of my laptop. I hadn't wanted to respond to his text right away, lest I appear sex-crazed and obsessed with him, which, of course, I am. But also, I am not quite sure how to respond because, despite our behavior at his pool party, we are not exactly a couple.

He has done nothing to woo me or let on that he is interested in anything beyond sex. I prefer to be, I don't know, courted? Is that the right word? I'm not interested in being one of many or simply a conquest for him, and so far, I'm not sure where I fall on that spectrum.

It had been like severing my arm when I left his place on Saturday night, but I needed to establish that I was not like all the other women who rotate through his front door. Sex is easy, but emotions are not so freely handed over, and I am unlikely to proceed with one in the absence of the other.

Anyway, like I said, his text sucked the productivity right out of my day and rendered me nearly useless. It also set me back a quantum leap concerning my steely resolve. This is what it said, all twelve times I read it:

Justin: *I can't stop thinking about you. About how badly I want to run my lips down your body, stopping to tickle the inside of your thighs with my day-old stubble. I think about your broken moans and how your back arches and your legs shake against me. Then, I think about how I would tease you until you beg me for more. How I would hold your arms above your head, pinning your wrists and looking you in the eyes when I find your eagerness. About how, when I enter you, you'll feel every inch of me as I let you adjust, inch by exquisite inch. About how you'll gasp in my ear with my first thrust. Then, I think about moving and grinding, making your body writhe in ecstasy. And how I will take you slow and sweet, then hard and fast. After that, I think about how you will call out my name and come so hard that I can almost see your soul leave your body.*

What? Damn auto-correct! I meant, 'Good morning, Beautiful.'

See what I mean? That's tough to ignore, no matter how much I want to know him better and develop emotional intimacy before going any further down that road. I suppose it wouldn't be the worst thing—to go ahead and throw down with him, and forget about a relationship, but it's not my usual MO.

I attempted and failed to type a sexy response no less than eight times. I tried something as trite as *that sounds hot.* After that, I attempted to swing wildly in the other direction with, *I wish I had you in my mouth right now.* Then there was the, *you should come over here and do everything you described.* But nothing I came up with sounded good. All my responses were horribly amateur when held up in the light of his erotic dissertation. I mean, how *does* one counter that? It's like he is trying to start a sexual revolution between my legs. He really is, but now the militia is beginning to lay down their arms because they are no longer interested in fighting. There is very little to no resistance left in me against Justin and his filthy, talented mouth.

I give up trying to be sexy because, frankly, it's of no use. He and I are in vastly different leagues. So, I text back: *That's a little heavy-handed, isn't it?*

Justin: *Did you just say you like a heavy hand?* Of course, his reply is instant because he doesn't need to draft twenty responses to find a good one. He didn't even have much time to think about it before firing a response back.

Me: *Sorry, I'm not paying attention. I'm too busy thinking about having sex with you.* Well… with that, it looks like I'm going all in. But screw him *and* the horse he rode in on because I'm squirming in my chair, and *he* is probably sitting at his desk…laughing.

Justin: *Me too! In fact, my imagination is fucking you like crazy right now. I mean, CRAZY.*

Me: *…*

Justin: *Norah?*

Me: *What?*

Justin: *I'm fucking you like all your ex-boyfriends are watching.*

Me: **Sigh.*

Justin: *Come over tonight?*

Me: *I can't. I promised Sophia I'd go with her to get the rest of her stuff back from her loser ex-boyfriend.*

Justin: *Ok, tomorrow night?*

Me: *Can't. I'm going to the baseball game.*

Justin: *Damn, Woman.*

Me: *But Friday, I have poor, sweet Mr. Abernathy at the very end of my workday. I'll bring the wine, you cook dinner.*

Justin: *You got it. I hope you like Pop Tarts and chicken nuggets.*

Me: *Mmmmmmm, delicious.*

***

So, I spent the last five days wrought with muddled thinking and dodgy expectations, and I'm not too sure if, or where I've landed. Sex tonight is a guarantee. That portion of my fate is sealed…in granite, and I have never been happier—or hair-free, lotioned, and polished up.

Justin and I have been texting during the work days and talking on the phone like two teenage girls every night. His texts and calls have mostly been playful. In fact, some of them have bordered on sweet, and surprisingly, they haven't all been sexual in nature. Some, sure—but not all. He threw me off when he wanted to know about my family and my goals and aspirations. Really, his interest in me as a person put a pin in all the sexy talk and spun me on my head.

Does he want to get to know more of me than just my O-face? At first, I would have said no, but now? Now, he is different. He is opening up to me and sharing parts of himself much more fluidly than before. Don't misunderstand, he is still a big, fat mystery to me, but the crack in his armor is expanding.

I don't know what to expect once I go inside. Will he pin me up against the wall before even saying hello? Or will he envelop me in a sweet hug and ask how my day was? The fact is, I haven't the foggiest idea. He knows I'm free for the rest of the evening. He also knows that sex is a green light. So, wherever Justin falls within the gradation of his moods will be a surprise to me.

It turns out, he's neither of those two extremes. When he opens the door, he's on the phone. He gives me a wink and then turns around to pace the living room, still grappling with whoever he is on the phone with.

I walk into the kitchen to put the wine in the fridge and notice the bin of cleaning supplies on the counter. How cute, he cleaned for me. The guy lives alone, so I'm not sure why it catches me off guard that he cleans his house, but it does. Also, he has told me quite a bit about his mother, and it sounds like she may have had a little streak of OCD in her. At the very least, she liked things in order. Some of that must have trickled down to Justin because his house is always clean. Seriously, always.

After hanging up, Justin comes behind me and hugs me while nibbling on my earlobe. His breath in my ear canal makes me shiver before turning around.

"Hi, Norah."

"H—" I can't respond because he grabs my face and gives me a hot yet abbreviated kiss. I can taste his minty gum, and for some reason, it makes me wish he went with option one, to pin me up against the wall before even saying hello.

I can sense the shower on him. It smells like an Irish glen that I want to roll around in. He's wearing a blue and white Henley, beat-up Diesel jeans, and he is barefoot, which is somehow even sexier. He is comfortable and at home—and he's about to make me feel *really* comfortable, too.

"I see you cleaned the house for our date," I tease, even though I'm happy he wants to impress me.

"Nah, the cleaners were here this morning. Do I get you all to myself tonight?" he asks while glancing down at his watch. I nod my head as a big, stupid grin overtakes my face.

"Perfect. But I need to jump on a conference call real quick. Can you entertain yourself for fifteen minutes or so?" he asks, before adding, "I'm sorry, this wasn't scheduled, but I still have to deal with it." Then he waggles his eyes, "I'll make it up to you."

"It's ok, go. I'm sure I'll find something to do." This time, his kiss isn't so rushed, and I can feel myself unwind against him.

With a parting kiss, he steps back and then charges up the stairs to his new office. I pour myself a glass of wine and then sit on the couch. I'd rather watch TV than snoop around his house. Too bad his remote controls the International Space Station. Why do guys need all these electrical components? I don't even know what half of this stuff is.

Once I succeed in turning the thing on, it comes as no surprise to me that the ESPN channel is the one that lights up the screen. After some initial trial and error, I finally navigate to something with fewer announcers caught in heated debates about athletes and their tiresome stats. Then, I settle in and make myself comfortable. The wine is smooth and buttery and goes down far too easily, but if I'm to keep my wits about me, I better hold off on becoming the wino my palate seems to demand of me lately.

After I get situated, but before I get sucked into the home remodeling show, I notice little handprints all over the bottom of the expansive front window. The whole image strikes me as odd and completely out of place for Justin's house. I would expect to see baby gates and cabinet safety latches accompanying such prints. Justin has none of that, not even a single outlet cover. Maybe he hasn't lived here that long, and they are left over from the previous owners. It's odd, though, because the rest of his house is so clean, and let's not forget the speckle of obsessive-compulsive disorder that ran through his mom.

Now that I've noticed the handprints, it's distracting. He has actual cleaners that come to the house. I can't believe they missed them. I can't believe Justin and his OCD mom missed them. Are people so preoccupied these days? I mean, I'm no neat freak, but the messy prints would have driven me crazy on at least a bi-weekly basis.

As I'm wiping the glass cleaner off the window pane, I hear Justin roar, "Norah! No!" It startles me so badly that I jump away from the window while he charges toward it. I'm shocked and angry that he would scream at me like that, but the indignance drains straight out of me when I see him pressed up against the glass, his palms resting against the remaining handprints.

He is sobbing and pawing at the window. I have never seen a man come so completely unglued. It's disorienting for me. Justin doesn't even seem like himself. All that cocky swagger and good-natured teasing—vanished, gone. All I can do is stand here frozen, with my hand over my racing heart and my eyes as wide as they can get. The intensity of the atmosphere in the room is like the sudden deafening roar of trumpets.

"Jax, honey, I'm so sorry. Please, God, no. You have to stop. Stop, those are my baby's handprints. Jax, I'm sorry. I'm so sorry." Justin is weeping, and as his grief-stricken words penetrate my consciousness, I, too, begin to cry. "Jax, don't be sad, I didn't know. I'm sorry, son," Justin snivels against the glass.

Burning hellfire! This man lost his son. And I just managed to wipe away half of his precious child's handprints. Now, my tears truly let go.

Justin isn't mad at me. He is completely and totally devastated. The scene of his desolation anchors me in place. I want to go to him, but I don't think he even registers that I'm here.

Annihilate:

Verb

To destroy utterly. To obliterate.

Chapter 21

JUSTIN

It's dark by the time I can get myself under control. Sharp intakes of breath now take the place of the baleful sobs that wracked my body for what feels like the last century. My eyes are swollen, I know that much. I also know my face is slick with drying tears. It feels like I'm in a suspended coma, yet awake. I blink slowly.

On some level, I'm aware that my head is in Norah's lap as she tenderly and repeatedly brushes the hair away from my face. It's more of a caress, really, it's soothing and gentle. I feel empty and wrung out from what had to have been a pretty substantial mental breakdown. I must have scared Norah because I haven't been that distraught in a long time. Usually, I can hold it together enough to exist in life, but that—that wasn't holding anything together.

I should have told her. How could I not have told her? It's too much a part of who I am to hide it. I wasn't exactly hiding it, though.

I just wanted to keep her a little longer before I drove her away. She's different. I wanted this to be different.

Everything was going so well. I was genuinely doing better, and I could see a light in my future for the first time in three years. For all those years, the heaviness had been so oppressive I thought I would never crawl out from under it. But then there was a glimmer. A tiny glimmer. As small as ground up pixie dust at first, but it was there.

Then, the tiny glimmer of light started to grow—incrementally at first, but I noticed it just the same. I caught myself smiling a few times, my cheek muscles stiff from neglect. The pain etched into my face seemed to be lessening—the dark circles, lightning. The agony will never go away; I don't expect it to, but for once, there was the tiniest sliver of hope that I might live again.

But now, that tiny sliver is starting to fray. She won't want any part of this life, and who could blame her?

And yet, she is still here. It's been hours. At first, she held me against her. She was also crying because the magnitude of what she had done was too much to bear. I think she spoke in the beginning, while she held me, apologies or endearments—I'm not sure anymore. Or maybe she sang? I'm pretty sure she rocked me too. Dwarfed by my size, she had simply swayed while holding my head to her chest. I remember focusing on her heartbeat while trying to get my breathing back to a normal rhythm. It was soothing. She was soothing.

She feels me stir, then stops toying with my hair, instead gently caressing my cheek with her thumb. The tenderness of the act gets caught in my throat, where it feels like brittle sticks have lodged.

She is still here.

I move my free arm around her waist, wanting to hold her instead of the pathetic other way around. I need to reverse our roles and negate this pile of weakness on her lap. Whatever the last couple of hours have reduced me to is an unwelcome intruder. I am not this guy. I am not a blubbering mass of hysteria. I don't let people see me lose my shit. I am a man for fuck's sake.

When my palm brushes against the skin at the base of Norah's shirt, it's not enough contact. I crawl up her body, backing her down against the floor and raising her shirt as I go. A few fevered kisses land on her chest and neck before I descend on her mouth.

She cups my face in her hands, pushing me away from her lips, and whispers, "Justin, I'm so sorry." Her eyes fill with tears again before they breach the lids and trickle across her temples. I'm upset she did what she did, but not angry. I'm only sad—sad that some of Jax has been erased. It's not her cross to bear, though; it's mine.

I don't answer her because there is nothing to say. I only work her shirt the rest of the way up and over her head. The last few hours have been strangely cathartic. If catharsis is even possible for people like me. My connection to her feels stronger, more hopeful, perhaps even fated. I can't explain it well, but now it almost feels like she shoulders my burden with me.

I'm pawing at her bra, all of a sudden not sure how to remove it, while she tugs my shirt over my head. Giving up on the bra but needing to feel her skin against mine, I yank the lace down, freeing her breasts. I drop my mouth, sucking and tugging harder than I usually would, but her frenzy matches mine.

I kiss a savage trail up her neck, hungrily finding her mouth as my hands move to her breasts. She groans into my mouth, emboldening me. I shift to one elbow, so I can unbutton my fly and shove my jeans and boxer briefs down my thighs. My erection is painful and engorged, thick and delirious.

Norah starts to shove her shorts down, then stops to palm my raging hard-on. The touch is reckless and determined, it makes me hiss and then groan with desperation.

"Justin, I need you," she gasps as she runs her palm up and down my length. I almost explode with the declaration. The words mark her as my prize, and I'm ready to claim her. I tug her shorts the rest of the way off, and I'm not gentle when I do it, either. Norah is not looking for gentleness right now. She is just as rabid as I am.

I settle between her thighs, swiping her readiness with the head of my dick before pressing forward. The clench of her body is rapturous, and I ache for the full, encompassing promise of it. I bore into her, stretching her, filling her.

Her moan is one of pleasure, but it's laced with pain. *Shit!* I'm hurting her. I haven't given her time to accommodate my fervor. I should have ensured she was ready for me instead of rutting like a bull.

"I'm sorry, Norah," I pant as I pull out. She says something, but my kiss swallows it. This time, my advance is not that of a barbarian. I ease in, only a couple of inches at first, and then drag myself back, feeling the euphoric suction her body provides. I press in a little further this time, then drag myself out.

"Justin, do it. I need all of you," she groans as she starts to writhe beneath me. My plunge is deep this time, but I've yet to bottom out. Her little vocalizations are driving me mad with need. I ramp up, my slide getting faster, harder, and deeper.

She brings the back of her wrist to her mouth and bites down on it while the fingernails of her other hand tighten against my back. She loops an ankle over my ass, pulling me tighter against her with each thrust. I can't get deep enough for either of us—like I'm not enough of a part of her yet.

I slap her hand away from her mouth and grin down at her, "Don't do that," I pant, "I want to hear you." The sweat beads up on my forehead as her face begins to twist into a familiar expression.

"Justin, it's so good," she breathes right before she lets out the sexiest moan. Her moan quickly evolves into a raspy cry, like her throat is scratched apart, "Yes! Like that—" the rest of her words garble into the crook of my neck because she squeezes me tightly against her sweaty body.

When she comes, I ride out the tight pulses that methodically clamp down on me. Then I grind my pelvis against her for a few seconds before emptying myself in deep, coursing surges. It's only when my teeth clench in a riotous climax that I realize I should have pulled out first. For that matter, I should have put on a rubber.

We lie together in a crumpled heap on the walnut floor with our pulses still racing. After a few minutes of throaty breathing, I roll us to the side, hugging her to my chest. I cradle her against me and then tip her chin up.

I kiss her with a sweetness that wasn't present while I pumped and slammed into her. It's the tenderness she deserves. I kiss her until I'm unsure whose breath fills my lungs or whose blood courses through my veins. I need this woman. And that scares me to death.

Upon further reflection, that is *not* how our first time should have gone down. I don't exactly regret it, but I certainly have some atoning to do. The next time will be better.

Chapter 22

Norah

I literally have sex dripping out of my body. For the first time in my life, too. Usually, it's neatly contained and then properly disposed of. I can smell the warmth of it—it binds us together. We lie still for a couple more minutes before Justin starts ramping up again.

The desperation is not present this time. Now, it's as if he is apologizing. He has nothing to apologize for, though. That was the grittiest, most real sex I have ever had, and the amount of emotion poured into it felt, I don't know, transformative, maybe?

Something huge just happened, and I don't mean the sex—not even the unprotected sex. I mean, I feel like he will finally let me in. It's like a wrecking ball crashed through him, and now I can see his soul from the inside. He may not have wanted to let me in initially, but I can see a shift in his disposition. It's almost like he is *relieved*.

I can't think of why losing a child needed to be such a closely guarded secret, but now Davis and Grouse's conversation about Justin being happy makes more sense. He must be so sad, so broken.

While he kisses me, his hand slides down my body, finding the slippery remnants of our sex between my legs. He glides his fingers through the mutual wetness, then teases me as he dallies with both my body and my self-control. When he slides a finger in, my eyes flutter closed.

"I'm sorry, I should have asked earlier. Are you on any kind of birth control?" Though a day late and a dollar short with his question, I can't answer right away because now his fingers move in earnest. When I roll my head back against the floor, arching my back, he shifts his position to add his thumb to the mix, rubbing silky ejaculate over highly sensitized flesh.

I find his erection, already at full salute, and begin stroking it. After a few indulgent seconds, he stops me by leaning in and whispering, "Norah, this is for you. Lie still."

"I am," I wheeze.

"Lying still? Or on birth control?" he chuckles, but it seems like a silly question because I'm clearly not being still. I'm squirming like an upside-down hamster. Justin can get my body humming faster and better than anyone ever has. He is gifted, he knows all the right spots, and the fact that he obviously enjoys getting me off is another tantalizing perk to this man.

"I'm on birth control," I grind out. It's the last thing I say before pinching my lips together, effectively silencing myself against the building turmoil. I know he's watching me, studying every sound and taking in each facial expression. It makes me self-conscious for him to inspect me this closely while working me up like this.

He leans down, bringing his lips close enough to brush against the pinch of mine, "You have to stop that, Norah. I told you I want to hear you when you come. Just thinking about your little sounds and vocalizations gets me hard."

I scrunch up my forehead and nod enthusiastically before crying out something about his name and God and then anointing his industrious fingers.

Twenty minutes later, he breaks our kiss and rises to lean on his forearm. He keeps his hand on my breast, thumbing my nipple while looking into my eyes. The savage look from earlier is gone from his face. Now, he looks peaceful. Content.

"Norah, there is something I need to tell you. It's not fair for me to keep eluding it," the pinch in his forehead reads crestfallen, and it breaks my heart.

"I know," I whisper, bringing my hand up to his face. He grasps it, holding it against his lips to softly kiss. "I know you lost a child. A son." Now it's my face that scrunches. I'm trying not to cry again, but my heart breaks for him. I can't even imagine how much he has suffered.

"No. I mean, yes. But that's not all of it," he says, resigned to telling me more. As much as I want to know everything, as much as I have tried to decode him and figure him out, I don't want to hear it. Not now, when he feels like he *has* to tell me. I don't want to know anything more until he is truly ready to divulge it.

"You don't have to tell me anything, Justin. I know you will in time."

"I don't feel good about sucking you into my life without having all the information. As much as I want you here, with me, it has to be your decision, Norah."

"I've made my decision. I want to be with you, too. Justin, I don't care what you have done, what accident you feel responsible for, or whatev—"

"Stop. I know what you're thinking. I was not responsible for my son's death. Not directly, anyway. It's something bigger than that, and you need to know…so you can decide for yourself," he states plainly.

"Ok," I whisper, trying to swallow a lump of saliva down my suddenly inhospitable, dry throat.

"I will tell you everything, but can we get off the floor first? My knees and elbows hate me," he says as he starts to get up. "I'm not trying to buy time either. I have finally yielded to the notion that I'm being selfish by not telling you. I fully plan to lay the whole messy thing out there for you. Just not here, on the floor."

"Should we eat something first? Or have some wine?" I ask. Now I'm back peddling, afraid of what he'll say. Avoiding this monumental declaration might be in my best interest. Why would something change my mind about wanting to be with him? This is only the beginning of a relationship. What could possibly be so bad that he needs to unselfishly confess it to me? Whatever it is, it hasn't stopped his friends from remaining by his side. Why should it affect me any differently?

"If you want to. Are you hungry?" he asks a little timidly. Maybe he is afraid of losing his nerve with a momentum change.

"To be honest, I'm not hungry at all. Let's go talk in your bedroom," I say, wanting to forget this hardwood floor and the scuff of it against my back. I also think it's a good idea to talk in a different space. We need to get away from tiny fingerprints and the lingering haze of both desolation and carnality.

I hope he is blowing everything out of proportion, and whatever he has to say is not that bad. I can't think of anything that would make me want to bolt, but clearly, he expects me to. Maybe if he has some sort of felony charge against him or something, but even then, I would still consider dating him. Well, depending on the charge, I guess. But the guy is not in prison, so the crime couldn't be that bad. Right?

"I'm not hungry either. Get dressed, and we'll go upstairs," he says as he fastens the row of buttons on the fly of his jeans. It's true, what he says, that he is not hungry. In fact, it looks like he's going to throw up.

Chapter 23

JUSTIN

We walk into my bedroom, and I close the door behind us. I'm not sure why. Maybe I did it subconsciously because I don't want her to leave. If there were a lock on the door, I'd lock it too. Her suggestion to come to my room caught me off guard because being in my bedroom makes the whole confession more intimate. It's not as sterile as sitting on my couch, which is where I planned to take her.

It's nearing ten o'clock, and I was supposed to cook dinner tonight. I have everything I need for bacon-wrapped pork tenderloin and roasted vegetables. That was my mom's favorite. I think I chose that meal as a way of including her in my budding relationship with Norah. The budding relationship that's about to crash and burn.

"Can I say something first?" she asks as she sits down tentatively on the foot of my bed. I cross the room to her and take her hands in mine as I sit beside her. She looks the way I feel, like everything is perfect right now, but in a matter of minutes, everything's going to implode.

145

"Of course, you can." It breaks my heart that she is so nervous right now. I'm not sure what she expects to hear from me, but I'm not a serial killer or anything.

"Justin." She stops and clears her throat, "I'm so sorry I cleaned some of his fingerprints off the window. I will never forgive myself for taking that piece of your son away from you," her throat hitches, and I realize how hard she is taking the whole thing. I pull her against me. I'm beside myself that some of Jax's little handprints are gone, but being angry won't get us anywhere. I certainly can't rage-force them back onto the window. I'll adjust to it. I have to.

I sigh, "Norah, you didn't know. It's my fault, too. I should have told you."

She crumples into her palms, crying while I rub her back. I don't know what to do because we are both upset about it. My touch is ineffectual, but I have no idea how to soothe her, not when it comes to this. I can't soothe myself about Jax—never will be able to, let alone another person.

"It's not only what I did," she sniffles as she sits back up, "I'm just so sorry…it's so sad… that you lost your son. I can't even imagine the hell you are in, and I want so badly to take that pain away from you," she says while swiping her fingers under her eyes to wipe away the tar from her weeping mascara.

I drop my head, but the tears don't come. The well is dry. One thing I notice immediately about her words, though, is that she acknowledges *the hell I'm in,* as in, currently and forever. Most people are sorry for *what I went through,* as though it's over and all in the past. She gets it. I don't even need to explain it to her.

"It's the worst thing in the world," I manage. Then the tears do come.

***

We are lying on my bed. I'm in nothing but my jeans, with both knees bent and my feet on top of the comforter. Norah is next to me. Both of us stare at the ceiling in affable silence. Our hands are clasped together, her right and my left. It's been at least twenty minutes since either of us has uttered a word.

Norah doesn't seem pushy or demanding—not like other women. She is fine lying here with me in a supportive role without having to fill the silence with some sort of brilliant epiphany.

I'm drawing more strength from her than she realizes. Not strength to get over my loss, but strength to look toward the future with some semblance of hope. She is that speck of light in a world of darkness. And that speck—that glimmer, is starting to gain traction, which is why I'm hesitant to pull the pin on the grenade. I want to keep her. I want this glimmer of hope to eventually spread into genuine happiness. I deserve to be happy because, most assuredly, my despair didn't bring my son back.

I squeeze her hand, suddenly worried that she had fallen asleep in the stillness. She responds by adjusting her position to rest her head on my chest and lightly stroking my ribs with her fingers.

"Justin?" she says quietly. Will you tell me about him someday?" I raise my hand to play with her hair as I ponder the question. I just hope there *is* a someday.

"Yes, I will." She seems content with my answer, and I love that she wants to know about him. One day, I will tell her how he used to lay on my chest in the bathtub as a baby. And how he had the tiniest lisp when he talked. And how he would hold a hula-hoop at his waist and spin himself around. And how I used to call him a Jabberwalkie because once he learned to talk, he never stopped. She should know those things about him.

"Norah?" I say. She doesn't answer, but she kisses my chest and hugs me with her free arm. "I'm agoraphobic." The word tumbles from my mouth like a cartridge of Sarin gas. Now, the deadly nerve agent is filling the room, and it's too late to take it back.

She doesn't say anything for a bit, but she also doesn't loosen her one-arm hug. Right now, I'm clinging to that hug. That hug represents hope for me. If her grip loosens, it's a sign that that's it, it's over. Her arm is all I can think about because she can choose to hang on, or she can let go. For me, her grip is symbolic of so much more. If she releases me, I know we are done, but the longer she maintains her hold, the more I dare to hope.

"I don't understand. I thought agoraphobia was when someone is afraid to go outside?" she says as she looks up at me. "You go outside." The look on her face reads curiosity, not revulsion, so I take a tentative breath.

"Not exactly. That's a common misconception, though," I start to twist her hair around my finger. She is still here. Still hugging me. In fact, she scoots up the bed to rest her head on my shoulder and then raises her arm to a new hugging position that encompasses my other arm. Her hold on me is still snug, so the glimmer swells a tiny fraction more.

"Agoraphobics are not afraid of being outside. We are afraid of being triggered in public and of losing control. So, we avoid those kinds of situations. We feel in control in a familiar environment." It sounds just as bad out loud as it does in my head. Right now, she is weighing a life indoors with a normal, happy life. She will cut her losses because no one would choose to live this way.

"What happens when you get triggered in public?" She has the grace to lift her head and look me in the eyes. That means something. I think she still sees value in me.

148

"It's hard to explain. It's the sincerest—rawest form of fear and imminent doom…it's perverse in its intensity. Words don't do it justice. The feeling is so profound, so…so, heinous, that I would do *anything at all* to avoid feeling it."

"Like stay in your house." It's a statement, not a question.

"Norah, I would live in squalor, chained to a vintage radiator to avoid that feeling."

"Have you always been like this?" she asks. She uses the tips of her fingers against my chin, turning me to look at her. I'm ashamed to be so weak, I can hardly even make eye contact.

"No. It's been about three years."

"What would happen if you went outside right now?"

"I would get all sweaty and anxious. I would feel out of control. I'd tremble violently and feel like I was dying."

"So, you would have a panic attack?" she asks. I can only nod, awash with self-loathing and righteous shame.

"And that's if you get triggered? Or no matter what?" she asks, trying to get a little clarity.

"No matter what. The possibility of being triggered is enough."

"What kinds of things trigger you? Or do you even know?"

"Barking dogs, the sounds of kids crying or screaming or even just playing, sirens, flashing lights, agitated people or distressed conversations…stuff like that."

"Justin?" she lowers her head so I don't have to face her. "What happened at work to make you feel this way? You told me you changed jobs after a particularly bad call…did that call…did it have to do with your son?"

"Yes," I force the word through my teeth. It comes out hoarse and ragged. I feel a tear streak down my face. This is when I have to relive the day my soul went dark.

Chapter 24

Norah

This whole thing has been a fiery train wreck I can't extract myself from. The problem arises because I don't think I want to extract myself. Well, I do, because I'm neck-deep in shit right now, but that doesn't change the fact that I doubt I'm going to.

The phrase *trial by fire* jumps to mind. Justin will throw everything at me and then sit back and wait to see if I emerge from the flames. To be absolutely fair, I don't think he expected to be so forthcoming this evening. Dinner, wine, and all night sex had been our agenda, but I inadvertently forced his hand.

Bring on the fire. My first layer of fiery soot was the handprints and his subsequent breakdown. The next layer was the knowledge that his son passed away. Then, the layer after that turned out to be more than just smoke and ash, that one also charred my lungs. That one directly involves me, and it's hard to breathe through papery, crispy lungs.

Do I want to be involved with someone who doesn't leave the security of his own yard, ever? How long would it be before I started wanting more? Dinners out. Vacations. Happy hour and live bands. I'm the furthest thing from a homebody. If I don't get out of my apartment, I get all squirrelly and start making bad decisions—like bar hopping and drinking too much, or dating Daniel, or $200 cute as hell, Sorel boots when it only snows here four times a year. Can I trade all that for the monotony of Justin's life? Sexy, charming, funny, Justin. Can I give up a vibrant life to join him in the ghost town of his home? Especially with the whistle of melancholy clinging to it?

Can Justin change his behavior—Does he even want to? Because even the gluttony of inexhaustible Netflix and long, sweaty sexathons have their limitations. His lifestyle would swallow me whole. It would grab me and pull me under with him.

This is a tipping point for me, do I run? Or do I take a risk on something that could be amazing? Justin is phenomenal, and though we have only scratched the surface of a relationship, I feel he might be worth the risk.

It's a far cry from cooking me dinner, I'll tell you that much. I should probably run away screaming, but truer to form, I will choose reckless.

I'm going all in.

Chapter 25

JUSTIN

"His name was Jax. My son…was Jax—Jaxson," I look away, not sure I can go any further. Then, after a shaky breath, I forge ahead. "It was a day just like any other. Vivian, Jax's mom, was typically out of the house by five-thirty for work, so I always had the mornings with him. I would make us breakfast while Jax emptied the Tupperware cabinet. Sometimes he would get inside and then try to scare me by popping his head out and yelling *Boo, Daddy!* To which I always put on a big show about being surprised to see him. He thought that was the funniest thing and would laugh and laugh at my dramatic antics. If he didn't try to hide in the cabinet, he would kick the Tupperware around in the kitchen like a little soccer player. Anyway, after breakfast, we always went upstairs to get ready. Jax would stand on the counter next to me and mimic everything I did. When I shaved, I would put shaving cream on his face, and he would scrape it off with a plastic kid's razor. He wanted to do everything I did. He was my little guy." I stop to see if all this is too much for her.

"How old was he?" she asks. She is lightly swirling her finger in a circle on my chest. I'm going to focus on the feel of her finger and only that. I need to tell the story as if it wasn't me that it happened to. A certain amount of detachment is necessary for me to continue because I never share this with anyone, ever. The people who know about it lived it with me. I never had to repeat it.

"Fourteen months. He had only been walking for a few months." I feel like I have to step even further outside of myself to tell her about this day. It's not healthy to separate myself from it, according to the myriad of therapists I've seen, but I can't even think about that day, let alone give the play-by-play if I can't block out my feelings and emotions. Giving a voice to the whole nightmare solidifies it as my reality, and I can't stomach that, even still. I need to approach this like a robot, or there is zero chance I will get through it.

"I dropped him off at the sitter's house, kissed his head, gave him knucks, and told him I would see him in two days after my shift. That was it. The last time I saw him alive was as he walked away from me to play with his trucks." I can feel Norah's warm tears on my chest. I wish I could stop the story here, it's bad enough already.

"Anyway, like I told you before, as first responders, fire gets called out the same time the medics do." I stop and clear my throat, or try to. "We got a call about a dog bite. It was nothing unusual until we pulled the rig into the sitter's neighborhood. I knew the call was for Jaxson. That was the *exact* moment I knew."

"Oh my God. A dog," Norah breathes.

"Jax's sitter had a dog. He was affectionate and playful, so I trusted him. He never showed any signs of aggression in the three years she owned him. Not to other animals. Not to people. Not ever.

In fact, he used to lick Jax's face when he was in his infant carrier. Once my son was mobile, the dog would play with him. He knew Jax. I would even have said he loved him. My son went to the same sitter's house for his whole life…over a year." I stop the dreadful story to gather my thoughts for a second.

"Norah, I trusted the babysitter. I trusted the dog. For three years, that dog was sweet and predictable. Loving even. What's worse is that no one can explain what provoked it to attack."

"Justin, I'm so sorry," she whispers.

"Before we even pulled all the way up to the house, I was out of the rig, sprinting to my son. Medics were already on scene, and as I approached, a few of them ran to me and started pushing me back. They were like determined linebackers, not only keeping me away but physically removing me from the scene. I was fighting like crazy and screaming for Jax, but I had four guys on me. Norah, I could smell the blood. I'll never get that smell out of my nose as long as I live. I could see it, too, in the snow. It seemed like it was *everywhere*." I pause here, transfixed in the moment.

It's like I'm right there all over again. The smell, so pungent and excessive I can taste it like a penny in my mouth. The sweat dripping in my eyes while trying to fight through the medics. I can feel it all as I lie here, wooden and cold.

After a few minutes, I continue the atrocity. "The call wasn't just a dog bite. It was a dog mauling. Everyone was frantic, which was out of character because we know, as first responders, we control the scene. We are *always* calm and collected, even if we are shitting ourselves on the inside. But that day, the agitation and frenetic energy level was off the charts. We would always work extra hard when an accident or trauma involved a kid, but this time was not usual. I knew it was bad. Norah, I knew," I finish in a whisper.

"You've been through so much, Justin. No one should ever have to endure even a fraction of that. I'm so sorry." She makes her way up my body so we are face to face and hugging on my bed. I bury my nose in the crook of her neck and breathe in life. My eyes and throat are dry. I feel like I've told that story a trillion times, but I never have.

"You know all the nine-eleven footage of the World Trade Center collapse? Remember the sound? The shrill sound of the alarms from hundreds of firefighters' PASS devices? You never forget that sound. For me, it's the sirens. It was all I could hear. I could see people shouting, but I could only see their lips moving. I saw the officer shoot the dog in the face but didn't hear his firearm discharge. Nothing— nothing but the sirens. I can close my eyes and still feel the flashing lights on my skin and smell his blood in the air, but in my head—it's the sirens."

I feel empty when I'm done with the hellish retelling, but empty in a different way than normal. I'll always feel empty without Jax, but my emptiness now feels like I've taken a shovelful of pain and cast it into the furnace. I'm still utterly empty, but maybe a tiny bit less so.

"Norah?" I say into the hair at her neck. "Do you want to take a shower with me?"

Chapter 26

Norah

When he pulls the shirt over my head, I understand why he wants to take a shower. It feels symbolic. The shedding of something for the purpose of purification and cleansing. The weight and the filth of his story feel like our own nine-eleven rubble we need to climb out of. He is looking for light in the darkness, and I want to give that to him however I can. It's the middle of the night, but neither of us is tired.

When he turns back around after starting the shower, I unbutton his jeans while kissing his neck and chest. After everything he has been through, all I want to do is bring him joy—in any form. I sit down on the tiled edge of the tub while I tease his ticklish waistline with feathery fingers. His erection is straining for release, but right now is all about the build-up, about taking his mind off the heaviness of his life.

I slowly work his jeans down, nibbling at his hip while I drag my fingernails back up the sides of his thighs. I can feel the warmth of him, stiff against my neck and jaw. His skin feels like delicate satin, and he's nothing like the fanatical beast from earlier tonight. As he heats up, I can smell the provocative scent of his bodywash faintly against his skin.

This deviation from our evening is a welcome escape, and though I face a legion of obstacles by choosing to stay, I can no longer fight my circumstantial uncertainty. His scent, his magnetism, his well of emotions and painful truths—all of it. I want all of him.

When I tease him with my mouth, he whispers, "Norah, make me forget." It's a plea I intend to champion for the rest of the night, but in my heart, I know forgetting is not the answer. I take him slowly with undivided reverence until I can feel the anchor, rooted in sorrow, start to lift.

He indulges in that lift—his ascent, and soon, he no longer recognizes the act as a diversion. He slides his fingers into my hair and exhales with pleasure. I take my time, willing him to relinquish the past for a few minutes and be in the moment, here with me.

It's a gentle, steady climb, but he stops me before he summits. Then he pulls me up from the edge of the tub to stand before him. "I'm tired of feeling broken," he ghosts into my ear as he unfastens my bra. The tickle against my ear canal, accompanied by the assertive way he undresses me, pushes any lingering doubt I may be harboring right off a cliff. This man is shattered and dejected, but I'm powerless against his lure.

"You'll always feel broken, Justin. Without Jax, you'll never feel whole. But you can still be happy," I say, with my hand on the back of his neck, before drawing his contemplative face toward mine.

He stops short of making contact with my mouth. Instead, he presses his forehead against mine. He's conflicted, and I can read it plainly on his face. I don't know if I've said the wrong thing, so I try again. "Expecting yourself to feel completely whole only sets you up for failure." I try to kiss him again, but he backs his head up. It's obvious now that he's avoiding my kiss. I'm not sure what to make of such a bold rejection.

"Norah, right now, I'm going to take your body because we both want it. But I don't want you to kiss me unless you're ready to give me your heart," he says. "I can separate myself from sex, but not from affection." The ache in his words absorbs into my skin like the growing humidity in the bathroom. There is a part of me that is terrified he won't ever leave his home. But there is *no* part of me that doesn't want to give him my heart.

"I'm going to get a condom," he says as he disappears into the bedroom. I remove the rest of my clothes and adjust the water temperature before getting in.

He steps in, facing me, and without a second of hesitation, he grabs my thighs and lifts me to his hips. The gravity of the evening momentarily forgotten, Justin reclaims the tenacity of his spirit right here in the shower. The way he owns me is confident and full of arrogant swagger—so much more recognizable than the shattered part of his identity I've only just learned about.

He presses inside me, kissing my neck while advancing his claim. It's the second time tonight he has entered me in this way, but the distention is the same as my body slowly yields to his girth. The breath catches in my throat and remains suspended because I'm unable to focus on anything except the steady advance of his penetration.

This feels amazing. He's wrong about thinking he can keep the act of sex separate from affection, though, because there is so much intimacy between us. His actions are tender and devoted—it's almost restorative, becoming one with him. I don't think I'll ever get enough.

"I'm going to do this the way I should have the first time, and then I'm going to cook dinner like I promised," he says, with playfulness in his eyes before pinning my back to the cold tile.

His mouth's singular focus is my neck, reminding me how he doesn't want me to kiss him unless I am ready to give him my heart. He has no such qualms about fucking me up against a shower wall because he needs to separate the two. Perhaps for some, sex can be about the raw carnality of the act—feelings not required, but he isn't very convincing. Everything about this defies his statement. There is no way to extract the affection between us because we are both too deep in our feelings for one another.

Then I remember how he kissed that woman when she left his house and figure that he must have shared a certain level of intimacy with her. Right? Curiously, he has made no mention of her and has already lobbed a volley into my court regarding giving him my heart.

Not a whole lot hints at him being someone to juggle women, but my impression may be because now I know he was such a doting father. It doesn't seem like guys who cook breakfast for their child every day also like to burn through women. Maybe I'm wrong, but I hope not.

It's also touching that he would even suggest giving him my heart. Many guys would be happy to kiss or even screw while requiring *much less* from me. I think Justin is different. Of course, he is sexy as hell, but he also has a sweet side, and I intend to get to know that side.

A moan rips from my throat in response to his eloquent strokes, and the sound is served back to me in the resonating hollowness of the shower. He pauses his mouth over the slope of my ear and murmurs, "I'm crazy about that sound, Norah."

The thought of him being crazy about anything regarding me only adds nails to the coffin of my decision. It's reckless and probably naive of me, but I never said I make good decisions. With my arms crossed behind his neck and a building sensation starting to tickle my core, I grip the back of his head and bring his mouth to mine.

His reaction is instant. He slows the ferocity of our sex, kissing me sweetly with a tone of reverence that twists at my heart. After a few minutes of this, he adjusts his hold on me, moving one hand from the grip of my thigh to ring his arm around my lower back. He sits down on the built-in shower bench and, with his hands on my hips, helps me to grind against his pelvis.

When I need more of him to chase my orgasm, I lengthen my movements and increase the intensity. He slows my tempo with his mouth on mine. With one hand against my ear and his thumb stroking my cheekbone, he says, "Slow down. We have all night."

As luck would have it, 'all night' only meant another twenty minutes of sensuality in the shower before the water started to rapidly cool against my back and his legs. Now, with time running out before the water gets cold, he turns me around so my back is to his front. Then he lowers me down while guiding himself back in and spreads my legs. The water spraying against the front of my body isn't cold yet, but it will be soon.

Reaching from behind me, he lowers his fingers between my legs to dally while I grind slow circles on his lap. He happens to be incredibly efficient with my body; no touch is wasted, and everything he does is for the sole purpose of pleasing me. His pleasure is by proxy of mine and a distant second on his priority list.

It's refreshing. So many men are selfish lovers. They assume that because it feels good for them, it must feel good for us. They don't even realize that women are built differently and require a little more coaxing. Justin understands this with stone-cold precision, and it's intoxicating.

"I want to hear my name on your lips before the water gets cold," he says, almost deviously, while his circling fingers work in earnest.

As it turns out, my orgasm comes at the same time the cold water does, which offers quite a dichotomy of sensations. On one hand, the chill against my breasts and open legs attempts to slow the rolling thunder, but on the other hand, the thick graze of him inside me and the erotic shifting of his fingers make it impossible to deny the impending release.

His name on my lips comes in a growly, raspy groan instead of a shouted climax. Which, based on the answering groan of my name and his heaving release, was exactly what he was looking for.

It's nearly dawn when we reenter his bedroom wrapped in asphalt gray towels. We both look at the other in wonder. We have spent the whole night bathed in emotions, both happy and sad. We've talked and had sex all night. Now, with the prickle of exhaustion at the backs of our eyes and the rumble of hunger in our bellies, Justin asks, "Should we eat? Or sleep?"

I bounce the options back and forth in my head and finally decide, "Sleep." He said he planned to roast a pork tenderloin, which sounds better for lunch than breakfast. Besides, waking up later only to lounge around, eat, and watch movies while wound up in Justin Abernathy sounds like the perfect day. Then, with a nagging pang of discouragement, I remember. *I just hope that's not all our future has in store for us.*

"My thoughts exactly," he says as he pulls the curtains shut, soaking his room in darkness. "Now, drop that towel and get in here," he says while flipping back the comforter and easing himself into bed.

When I join him, he pulls me into the tuck of his arm so I rest my cheek against the water droplets still clinging to his skin. He rolls the rest of the way toward me, embracing my body against his nakedness. I throw a leg over his hip, which, in my state of undress, may be a bad idea because of the close proximity of intimate flesh. I can feel every inch of his body pressed up against mine. He feels warm and safe—it's an illusion, though, because, as I've said all along—this man is dangerous for me.

"Thank you," he says as he lowers a kiss to my forehead.

"For what?" I ask, is he thanking me for the shower sex?

"For not running away."

What I want to say in reply is, *please don't make me regret it.* What I actually do say is, "You promised me dinner, and I'm not going anywhere until you feed me." He chuckles into my hair, and within minutes, we are both sound asleep.

Chapter 27

JUSTIN

There is a comfort level with Norah that I haven't felt before. Maybe it's because she knows all my jagged edges and still looks at me like I'm a worthy person. The other women I've been with don't know about Jax. They don't know why I am the way I am, only that I'm broken or incomplete because I don't leave the house.

The crippling anxiety that stems from having my son violently ripped from my life, and the paralyzing inability to do anything to change that fact have always lurked beneath the surface. Until now, I haven't let anyone close enough to try to understand my agoraphobia. Maybe I should have let some of them in sooner, but I wasn't ready. Or perhaps the others weren't the right person to try to understand it.

This morning, I woke up before Norah. She was sleeping on her stomach with the side of her face lost to the down of the pillow. Her hair was unruly, but her face was tranquil, angelic even. The whole time I stared at her perfect sleeping face, I thought about how I had lost my shit last night. I couldn't bring myself to feel shame, though. Norah saw my truth. It's ugly and unrestrained, raw and abhorrent. But now, I'm finally free of the mask I donned like a death shroud.

Maybe, finally, being honest is part of my process. I hadn't wanted to share Jax with any of those other women. They felt like interlopers treading on my relationship with him. Now, with honesty comes a level of freedom I'm not accustomed to feeling but also a certain accountability.

I think Norah was right when she said I'd never feel whole without my son, but I could still be happy. I don't think she meant to be quite so prophetic, but the truth of her statement hit me between the eyes like a practiced kill shot.

Living a life of emptiness and chronic despair will never bring Jaxson back, but being happy also doesn't have to mean I loved him any less. I think I felt that hanging on to the sorrow would be my tribute to Jax and a testament to how much I adored him. But the true testament to my love may be allowing myself to feel joy again. I can give Jax that. I can allow his father that peace—that permission to feel happiness again.

Norah's statement was a profound realization for me. I don't have to wait until I feel whole to be happy—because that is an unrealistic expectation. I can miss my son to the depths of my soul and still live a happy, fulfilled life.

It's crazy because all of this occurred to me while watching Norah sleep this morning. It also happens to be the reason I'm at peace with her seeing me like she did. Perhaps she realized the sobbing, hysterical shell of a man before her was just preparing some space in his heart for another.

Last night was more powerful than all my years of therapy. I didn't exactly know it then, but I was ready—ready to unburden myself. Norah will probably never fully comprehend her role as the precipice, but my first act of gratitude will be to finally prepare this dinner for her.

Right now, she is sitting on the kitchen counter wearing one of my dress shirts, now a bit rumpled and rolled up at the sleeves. Her legs are bare except for some of my heavy wool socks, and her hair is a mass of wild anarchy. The savageness that is her hair is especially endearing because she doesn't give two shits about its restless state.

I've dated too many women who kept up the pretense of constantly being put together. They thought they fooled me into believing their goopy eyelashes were their natural state and that they woke up with minty, fresh breath. I suppose that spoke to their insecurities. For me, though, there is nothing hotter than a fresh faced, snarly-haired woman wearing my clothes after emerging from my bed.

"Are you sure I can't help with anything?" she asks over the rim of her coffee mug as I slide the tenderloin pan in the oven.

"Norah, I don't want you to ever move from that spot. I want you to stay looking exactly like that forever." I can't help the spirited grin that pulls at my face. Sexed-up looks so damn good on her.

"That's ridiculous. I'm a hot mess," she laughs while indicating her recklessly abandoned hair. It's disheveled, I'm sure, from sleeping on post-shower, wet tresses. "Why would you want me to look like this forever?" she asks.

"Because it reminds me that I had a hand in making you look that way," I say as I stalk over to her and settle between her thighs. She drapes her arms over my shoulders while mine circle her body, pulling her closer. Her kiss tastes like my toothpaste laced with the vanilla cream in her coffee. Is it weird that I thought nothing of it when she asked if she could use my toothbrush? Sharing oral hygiene products only made me feel more connected to her, though I can't say I would share a toothbrush with a single other person on the planet.

"I look like a homeless woman. Are you sure you want to mix with such a degenerate?" she asks.

"I'm sure I want to mix with you," I say, piecing the words together as part of our kiss. "Not homeless, just sexy as hell."

"How long does the tenderloin need to cook?" she asks as she tightens the squeeze of her thighs around my waist.

"Forty-five minutes," I answer while picking her up off the counter and holding her against me as I walk out of the kitchen. "I need to get you out of this shirt; the size is all wrong for you," I say as I ascend the stairs two at a time.

This time, I take her gentle as a lamb. With one of my hands clasped against both of hers and held above her head while we kiss, and I slide rapturously in and out of her warm embrace. Right now, our sex is intimate and sensual, nothing like the first time. I think I had fucked her so many times in my head that I almost needed to blow out the pipes before this kind of tenderness was possible, but after last night, I also feel closer to her than any other woman. Even Vivian and I had a kid with her.

When I look into her eyes, I don't see the feisty, snarky woman who marched into my house all those weeks ago, filled with venom and accusations. That chick was fun to tease and get all riled up, but this one—this one is so much more.

I change up my stroke, this time rolling my hips more and grinding against her as I whisper into her ear, "You're so perfect. So, so perfect for me." She smiles and cups my jaw with her free hand. Just when I think she's about to return the endearment, she surprises me.

"Your penis—Aahhh." Great, I tell her she is perfect for me, and she tells me she likes my dick. That ought to knock me down a few pegs.

"Ohhhh. Justin… *you're* so perfect," she says as she strains her head back, arching her body against the grind of my pelvis.

"You mean my penis?" I tease, nibbling on her chin and jaw.

"Your penis is amazing, but I can't concentrate when you—but Justin…you. Ohhh," she finishes with a long, drawn-out moan while her body pulses around mine. I think it's how she sounds when she comes that triggers my orgasm. I mean, the feel of her contracting tightly around me probably helps, but her sex noises are lyrical.

I'm laying on top of her with my cheek against her chest as she combs her fingers gently through my hair. I bask in the smell of her warm skin and love the feel of her naked body beneath me. I'm perfectly content to stay like this forever. This is when she starts giggling.

I smile at the ripe sound of it, "What's so funny?" I ask. Her giggles start to roll into something more, a heartier laugh. Then, before long, a full-blown one. I raise myself on my forearms above her and study her face. She is still glistening from the sex, and she is also not holding back her boisterous reaction.

After she calms down a bit, she explains, "I was trying to tell you that I couldn't concentrate on stringing words together when you were doing that with your penis…" More laughing; in fact, her chest is rumbling so much with her laughter that it makes me crack a smile. I cock my head to look her more directly in the eyes. She has tears streaming from the corners of them, and the whole scene makes my own laugh tumble out, light and unfettered.

"So, it sounded like I was saying—" Full, unadulterated laughter now, as she brings her hand in front of her mouth to try to temper it. She still can't stop long enough to finish what she was trying to say. I smile broadly at her amusement but also a little because she wasn't voicing what I thought she was.

"So, instead of telling you that, I totally demonstrated it in the most *epic* fashion!" she chokes out. Now, I fully join her in the laughing—I love the easiness of it. It feels limber and carefree. I roll over, bringing her on top of me so I'm not crushing her anymore.

After the mirth dies down a little, I look at her seriously while I smooth the hair away from her bright eyes and smiling face. "So…my penis is not perfect, is that what you're saying?"

She crumbles on top of me with a snort. "Justin, if your penis were any more perfect, it would belong in a museum."

Chapter 28

Norah

"Spill," Sophia says as she hands me a glass of iced coffee and then sits cross-legged on the foot of my bed. "I need details. All of them." It comes as no surprise to me that she is perfectly showered and done up, while my feet have not yet touched the floor today. I got home around three a.m. and did nothing but smile at the ceiling for forty-five minutes before I got tired enough to drift off to sleep. The all-nighter on Friday seems like forever ago, but it successfully threw my circadian rhythm out of whack. I need to get up now just so I can fall asleep tonight and salvage a decent sleep schedule for my work week.

"It's crazy, Soph—"

"You whore."

I snort. "I'm serious. There are a lot of layers to this onion."

"Thanks for the heads up. Now, get on with it."

"Ok, well, Reader's Digest version…" I run my fingers through my hair and start.

"No, screw that. I've seen him. I don't want the Reader's Digest version. Give it all to me." She is adamant, but this is Justin's life, it's not trashy gossip to divulge. "Norah, I put lashes on for this," she blinks a few dramatic blinks before leaning forward with wide, dopey eyes.

"Ok, here goes. His son died in a dog attack, so he's riddled with anxiety, and now he's afraid to be triggered, so he doesn't go outside of his yard, and he can't be a firefighter anymore because lights and sirens are some of his triggers." I take a breath, "Oh, and we had sex." I fling the comforter off of me so I can go to the bathroom, but I get hung up on Sophia's gaping mouth.

"What? Soph, I have to pee."

"Stop right there." She holds out her arm as if it's an effective barricade for my distended bladder. I ignore it and walk into my bathroom. I leave the door open while I pee because I know with certainty she is only getting started. "We'll get to the sex in just a sec," she says, "Was his son really killed by a dog? And is he really a shut-in?" she asks as if she's not sure I'm a reliable source. Then, with a shouted epiphany, "Cheese and Rice!" her words, instead of the other, sacrilegious option of *Jesus Christ!* "That's why he hired Hand to Heart!"

"Good job, Sophia," I tease as I sit back down on my bed. She stares at me. I swear I can hear the audible blink of her wide eyes. Blink-Blink-Blink.

"When? How old? Really, never? What are you gonna do?" She is stumbling over her words in a very uncharacteristic turn of events. Questions are rolling out of her mouth unchecked and falling like rain.

"Three years ago. Fourteen months. Yeah, never. I don't know because I've already got it bad for him." I say, trying to keep up. She launches off my bed, returning a millisecond later with her laptop. This time, she joins me at the head of the bed, settling back against my pillows like a spouse.

"We gotta figure out how to break the whole indoor cycle. There has to be special therapy for arachnophobia, right?"

"Agoraphobia."

"Same thing," she says as her fingers fly over her keyboard.

"Not even close."

***

After an hour or two of consulting with Google, I have a better grasp on Justin's issues. I'm more familiar with terms like *visual kinesthetic dissociation, systematic desensitization,* and *cognitive restructuring*, though I am nowhere near qualified to apply them. I also understand the disorder better.

Based on what Justin himself told me, as well as the omnipotent internet, it sounds like he may have had a few panic attacks while out and about, and now he is afraid to appear distraught or lose control in public. Now, I think his fear of being triggered is enough to make him avoid the anxiety altogether. Simply put, he no longer feels safe in public and probably worries about being unable to escape if something happens. Agoraphobia is nothing more than a big, fat anxiety disorder.

I can do this. I can help him with feeling anxious. The trick is going to be not creating more anxiety by pushing him to change his behaviors. And I definitely don't want him to get the impression that he is not good enough the way he is because that will provoke a whole different stream of anxiety.

"Are you sure you want to take this on?" Sophia asks. "Phobias are no joke. It's not like he can just snap out of it. You have to be willing to accept him exactly as he is *right now* because he may never change." She's right, I can't approach Justin as if I can bend him to my will. If I'm honest with myself, I would admit that even when he told me about his disorder, I didn't think of it as something permanent. I kind of figured he would eventually get over it.

"Can you accept it and live that way, never going out with your boyfriend?" she asks. "I mean *really* accept him how he is. You don't get to romanticize this, Norah. It will have a huge impact on you. On your life. And, I can't believe I'm about to say this…but, it doesn't matter how good he is in bed, you can't be blind to the truth."

"I know. You're right, and now that I'm free of his sexual magnetism, I can think clearly. I don't know if I *am* ready to take this on," I admit. My statement is authentic, though it feels like a betrayal and burns in the back of my mouth.

"Well, Girl. You probably shouldn't have slept with him. It clouds the reality of the situation too much. But you don't *owe* him anything. Guys tap and run all the time. He's a big boy, he can handle it. He has already dealt with much worse. Good lord, could you even imagine?"

"No, I can't imagine. It's too horrible to even think about." My mind starts to get foggy just thinking about everything Justin has endured. "I'm going to jump in the shower, Soph. Make the bed when you get out of it, K?" I throw out over my shoulder.

I need to be alone with my thoughts right now. What the hell was I thinking? It's not like Justin has a touch of the flu, and he will be fine in a couple of days. He may never change. We may never go out on a real date. And what if, down the line, we get married? Would the wedding have to be in his living room? What about babies? He wouldn't even be able to come with me to the hospital—and I am *not* having my babies at home, I'll need the drugs. What have I gotten myself into?

I close the door to my bathroom and sink to the floor with my back against it. Everything Sophia said was dead on, and she's right about most of it, even though I wish she weren't. She's wrong about one thing, though, I do owe him something.

I owe him my heart.

Chapter 29

JUSTIN

When Norah left last night, I felt like I'd hit the lottery. I'd been so giddy I didn't even recognize myself. Not to mention, for the first time in forever, I didn't need to jerk off before going to sleep. The fresh new optimism buzzing around me made me feel invincible. Now? Now, that buzzing has turned into a field of locusts.

I am halfway preoccupied with a work project due by nine a.m. tomorrow and halfway terrified that Norah will gather her wits about her and vanish from my life. In my defense, I have never laid myself out there like that, so I'm not even sure I did it right.

Poor Norah walked in here on Friday with a twinkle in her eye so shiny that I felt the possibilities rumbling in the base of my nut sack. She had no idea what the hell she was walking into—how bad of a shit storm was headed her way. To be fair, neither did I. Then I steamrolled her under mountains of crap, peeled her up from the carnage, and had sex with her before she could make sense of any of it. What's worse is that I hardly gave her a chance to process anything before I threw her in the shower and did it again.

If I had time to think about everything first, I never would have involved sex. I knew she was hot and ready because I'd been watering that seed for weeks. But, I let that animalistic need cloud her judgment, and now here I am—feeling like an emotional rapist. I'm disgusted with myself, and I have no idea what my next step with Norah is. Usually, by now, we would have at least shot a few texts back and forth. The silence is uncharacteristic and rather foreboding.

I would let her go if I were a stronger man and much less selfish. I forced the perfect storm on her when the forecast hadn't even predicted rain. Now, I know once she thinks about the gravity of the situation, she will realize I'm not worth the collateral damage. What sometimes looks good on paper isn't always good when you view it in the light of day. That's me, and I took advantage of her before she could assess her predicament in the light of day.

I ignore the mounting work emails that are starting to collect and buckle my weight belt around my waist. Forty extra pounds added to my pull-ups should be punishment enough to at least get through this marketing project.

***

Somehow, I limped my project through to completion, although my fee is at least double what it should be for the lackluster work. I haven't heard from Norah today at all, and because I've left the ball in her court, I've not reached out to her either. It's been tough. I've gotten used to all the fun banter that got me through the day in a house I'm trapped in and a job I have no passion for. Even her texts have dried up and completely ghosted me.

I thought about having Davis over, but I can't face all the questions that will bubble to the surface, and he doesn't back down. He has some self-righteous delusions of grandeur that make it impossible for him to drop something once he decides he should know more about it. He would only poke at my bruise, so I let his invitation die before the thought came to fruition.

I eat leftover pork tenderloin—the same one I made for Norah, and drink four beers before I decide seven-thirty is a perfectly acceptable bedtime for a grown man. There is not a damn thing I want to do except talk to Norah. At the very least, I should apologize to her. Since that is not an option right now, I'll go to bed.

I need a shower before I check out for the night, but I can't bring myself to use the one in the master bathroom. There's too much familiarity with my recent heartbreak in there—it's pressed all over, up against the shower walls and the tile bench. I'll use the shower in the other upstairs bathroom and try not to think about Jaxson's bathtime ritual with his foam fish and plastic fishing pole.

I clean myself quickly and then try in vain to beat off, but I don't allow myself to think about anything Norah related, and my dick never fully rises to the occasion. When I step out of the bathroom, I can hear someone pounding on the front door. Fucking Davis, he's like a goddamned bloodhound, and he's caught the scent of my misery.

I swing the door wide open, angry I'll have to tell a pushy Davis about everything after all. I'm wearing only athletic shorts, water droplets, and a scowly frown when I realize it's not Davis at all.

"Hi," I say, but the rest gets stuck behind my lips.

"Hi," she says. The look on her face is morose at best. I hate that she feels the need to sever ties in person. I don't even invite her in. I don't want to make it harder on us than it has to be.

"I just need to know one thing," she says flatly. Great, this is where she unleashes on me about everything I kept from her, and what a scumbag I am, and how I should have told her about my issues before luring her into my bed. I guess this is where I should insert my apology, but I can't seem to find the right words.

"Do you want to live this way? I mean, *really* want this lifestyle for yourself—for your future?" she asks. Her eyes are pleading with me. She is very much in self-preservation mode, but she looks as gutted as me. I take a deep breath and answer her honestly.

"No. I don't."

It feels like entire minutes pass after I give her my answer. She seems to take it in and then sucks on it for a while. I'm not sure what to do. I still haven't invited her in, and it's getting increasingly harder to keep looking her in the eyes. She has no idea how hard I have fallen for her. Absolutely no idea.

She surprises me by stepping forward and wrapping her arms around me. I'm standing here like a jackass, one hand gripping the edge of the door and the other forearm on the doorjamb. At first, I'm too stunned to do anything except stand here like she's nothing but a handsy solicitor at my door, but then I allow myself to wrap tentative arms around her. She tucks her face against the crook of my neck as I choke on the lump in my throat.

Is this goodbye? Is she submitting? I'm still too afraid to let my guard down, but I squeeze her to my still-wet chest and hope against hope that she will at least try. Try to see if I'm worth it.

Please, Norah. *Please* find me worth it.

Chapter 30

Norah

He smells crisp, like testosterone scrubbed with manly soap, and the fact that I want to lick him from stem to stern is starting to cloud my judgment. He gave me the answer I was looking for. He doesn't *want* to live like this, so that gives me hope for the future. If he wants to break free from his self-imposed prison, then that means he is open to change. That's good enough for now. He is good enough.

I'm not sure he knows how to interpret my hug, so I raise my chin and kiss his neck. I can feel his pulse pounding against my lips. He raises one hand to cradle my head against his chest and eventually lifts my face for a kiss. He appropriately interprets the passion in my kiss because he backs us up and shoves the door closed.

"I know it's too much to ask of you, and I know I shouldn't, but Norah, I am crazy about you. I don't know how to navigate this. I want you so bad, but it's completely selfish because I know I will slowly poison you."

"Justin," I say, "We will figure out how to navigate this together. For right now, it's enough that *you* know I will eventually want more, and it's enough for *me* to know that you don't want to be like this forever."

"Thank you," he says, and he sounds a little choked up as he buries his face in my hair.

"But you do need to know that one day, I want to travel with you; I want to go to fancy restaurants and seedy dive bars. I want to go to concerts and beer festivals. I want us to go camping. I want to hike fourteeners in the summer and ski in the winter. I want to go on road trips where we can listen to erotic audiobooks on long stretches of highway." He stops me by dusting his mouth over mine. His kiss is hopeful.

"I want all those things too, Norah, but even more than that, I don't want to deprive you of having them. And I will be damned if I'm going to let another man do all of that with you instead of me," he says, cradling my face with both hands. His eyes are earnest, and he sounds committed to those experiences. It's everything I want to hear. I'm on board as long as there is hope. I can handle a challenge, but not a lost cause. I know I need to accept him like he is, and I do, for now, but I can't shy away from what I need out of life, either.

I grin mischievously into his reassured face, "And I want to have sex with you in swanky downtown hotels, in European hostels, in my apartment, on mountain tops, and on beaches." He visibly relaxes at my words, then lifts me to his hips, walks to the couch, and then sits down with me, straddling his lap.

"I certainly don't want to deprive you of all *that*," he says as his hands slide up the back of my shirt, caressing me with relief. It's palpable, his relief. I can taste it on him. After not being in contact with him all day, which is highly unusual at this point, I can tell he was waiting for the other shoe to drop. The worry was etched in his face when he opened the door because I didn't think he ever expected to see me again.

I've been true to myself, too. I haven't given him any empty promises because to do so *would* slowly poison me. The only thing is, and it's niggling at the back of my mind even now, is how the hell will I be able to let him go after I've fallen in love with him? Will I be able to cut my heart out and lay it at his feet, only to slowly rot inside of his house while I try to move on with my life on the outside?

That instance is the single most dangerous thing about Justin Abernathy. It scares me more than I want to acknowledge, especially while his hands are on my body.

"We can slow things down if you want to," he offers. I think he is serious, too, because he has not yet made a play for the clasp of my bra. I press myself into the thick post between us and slowly grind against it.

"Sure, we can slow things down," I tease into his ear as I slow my grinding hips almost to a stop, but not quite. If he thinks we can back this train up after we've already had sex, he is crazier than I thought.

"I'm serious. I want to build something with you without the physical aspects getting in the way. I want to push my limits and take off my shackles, but—" he drops his head in shame, "But if I can't, I want you to move on. We don't have to have a sexual connection if it will make it easier for you to move on."

"That's very noble of you, Mr. Abernathy," I whisper in his ear between feather light kisses, "But I've already sampled the goods, and I have no intention of giving them up."

My shirt is over my head before I can register the neckline of it against my face. He presses his hips up enough to shove his workout shorts down his thighs, and in the process, he raises me enough to take the hint and lose my own shorts and panties.

When I straddle him again, we are both bare, and the feel of him between my open thighs is enough to give me the shivers. He divests me of my bra as quickly as he did my shirt, and when I fuse my torso against his, we melt together for a sexy, lingering kiss. Our lips divulge each other's secrets and confess how much we missed one another today.

"Are you clean? I want you like this." I ask, ridiculously naive yet still hopeful.

He groans at my implication, and if it's even possible, his erection swells and becomes even more imposing while pressed between us. "Norah," he pants as if that's the sexiest thing he has ever heard. "I've always worn rubbers, but it's been a few years since I tested."

I want him bare. I've always used protection before as well, and I've been on the pill for years. Also, lest we forget, the first time we were together was skin on skin, so I've already thrown caution to the wind.

"Then I want you…just like this," I murmur against his mouth. He has one hand in my hair and the other one on my breast. After I say that, he tightens his grip on my hair and nips my throat with his teeth.

"And I want *you*…just like this," he breathes back. His words drip with raunchy sex appeal before his mouth takes my nipple. He flicks it roughly with his tongue while his fingers tease the other.

After a few minutes of pure indulgence, he flicked, tugged, and sucked my nipples into radiant, throbbing beings with their own heartbeat. My body is alive and singing for him because his touch is nothing short of rapturous.

"Let me look at you," he says as he eases me back to sit down on his thighs. He stares at me, my face, my breasts, my open legs, everything, long enough for insecurity to creep up my neck and shyness to powder my cheeks with a heated blush.

"Norah. You are the sexiest thing I have ever seen," his eyes are ravenous, and his clipped breath is enough to dissipate my insecurities and strum at my heartstrings.

"You like what you see?" I ask, emboldened by the hungry stare that has landed once again on my showy nipples.

"No, baby... I love what I see." He drags his eyes up to meet mine and then places his flattened palm against my chest, on my pounding heart. He seems to be quieting himself for something big.

"Norah, I promise you I will *try* to get better. I will try harder than I ever have before. *I want this so bad.*" I think he refers to my heart—still covered by his hand, and not my body, offered so blatantly. He wants us.

I place both my hands on top of his and say, "Justin, it's not going to be easy for you, but it will be worth it." Tears flood his eyes, but he blinks them away before I can be sure. Then he wraps both arms around my lower back and pulls me into his body. I rise up on my knees and, with one hand, guide him into my body.

"Say it again," he whispers.

"It will be worth it," I murmur as I sink down.

"Again."

"It will be worth it."

Chapter 31

JUSTIN

When Norah left last night, I didn't want to let her go. I can't remember the last time I was so afraid to lose something or someone. After Jaxson died, it wasn't six months before Vivian left, and as crazy as it sounds, I couldn't scrape up two tears to rub together about her leaving. Part of the problem was that my pain was so oppressive I literally could not have been any more destroyed than I already was. The other part of not missing her was that I don't think I was ever in love with her in the first place.

When we got pregnant with Jax, it was because she was a scheming, devious person who wanted to trap me in our relationship. Back then, I wasn't ready to be a father. I was militant in my use of condoms because I didn't trust anyone else to handle the birth control. It turns out my instincts had been right because once we were already pregnant, Vivian admitted she hadn't been taking her pill for months. It wasn't until after Jax was gone that she confessed she'd also tampered with the rubbers. At any rate, I knew enough not to marry her, but I was willing to make a run at being a family.

Anyway, that was Vivian in a nutshell, and no, I never worried about losing her. Last night struck a nerve when Norah left, though. I am terrified I will never conquer my demons, in which case, it will only be a matter of time before Norah leaves for good. I hope I don't wonder if it will be the last time I'll see her every single time she goes. I already have enough anxiety. Any more would just be cruel.

After Norah and I had sex on the couch, we went up to my room and lay naked in my bed for a couple of hours while we talked and laughed and kissed. The feel of her in my arms was so natural and easy, it was like she belonged there. When she shimmied down under the covers, it only cemented the idea that she belonged with me. Before heading home, she assured me she would be back tomorrow after work, and I fell asleep smelling her on my pillow.

In an effort to keep my word to her, I put myself back on my therapist's schedule. Twice a week this time instead of once a month. I feel like my progress before was hampered because I only cared about getting by. I never really had anything more to lose. I didn't care about my job, my friends, women—nothing.

The fact that everything I needed was at my fingertips made it hard to strive for more. Groceries were delivered, and there was Amazon for everything else. As much as my friends wanted to help and be there for me, they probably only enabled me to dig my heels deeper into my agoraphobic existence. Basically, there was never anything outside that convinced me the panic attacks were worth it. I still had my friends and women when I wanted them, and when things started to go south with Vivian, my mom moved in, so I had her, too. For a long time that was all I needed, but it feels different now. My lifestyle feels empty and desolate for the first time. For the first time in years, the outside holds the promise of a better future instead of the security of my home.

When Norah rattled off everything she wanted to do, it wasn't the traveling and beer festivals that appealed to me. It was the burning possessiveness that I didn't want her to do those things with some other dude. I don't need concerts and camping trips in my life, but I'm starting to think I need Norah, and the voracity with which I experience those feelings is entirely new to me.

My new reality is that I have to get out of this house, or I will lose the only thing I've cared about in three years. Just the thought of leaving my safe zone has my palms sweating and my heart racing. It's already fucking with my head. But I need to keep reminding myself of my options. I can choose crippling anxiety, or I can choose devastating loss.

I've already lost too much.

Chapter 32

Norah

This is my first attempt to get Justin to challenge himself, and it may go down like a fiery comet with a suicide cult following, but I'm going to push him anyway. I've done my research, and though I'm no expert, I have the unique ability to reward Justin for his advances. I think his disorder is fixable or, at the very least, pliable. I would think differently if he told me he was happy living as he was, but he didn't. Step one, admit you have a problem. Step two, be willing to change. I'm pretty sure that encompasses the first seven steps for Alcoholics Anonymous, so I'll consider his willingness a win.

At the distinct risk of appearing overconfident and unrealistic, I picked up a pre-made fruit and cheese plate, spread out a blanket, and chilled wine. I also have earbuds at the ready in case he requires a sound diversion to remain outside. Finally, I have something special that I made just for him. I'm hoping it will offer another layer of comfort once his panic tries to force a retreat. Now, *I'm* the anxious one.

I take the gift with me and head over to knock on his front door. He opens it and swoops me up in a hug while he kicks the door shut with the back of his foot. My giggle sounds muffled against his chest. I'm glad he is in a playful mood and hope he hangs on to it once he sees what I have in store.

"What's this?" he asks when he sees the gift.

"It's something I made for you. I want it to bring comfort and encouragement when you need it." He takes the box from me but sets it down on the coffee table so he can properly kiss me first.

Justin is expecting a relaxing night in—dinner, a movie, new-couple sex—I doubt he realizes that I'm going to stir up some shit first. When he suggested a 'Netflix and chill' night, I laughed and asked him if he knew that was code for meeting up for sex and had nothing to do with streaming movies. His quipped response was that he doesn't even like movies. For the record, I'm fine with a Netflix and chill night, but it will be *after* we take a trip outside of his safe zone.

"Hmmmm, and I didn't get you anything," he says, but his bright smile hasn't faltered a bit. He is not at all suspicious of my intent, which is good because his buy-in is vital, and I don't want his anxiety churning yet.

"Are you sure about that?" I tease as I palm the button fly of his distressed jeans. He is semi-hard until my hand makes contact, then, there is absolutely no doubt about his gift for me.

"Should I open it now, or should we order dinner first?" he asks, although he looks more like he wants to bend me over right here. To hell with gifts and dinner.

"Presents are always first," I say as I wiggle free and then go sit on the couch. He sits down next to me, and I watch as he slowly unties the bow. I would love to know what he thinks it is, probably a slutty outfit, if the look on his face is any indication.

When he moves the tissue paper aside, he stills. At this point, he knows it's not a slutty outfit, but I don't think he has figured out what it is yet. He stares at it for a bit without taking it out of the box.

"I can smell her," he says. So, he *does* recognize it. I'm hoping he doesn't take exception to the fact that I cut up his mother's flannel nightgown. Hopefully, he sees it as a tribute to her instead of sacking her memory by destroying her things. He gently takes the pillow out of the box and brings it to his face to brush his cheek against it.

This is an emotional moment for him, I can tell. Her death is still very fresh. I know that because whenever he talks about her, his eyes mist up before he can blink away the sentiment.

His eyes are closed as he whispers, "Thank you." After a few more seconds of feeling like a third wheel, I sit back on the couch. He opens his eyes and hugs the pillow to his chest. "Norah, this is the nicest thing anyone has ever done for me. Thank you." His voice is so sincere, I could wring it out into my lap. The sound of it makes my throat tighten. He cups my jaw and then tenderly kisses me. "I wish you could have met her," he says quietly. Now, my throat is not only tight—it seizes entirely.

"Me too," I manage to choke out. I want him to be reminded of his mom and comforted by her memory, but I don't want him to feel vulnerable for the next part of my plan, so I cut the nostalgia short. "Bring the pillow if you want, and come with me," I say as I stand up and reach for his hand. He looks nervous as I guide him toward the front door.

"Don't worry, Justin. It's just a date. Just the two of us."

He follows me outside, immediately noticing everything I have set up on the front lawn. "Are we going on a date in my front yard?"

he asks with a smile that doesn't look fake or painted on. His neighborhood is fairly active. There are cafes and art galleries within a quarter mile and a park two blocks away. Although there aren't any at this exact moment, people jog and walk their dogs by his house all the time. This will be a good first step because it's familiar, but it should also stretch his comfort zone a touch.

"Take these," I say as I put my phone and AirPods into his palm. If he starts to feel triggered by sounds, I want to be prepared. "It's my calming playlist on Spotify. Don't worry, it kicks ass."

"You think I'm worried about the music selection?" he asks, as he cuts his eyes and strokes his chin in bewilderment. I can tell he is fighting some anxiety, even though he doesn't outright show it. His inability to read my joking tone is only the first clue. The subsequent ones are the mild tremor in his hands, his darting eyes, and the stippling of sweat across his brow. All of which I expected.

"I want you to lie down with me. All we will do is focus on the clouds and breathe," I explain as I pat the blanket beside me, encouraging him to comply. I take his hand and entwine our fingers when he finally lies down. Our grip is tight and as damp as a used gym sock. "Do you need to start with the earbuds in? Or are the sounds ok?"

"Uh. I might be ok. I'll let you know."

"Good. Now, we are going to stay just like this until you start to feel your anxiety lessen. Let's pretend to be in a protective bubble, and the only things that matter are our clasped hands and those clouds right there." He seems fine so far, a little stiff but nothing too crazy.

"Have you factored in what will happen if my anxiety never lessens? Even in my front yard where I'm not exactly trapped, there are triggers everywhere."

"Then we will hang out and watch the stars. We will watch the sun come up if we have to, but Justin, your anxiety *will* lessen." He closes his eyes, and I can almost feel him withdrawing from the experience. It's essential that he remain present because distraction or denial will only slow us down.

"Justin, this is *supposed* to feel uncomfortable for you. Everything you are experiencing right now is exactly how you should be feeling. Your thoughts and reactions are a natural response to anxiety. Pretty soon, you will start to feel better. Once you realize you are safe and nothing catastrophic is going to happen, you will have taken the first step toward getting your life back."

"Ok," he says. I smile because he is willing. Not happy, mind you, but at least willing.

After about thirty minutes, he started to relax, but being the insistent woman I am, I began to push him a little further. First, I called his attention to the sounds around us, like the car door slamming, the panting conversation of two joggers, and the jangle of a leash as a man and his dog walked by on the sidewalk.

After the whole dog-in-the-vicinity incident, it had taken another thirty to forty minutes for his panic-stricken heart to beat normally again. I'm not sure if he expected the dog to attack us or what, but just the presence of the animal—tongue lolling out of its smiling mouth and the chipper greeting from its owner and all, was enough to leach the color from Justin's face.

After that round of anxiety lessened, I pushed him to sit up with me and have a sip of wine and some food, which equated to three grapes and a hunk of cheese for him. The meager attempt at eating was still good, considering none of it made it down his throat without quite a bit of coaxing.

Up until that point, I had tried pretty hard to anchor him to the moment by not talking or distracting him a whole lot, other than encouraging him to take deep breaths and reminding him that everything was fine. But once we sat up to the world around us, I began yammering about my day and, at one point, even undid a few buttons of my shirt just to reel in his racing thoughts.

Now, things are calm. It's late evening, and life on his street has lulled itself to sleep. Other than an occasional car driving by, it's quiet. Feeling especially encouraged, I snuggle into his side and hug his body with my free arm.

"Justin, I'm so proud of you. I know that sounds trite, but you did better than I expected."

"My behavior tonight was better than what you expected? I shudder to think what that was. I hate that you saw me like this at all." It's true, he spent the last few hours uncharacteristically fidgeting, stammering, hyperventilating, and trembling with impending doom— but he stuck it out, so as bad as he looked, my focus is still on the outcome.

"You did great," I say as I slide my hand down his stomach and tease my fingers under the waistband of his jeans. My creeping hand should indicate a certain reward system that he may like. "But there is still one more experience I want you to have before we go inside. Coincidentally, it hasn't happened yet."

"Does that experience involve your wandering hand? Because I'm pretty sure I can get behind that."

"That depends on how long we have to wait to hear sirens," I say. As his eyes widen with panic, I quickly add, "But first, let's make up a story about the emergency call the first responders will get called out for; then, when we hear the sirens, we can think about how it has nothing to do with you. It can be a run of the mill heart attack, or maybe a drug overdose?" I can try to spin the whole siren story as much as I want, but I know that particular sound will be the most difficult for him. Irrevocably woven into the worst day of Justin's life is the sound of a siren. That sound alone is enough to bring the horrific scene and all those feelings of helplessness and loss into *this* moment with vicious clarity.

It's no surprise he wants to avoid that specific trigger because anything that submerges him in a memory like that is a vile beast. The trigger brings him right back to that day, so his earlier comment about rather spending the rest of his life in squalor, chained to a radiator in place of re-experiencing that horror, makes a lot of sense now that I've done my research. It's not that he doesn't want to hear the siren. The poor man doesn't want to endure that godforsaken day again.

In a way, it's lucky we didn't hear the squeal of sirens earlier in this process. Justin has fought through multiple spikes of panic and blistering vulnerability, but he understands the concept that his feelings of anxiety will eventually subside. The path isn't pretty, and it takes a long time for him to calm down after each episode, but at least he recognizes that the anxiety won't peak indefinitely.

"Norah, emergency lights and sirens are my two biggest triggers. I don't think it's a good idea." I can already see the panicked thoughts stampeding through him, and his wide eyes are the color of electric fear. Even the suggestion of hearing sirens has ballooned Justin into an unstable, ticking time bomb.

I calmly remind him of an unavoidable fact. "Lights and sirens are never going to go away, Justin. You need to realize that the sight and sound of them don't indicate a personal cataclysmic event for you. In fact, I would be willing to bet you saved enough lives because of those lights and sirens to remind you that they often precede hope and rescue, right?"

"I don't think you understand. It's not because I think they deliver a personal cataclysmic event. It's because they remind me of something so horrific that it pulls me back to that moment, and I have to relive something I hardly lived through in the first place. I can still feel the lights flashing on my skin and hear the squeal of the sirens above all else…it brings me right back to—"

"*I know*, Justin. I'm sorry for that. However, it's critical to change the narrative. I understand how triggers work. I know how they make you re-experience that day, but we need to shift your way of thinking because lights and sirens are a part of life."

"I don't know, Norah. I don't think it's possible to separate one from the other."

Undeterred, I explain, "That is why we will devise an alternative story for when we hear them in the distance. We are going to rewrite the narrative. It will be a version that doesn't involve you at all." I speak calmly as I tug his fly, popping the buttons open. He's not hard yet, which is a testament to his anxious state of mind because the tiniest flutter of my fingers is usually enough to bring him to full salute.

"Norah, please. You can't fix this in a day." He wants to retreat, but I must keep him here until he can ride out those anxious feelings. We can't go inside until he relaxes again because it would only reinforce his instinct to run while trying to avoid the spike in his anxiety entirely.

"Of course not, but you *can* make progress each and every day. Right?" I ask. I know I sound pushy and unsympathetic, but if I coddle him through this, he will remain weak and helpless instead of finding his inner strength. I've read an atrocious amount about his condition, and change only comes from challenging oneself and learning to, first cope with, and then to overcome the discomfort. By constantly pushing his boundaries, he will eventually become desensitized to the process. Even I am not asshole enough to *constantly* challenge him, but I'll push—and then reward his efforts. Pavlov would be proud.

"Will you tell me the funniest, most ridiculous call you ever went on?" I ask as I coax his moderately interested penis from his jeans. "I want all the details, so I will keep going as long as you keep talking. Deal?"

"You are fully aware that we are still in my front yard, right?" he asks as he relaxes back against his elbows. Apparently, his concern for public indecency still comes in second place to a blowjob.

"I'll go turn off the porch light. Should I grab another blanket too? You know, to cover us and protect your delicate sensibilities?"

"A blanket won't be necessary. I still want to watch—even if I am in the middle of a level ten panic attack," he says, a little sardonically perhaps. After I run to the house and turn off the porch light, I settle in between his legs.

"I'm ready when you are, champ," I say with a wink as I eye him from between his thighs. He sighs, which is hilarious to me because he gave in so easily. He's not even thinking about the fact that we are waiting for the sound of his biggest, most fearsome trigger.

"Funniest, most ridiculous call, hmmm—there are so many. I don't know where to start."

"Better start somewhere," I tease as I suggestively lick my lips.

"Ok, ok. Off the top of my head, the funniest and most ridiculous calls were two separate dispatches. I'll start with the most ridiculous." He sucks in a sharp breath of air as I take him in, and then stays mute until I slide him back out of my mouth.

"We got toned out at like two in the morning…with the dispatcher reporting a medical alert with unknown status, ahhhhhh, which means we didn't get any patient information beforehand.

Fuuuuuck, that's good…" he pauses indulgently before continuing, "Anyway, the neighbors reported suspicious noises coming from inside the residence, but we had no idea what to expect. When we arrived on scene, we could hear this unusual groaning sound, but no one answered the door. Anyway, fire service can force entry in the case of an emergency, so we broke down the door and went in—*Jesus, Norah*, I can't concentrate—"

I lift off of him, "It's ok, I can stop so you can concentrate," I say, widening my eyes at him, urging him to go on. It's dark out, and I can't tell if he can see my face, but he gets my message loud and clear.

"So, once we gained entry, we followed the sound to a bedroom and found this dude in a full head-to-toe, tight latex suit. It had the whole zipper-mouth and zip-up flap for backdoor access and everything. The guy had a shiny red ball gag in his mouth, and he was bent over with his arms wrenched back and cuffed to the wall behind him," Justin stops. He's almost panting now, but I don't want him to come before he finishes the rest of the story, so I slow down and become less enthusiastic with my efforts.

"MmmHummm?" I hum, encouraging him to continue his story.

"The guy had this janky machine behind him, jackhammering a purple dildo into his ass." He stops the retelling as if I'm not fully invested in how the whole thing played out. I stop sucking. Message received.

"Davis unhooked the ball gag while a few other guys and I tried to figure out how to turn the machine off. The guy started begging us for water once the ball gag was out of his mouth. He didn't even care that we were all standing there watching him… get railed… by a piece… of plastic. Ooooooooo, baby…. I'm… I'm gonna co—" and that was the end of that story.

After Justin gets himself tucked back into his jeans, I crawl up his body and then snuggle against him, kissing his neck while he wraps his arms around me. The night is utterly peaceful. Were it not for the slight dip in temperature, I could sleep here all night. The smell of his warm skin fills every need inside my body, and I almost feel choked up at the fact that we are out here.

"Then what?" I ask into his neck. His chest rumbles beneath me before he continues his story. He's relaxed. And happy. And it makes my eyes feel raspy with the prickle of tears.

"Someone had welded the switch in the *on* position after chaining the poor guy to the wall, so we had to cut the power. It turns out he had been there for two days getting battered by the machine."

"Poor guy. That must have been mortifying," I say.

"From what the paramedics could piece together on route to the hospital, his lover had taken exception to the guy having sex with someone else." Justin lazily drags his fingertips up and down my arm as he talks.

"Wait, was that supposed to be your funniest call?" I ask, slightly horrified.

"No, that was the most ridiculous call I could remember on cue. Sadly, there are dozens more where that came from." His chest rumbles again. I think he likes talking about his past as a firefighter, so this is great news and an unexpected turn of events.

"The funniest one I can think of was actually a serious apartment fire. It's only funny because we got everyone out, and no one was injured or killed."

I sit up on my elbow to look at him. "Why is that funny? Did I miss something?" Short whiskers speckle his jaw, and the memory of them against my inner thighs is enough to make me want to abandon the cause.

"It's funny because we had a new guy on the deck gun, which sprays from on top of the tanker truck," he snorts and then laughs unabashedly at the memory. I smile and then giggle at his hearty reaction to it. I can tell he was happy back then. I bet he didn't take everything so seriously, either. I hope he can get that back because his unchecked laughter is everything. It sounds different from anyone else's, like he just took it out and dusted it off. I've heard him laugh before, but this time it feels free, or maybe like it has permission to leave his body. All that laughter *and* we are outside. It's more than I could have hoped for.

"Anyway, it's hard to have any sense of depth perception using the deck gun because it creates this huge plume of water fog. It takes a lot of practice to get good at hitting the target," another snort while he tries to hold back his laughter long enough to finish the story, "And Greenie…we call all the new guys Greenie until we settle on a nickname, he knocked down the entire hose team with one sweep of the thing," more rolling laughter, then he reaches up to wipe the tears from his eyes. "He took out several groups of firefighters and a bunch of bystanders before he finished. I almost peed myself in full turn-out gear, I was laughing so hard."

"Did he get in trouble?" I ask. I'm giggling more at Justin's laughter than from the story itself. The sound of it is completely melodic.

"Nah. He caught a rash of shit about it for *years,* though," Justin says, finally settling down. We lie here for a few long minutes before I start to slow-blink and then worry about falling asleep.

We haven't had a chance to push his siren trigger, and we didn't re-write the story either. I guess it wouldn't be horrible if it didn't happen tonight. At least he is relaxed and calm—happy even. Maybe this is the perfect way to end the exposure "therapy." A shiver runs through me as the night air whispers against my skin with a chilly breeze.

Justin notices and snugs his grip on me. "Do you want to know why I want to go inside right now?" he asks.

"Why?" I ask. I'm no genius, but I can guess it's because he doesn't want to sit out here waiting to hear a siren in the distance anymore. But his actual answer surprises me.

"I want to go inside because it's pitch dark out here, and your body tastes like sunshine."

Chapter 33

JUSTIN

The truth is, being outside with Norah last night had gone better than I thought it would. The other baffling truth is that some of what my therapist has been trying to get through to me is genuinely starting to make sense. Are the cogs suddenly beginning to fall into place because I am finally ready to jump back into life again? Or is it something more sinister, like already feeling jealous of the next guy— the one without any debilitating issues, who takes Norah to all the places I should take her?

Talking about the fire station and telling her those stories made me realize something that I feel in the depths of my bones, something that whispers in my ear—that I *hate* being a digital marketing strategist. My bulging inbox of unanswered and thoroughly ignored work emails drives home that simple fact.

In the beginning, once I realized that life would continue to drag me along for the deeply rutted ride, it had been the answer. I didn't have to face anyone, I could still get paid, and the work was mundane and ritualistic. I needed those elements back then, and I was good at the job. Do these ten things—get this result. Easy. Then repeat ad nauseam.

I think part of the reason my home became a self-imposed haven/prison was bigger than the fear of having another panic attack in public. Of being trapped in the world and unable to escape. Of spinning wildly out of control while everyone witnessed my unraveling. I think it was also because I was no longer interested in what life had to offer. There were no experiences I missed or even cared about anymore.

When Jax died, I had never felt so alone, even though I was surrounded by people. People who couldn't do a damn thing to alter my fate or bring my son back. The sun lost its glow. Love toward others or even for myself withered in my heart, and I spat it out destructively from my lips. I didn't want to live without him. Back then, the only thing that kept me from putting a gun in my mouth was the fact that I would doom my own mother to the same fate. I would rob her of her son.

I think my mom knew how close I was to the edge because she moved in even before Vivian left. She was the one who would peel me off the floor just to put a bite of food in my mouth. She was the one who joined me in Jax's room and held me while I sobbed into his crib. She placed the wet cloth on my lips to dribble water into my mouth in a desperate attempt to hydrate my withering body. She fought like a warrior to keep me alive, and I couldn't repay her by snatching my breath from her motherly grip. I knew how tightly she clung to me because that was how tightly I had clung to *my* son.

It's been three years since Jaxson died, and now my mother is gone, too. My heart is no longer obligated to beat for her. But nowadays, I don't have to fight the urge to disappear. For the first time in three years, I don't want to recede further and further away from society. In fact, with a strength that belies my wounded nature, I suddenly feel intensely as though life owes me something. Life owes me at least a shred of happiness, and I intend to claim it—even if it's by storm. My shackles no longer offer comfort. They dig into my skin and cause the very festering I designed them to repel.

I'm ready to break out of this glass castle—from its empty promises and false hopes. Life owes me this. God owes me this. I'm even starting to realize that *I* owe myself this. These feelings are all crispy and new for me, too. If you had told me a couple of years ago that one day I'd be ready to face the world, I would have told you to go suck a bag of dicks.

On her way out this morning, Norah told me there would be another picnic later this week. She dropped the statement like a bomb before casually adding that the next one would be at the park down the street. The thought she had inadvertently left ringing in my ears was that there would be a lot of screaming, loud, frolicking—highly triggering—kids at the park. I hope she realizes a blowie near a playground filled with kids would not work the same as it did on my front lawn under the cover of darkness. Plus, it would get us a few criminal charges—Just offhand, public indecency, disorderly conduct, indecent exposure, and committing a lewd act in public. Never mind the seared retinas of the children and the high probability of needing to register as sex offenders. Anyway, as determined as I felt this morning and as ready as I thought I was, I could still taste my heart beating in my throat.

Now, following one of my twice-weekly therapy appointments, with the door hardly shut behind my therapist, I stare at the bulky headphones he left with me. Apparently, in the interest of striking while the iron is hot, Dr. Edward decided I should do some homework to desensitize myself toward the sounds of kids. Kids—happy and alive kids.

I can't decide which is worse for me right now, answering all those blasted emails and committing myself to work or lying in bed with my head pinched between giant headphones. These things are legit, even heavy in my hands. Immersive therapy evidently looks a lot like a turntable spinning DJ at a rave.

I understand the theory Dr. Edward preaches, that exposing myself to specific triggers over and over will eventually lessen my undesired response to them. I get it, but can *any* amount of exposure succeed at unraveling my trauma? I want it to work, but my doubts remain undiluted.

Headphones and the triggering sounds of children? Or work that I loathe? Anxiety or disdain? How does one choose?

In the end, I decided to get back in bed and still myself for the racing thoughts and pounding heart. I guess I'll have to submit to the process because I can't exactly slow down a speeding freight train.

At first, there are no anxiety provoking sounds of children crying or playing at all. Only the quiet voice of a little boy reciting the Pledge of Allegiance, a little boy who sounds just like Jaxson.

***

I can't tell if it's been minutes or days inside these headphones. My initial reaction had drained me of any notable response to the rest of the sounds. As I focused on the orange peel texture of the ceiling, my cheeks streaked with tears, violent sobs wracked my body. Just the sweet, innocent sound of the little boy's voice reduced me to rubble.

But, after the well ran dry and my body overcame the shaking convulsions, I continued to listen. When it finished, I closed my eyes and listened to it again.

And then again.

Chapter 34

Norah

My next attempt at desensitizing Justin could explode in my face like a fiery bag of shit, or he could like it. Not knowing where he will fall on the spectrum of responses makes me nervous to knock on his door for the first time in months.

Sophia had gone with me to pick it out. She had also reasoned that it would continue to work its immersive magic even in my absence. Sometimes Sophia's no-nonsense delivery of her opinion makes a lot of sense, and sometimes I question if she is giggling behind her hand, just as unsure as me. In the end, I was lucky to get away with one and not two of the pricey little fuckers.

The question of Justin's level of responsibility was never in question, only his level of contempt. Which I will measure in,

5…

4…

3…

fuuuuuuck…one.

He swings the door open and steps out to smother me in an ambitious hug but then drops his gaze to my feet and stops short of the hug. He has to like it. Who wouldn't like it?

"Really?" he deadpans, with complete boredom stitched to his voice. "We're doing this?"

"Yep," I say with confidence I don't feel, as I fight the urge to put it back in my car and pretend this never happened.

"Is it housetrained?"

"Uhhh, nope. At least I don't think so," I say through a smile that must look an awful lot like the shape of guilt. He looks away from my eyes and back down to my feet. Then he sighs.

"Alright then, come on," he says with resignation as he squats down and picks the puppy up. The leash was completely unnecessary because the fluffy little thing was downright sulking at my feet after I set him down in the first place. In the eleven hours since I purchased him, Sophia or I have held him for ten and a half of those hours. He is a mellow little dude, too, because I did my homework about the breed. My single biggest requirement when I chose the type of dog was a gentle disposition.

Justin plops down on the couch with all four of the puppy's paws comfortably against his chest. "I only have one question for you," he announces. I gulp down a big lug of saliva, expecting him to say, *What the hell are you thinking?*

"Couldn't you have found a bigger, furrier breed of dog?"

After a short pause, I cough out a laugh. He is obviously joking because a Bernese Mountain Dog is a huge, hella furry breed. Justin beams at me while the dog tries to lick his face. He dodges the first few attempts, but his efforts are futile. He gets a better hold of the squirming mass of black, white, and brown fur, then lifts the puppy off his chest to discern gender.

"What's his name?" he asks.

"I don't know. I've just been calling him *Little Shit* because he peed in one of my gym shoes."

"How about Indy?" he asks, still holding the puppy up like he is presenting him to the tribe.

"Yes, I like that name. Indy." I smile warmly, but it has nothing to do with the name. It's because of the fat smile on Justin's sweet face.

"Ok, Indy. Time to go outside because the fastest way back to the puppy mill would be to pee on my Brazilian Walnut hardwood floors." Justin carries him to the back door, then sets him down and closes it behind him.

Indy turns around to face us, then slumps down with his face resting on his front paws. He makes no effort to do anything, let alone walk out into the yard to pee. He watches us watch him, a stare down of sorts, but I get the impression that he will learn to do his business quickly if he wants to come back inside. His breed is known to be sensitive, and they get their feelings hurt easily—which is exactly what we are looking at now. Sad, puppy dog eyes.

"I went for a walk today," Justin says offhand as he crosses his arms over his chest, never taking his eyes off the puppy.

"You what?" I ask incredulously. My mouth drops wide open with surprise, but Justin still looks at Indy, so he can't see my unattractive facial expression.

"Yeah, my therapist said I need to be careful about you driving the ship instead of me. He also warned about using you as a crutch, or more accurately, a security blanket. I almost told him I'll get fewer blowjobs that way, but at the last second, I kept that bit to myself." I roll my eyes at his summation, but mostly because he glosses over the momentous fact that he went for a walk today.

"How did it go? The walk, not the therapist's pity about you getting fewer hummers."

"I said I kept that bit to myself. So, it's true then?" Again, he glosses over the real achievement just to toy with me.

"I haven't decided yet," I grind out as I step into him and squeeze the side of his body in a proud hug.

"Oh, ok then, while you decide, I'm just going to tell you everything there is to know about my spontaneous walk. Actually, it wasn't spontaneous at all. In fact, my therapist and I chatted about it for an hour first, and then I visualized it while he talked me through the whole thing—start to finish. It was a pretty epic pretend walk." He concedes defeat and finally opens the door for Indy.

"What about the non-visualized one? How did that go?" I ask as I kiss his chest and then bite it when he pauses too long before answering me.

"Surprisingly, it went well. Did you know there is a Starbucks on the corner of Downing and Sixth now?" His smile is bright, and it gets brighter as I laugh about his discovery. Sixth and Downing is only a few blocks away, but it is still a huge accomplishment for him.

"Did you have a panic attack?" I ask.

"Attack? No. But did I sweat through my shirt? You're damn right I did."

"But did you die?"

"Not this time—" Just then, the doorbell rings, presumably with our dinner, and Indy attempts a vicious guard dog bark. He'll have to work on it, though, because it sounds more like a throaty cough than a bark, but whatever, his instinct is right.

Chapter 35

JUSTIN

Predictably, Norah left me with the furry little shit. At first, I was excited because it would be nice to have company on my doctor-prescribed walks. My therapist thought four a day was a solid number, but how he decided to go from zero in three years to four a day was a good idea, I'll never know. Anyway, like I said, I was excited at first.

That was before Indy chewed up my weight belt, crapped on the floor twice, rubbed his wet nose all over the glass patio doors, dragged toilet paper all through the house, and barfed on my bare foot. That was day one, and he was only getting started.

Now it's day two, and he's already started the day by peeing on the floor. Then, for good measure, he teepeed the house with an entire roll of toilet paper—again, then destroyed my remote and chewed up my phone charger. Asshole.

There is a little voice in my head that sounds an awful lot like Davis. It keeps chanting, *Bro, a bored puppy is a naughty puppy.* I hate that smug, know-it-all voice, especially because I've already taken Indy on three anxiety-riddled walks today, which he doesn't even seem to acknowledge before soundly trashing the place—again. And the way he just sits and looks at me while I try to work makes me think he expects me to quit my job and tend entirely to every one of his needs and desires.

Maybe I should toss Indy in the pool and let him swim off his boredom. Perhaps then he would lose his disenchanted, millennial stare. Better yet, I'll maroon him on a raft; that way, he couldn't get into trouble. Wait, who am I kidding? He would pop the raft, swim to the bottom, chew up the robotic pool vacuum, and then take a shit next to both filters.

I know what I *should* do, aside from tying him to a moving treadmill. I should take him for another walk, even though I have hardly calmed myself after the last one. As early as yesterday morning, the thought of taking him outside with me when I could barely handle myself tripled my heart rate and elicited bucketfuls of sweat. Every walk so far has smothered my fight or flight mechanism with a deluge of righteous anxiety, but I persevered each time.

My therapist told me I was supposed to react that way. All panicky and disconcerted. He said I need to put myself in uncomfortable situations to trigger the panic so I can "sit with it" until the anxiety starts to subside. I prefer the avoid-and-try-to-ignore approach, but I can't seem to swing any supporting votes in my direction. Theoretically, once I have done something dozens of times, it should become routine, and the anxiety should get easier to conquer.

Norah has become a terrorist regarding the whole thing, too. If she gets her unflinching way, which, let's face it, she will—as all terrorists do, we will be going to the dog park after she gets off work.

She has run out of sympathy for me and has jumped on my therapist's bandwagon entirely. The two of them in cahoots are borderline insufferable, and when they gang up on me, I don't even stand a chance. If they continue at this pace, I'll surf the panic wave 24/7 until nothing phases me. Exposure therapy, my ass, this is cruel and unusual.

"I know you did *not* just pee on the floor right in front of me, Indy. Please tell me you are smarter than that, dude." I stare down at him, and I swear to God, if he could talk, he would have just said, *I told you to go get the leash, punk. This one's on you.*

I don't have to go far for paper towels because I *do* happen to be easily trainable, so I have a roll right next to me on my desk.

"You see this? This is called 'anticipating the need,' you little squirt," I grumble as I soak up the second lake of urine today. Indy has the audacity to wag his tail and try to lick my face while I'm bent over. He has no clue what a dick he is.

"I'm selling you to the Gypsies first chance I get, you little turd." Clearly, he doesn't take me seriously because I already love him and smile through my threats, but he should at least have the grace to look contrite. Not Indy, though. Nope, he just snatches the flip-flop off my foot and runs out of the room.

I sacrifice the flip-flop to get some work done. He will chew it up and sprinkle it all over the house, but at least he won't pee inside again for a little while.

I haven't accomplished jack-shit today unless you count the psychotic doses of adrenalin repeatedly dumped into my system during my walks, and the eternity it took to calm down from such things. Now, I have to squeeze a nine-hour workday into the hour and a half before Norah gets off work.

I'm granted maybe forty-five minutes of productivity before I hear someone knocking on the front door. Indy, ever vigilant watchdog that he is, scampers toward the noise, wagging his tail so hard he can't even walk a straight line. After taking the stairs two at a time and glancing at my watch, I realize it's too early to be Norah unless something went sideways at work. Plus, it can't be her because she just walks in after a preemptive knock these days anyway.

I scoop up Indy so he doesn't terrorize my visitor with vicious licks and savage tail thumps, then open the door. It's Kate. I took the coward's way out of our relationship a few months ago by not calling her back or responding to her repeated texts. In all fairness to myself, though, she knew we were casual, and I wasn't looking for commitment. Not back then, anyway.

"Hey, Kate. What's up?" I ask. I'm not even surprised to see her at my door. Just last week, she made two attempts to rekindle our long-extinguished spark. Two texts; one was light and breezy, and the other I needed to delete immediately so it didn't stir up trouble for me. All I need is for Norah to stumble across a raunchy text like that. There would be no way to explain it, even though I've entirely moved on from the bleach blonde in the pic—not that you could tell she has blonde hair, mind you. Really, all you could see was her fake tan. Well, that and her open legs and shameless fingers.

"Hi, handsome," she tries demure on for size because obviously, the Hustler shot didn't get a callback. I don't even respond to her calling me handsome. For that matter, I don't invite her in either.

"Can we talk?" she asks.

"Kate, I'm seeing someone," I give blunt a shot because not responding to calls or texts may have been too subtle for this one.

"I only want to talk to you, Justin," she pleads, as her eyes well up with tears. "I just need some kind of closure, that's all." I try to ignore the tears that I have evidently caused because heartache is a tricky emotion for me. I prefer to deny the existence of other people's pain rather than jump in it with them. But, because I thought enough of this woman to sleep with her a handful of times, I suppose I can at least grant her closure. Closure I can do.

"Sure, of course. Come in," I step aside while she walks in. Kate moves as if she's walking over a bed of nails. She's too fragile, not at all like her former self—it's intensely annoying. I ignore her trepidation and sit down on the couch, still holding Indy. She sits next to me instead of on the chair, which makes more sense, but I don't worry about it too much because I think it's because she finally notices a puppy in my arms.

"Cute dog. What's his name?" she asks as she scratches Indy's ears, ignoring the nips from his puppy teeth. She should read his non-verbal cues, though, because Indy *hates* when people mess with his ears. Norah picked up on that right away.

"His name is Indy. Look, Kate," I pause because I'm not sure how to tell her to get on with this closure thing. Would it be rude to tell her to land the plane? "I know you are looking for closure, but—"

"Just tell me why."

"Why what?" I ask. Her question is too vague. Does she want to know why I didn't respond to her calls? Or why she couldn't get me to leave the house? Or why I wasn't looking for commitment? I could go on for hours.

"Why you don't want me anymore," she says into her lap. I can deal with a lot of things, but one of them is not Kate behaving like a broken China doll.

"Kate, I told you I wasn't looking for anything serious." I want to ask her how my couch dissolved her backbone, but I swallow that sentiment for now.

"That was in the beginning. Our relationship evolved—like all relationships do," she looks gutted, and I hate that she misconstrued our fucking as an evolving relationship, but that's on her. I was always very upfront with women because I never wanted the hassle—this exact hassle.

"I never wanted it to evolve from what it was. As wonderful as you are and as happy as you will make someone someday, I never wanted a serious relationship. I told you that multiple times, but I'm sorry if I ever led you to believe anything different. Truly, I'm sorry I hurt you. I never meant to cause you any pain."

"You used to like causing me pain."

"Huh?"

"You used to smack my ass while you fucked me," she smiles at this and even raises her chin with conviction. "And you liked to pull my hair and strain my neck back whenever I rode your hard co—"

"You should go," I say in response to her one-sided nostalgia. I think she believes speaking to me like this will somehow bring me to my senses and remind me of everything we had. She may even think I will throw her down and have sex with her right here. When she makes no move to stand or go, I pick up a sleeping Indy and leave the room myself.

"I need to let the puppy out," I say over my shoulder. Letting her inside was a huge mistake. Norah will eat Kate alive if she's still in my house when she gets off work. It's a good thing Norah is good at sniffing out bullshit, I'm not even afraid of them meeting.

Indy waddles off of the patio, still half asleep, while I shut the door and return to the mess I stepped in by believing sex could be casual. Kate could have any other guy eating out of the palm of her hand. I wish she would let it go and move on to someone who wants her.

When I return to the living room, I don't see her at first. However, my relief at thinking she let herself out crumbles around me and threatens to cave in the entire house when I see her. Her shirt is off, and she is in the process of stepping out of her tight jeans. Never the fuck mind about being fine with Norah and Kate meeting. This could detonate into something massive.

"What the hell are you doing?" I step forward and tug her jeans back up, lifting her off the ground in the hasty process. She stabilizes herself by clutching my shoulders with her needy talons and pressing her tits against my chest.

"Come on, baby," she attempts a sexy whine that only makes her sound more pathetic.

"Kate, don't stoop to this. Hang on to your dignity and go. Now." I pick up her shirt while she fiddles with her bra clasp and aggressively guide her to my front door. She clamors and tries to speak, but it doesn't penetrate my brain. With single-minded focus, I escort her judiciously out of my house and close the door behind her before Norah arrives.

Normally, I would feel like a dick shoving a woman out my front door with her jeans undone and shirt clutched in her hands, but not today, and not with Kate. She needs to hear me loud and clear. Our casual relationship is over. Don't come back.

I slide my fingers through my hair and tightly grip my head as I pace the living room. This will be a story I laugh about one day, but today is not that day. I need to get my breathing under control and unclench my jaw. Damn, why does my stomach feel like it's digesting a bag of Ninja throwing stars?

Norah's late, and that knowledge doesn't sit well with me. I storm through the house toward the back door. I need my dog.

Chapter 36

Norah

It's her. You have to be kidding me. If you told me yesterday that Justin was still sleeping with her, I would have thought you were crazier than a shit-house rat. But now, *now* I see it for myself. It's cute how he wants to ensure she is out of the house before I stroll in and discover his betrayal. She isn't even fully clothed as she bolts to her car, and he closes the door behind her. Time must have gotten away from him as he languished between another woman's thighs. Right now, he's probably wondering if he has time to shower before I arrive. Yes, Justin, take all the time you need to wash your filthy cock.

I have half a mind to take my dog back. Fucking asshole. I'm not even sad right now. I'm quaking with *white-hot rage*. My transmission tries to drop out of my car when I attempt to put it in gear without pushing in the clutch first. The wretched sound jolts me from my seething vehemence and gnashing teeth. I stomp on the clutch before speeding off down the street.

When I get to my apartment, I'm already peeling off my work clothes as I yell out to Sophia. She better hope she doesn't have other plans tonight because I just canceled them. I'm halfway in the shower when she finally answers me.

"I was Skyping with my mom. She says hello, by the way. Now, what the hell is all the commotion about?" She flops onto my bed, talking to me through the open bathroom door.

"Get ready, we are going out. Justin is sleeping with someone else," I say as I savagely rinse the shampoo out of my hair. It gets in my eyes, but I welcome the burn—anything to circumvent the pain threatening to crack open my chest.

"No, he's not," she says flatly. I want to shake her; I mean really shake her—rattle her teeth, shake her. I think I would know. I never would have guessed it, but I know what I saw.

"What the hell, Sophia? I saw him. Now, get ready. I need a few drinks and some really loud music."

"I don't believe you. There is no way he is sleeping with someone else. Davis suspects that Justin is in love with you. That doesn't sound like someone who's sleeping with another woman on the sneak." Her words shoot multiple harpoons straight through my heart, tearing through it with jagged gashes and barbing the delicate tissue. If I start crying right now, I'll never stop. I have to shut down the tears and remain angry. Still, she makes no effort to get up and get ready to go out.

"I don't care if you believe it or not. Who's playing at The Casbah tonight?" I quickly change the subject because I'm done thinking about it. I have to be, or I won't be able to draw a single breath tonight.

"It doesn't sound like it matters who is playing," she tosses out, while most likely twirling her hair around a manicured finger.

"You're right, it doesn't," I say as I jerk the faucet to turn off the water.

***

It turns out an eighties cover band is playing tonight. I guess it's better than the heavy metal, head-banging band that scorched my ears the last time we were here. My phone vibrates in my back pocket, and I pull it out only to decline the call and mute anything incoming. It's Justin, of course, because he doesn't know I busted him, so he's probably wondering why we aren't on our way to the dog park right now. I am confused by the string of texts I see from him, though. It's like he *knows*.

I'm going to have to change his contact information to LiarLiarPantsOnFire, because the current one doesn't work for me anymore. The texts started about twenty minutes after he was expecting me and then came again roughly every fifteen to thirty minutes after that.

SexyMotherFucker: *It's kind of a funny story.*

SexyMotherFucker: *It's not at all what you think.*

SexyMotherFucker: *Norah, please.*

SexyMotherFucker: *I'm begging you to listen to what I have to say.*

SexyMotherFucker: *Baby, you are killing me.*

He obviously knows why I didn't come over after work. He knows that I know. How is he going to try and spin this? Sophia watches me digest his texts as she snaps her gum and leans her back and both elbows against the bar.

"Told ya," she says with a knowing grin as the crowd swells exponentially.

Before I have a chance to respond to her, the bartender leans in and says, "Here you go. Do you want a tray to carry all of them?" That's hilarious. He thinks I bought a round of shots for my friends.

"No thanks," I say, my eyes daring him to challenge me, even for one fleeting second, so I can rip his head off. He wisely keeps his mouth shut and smile in place. I hand him my credit card. Hopefully, he reads between the lines and keeps my tab open.

"Bottoms up, Soph," I say, not even waiting for her before taking my first shot. We tap our shot glasses together for my second one, her first, as she gives me a disapproving look.

"Stop looking at me like that. You don't know what I saw," I say before number three burns my throat like some sort of unsolicited heartburn or something.

"Did you eat?" she asks.

"Huh?"

"Did you eat dinner? I need to prepare myself for exactly how big of train wreck you will be tonight," she blinks dotingly, but there is an eye roll disguised behind her friendly smile.

"I didn't have time to eat, I was too busy watching Justin push a half-naked, sexed-up woman out his front door." Shot number four. It should have been Sophia's because I only ordered six of them, but she doesn't seem to mind—and she is drinking them way too slowly.

"Really?" she is flabbergasted for some reason, not that I haven't been telling her that since I got home. "Why would he do that?" Now, she *does* pick up a shot as she ponders what I just told her.

"See? Now, do you get it?" I ask before I hop off my barstool. "I'm gonna go dance."

As I cleave through the masses, I can't help but think my hair is not nearly big enough to fit in with an eighties crowd. It seems this band has its own following. Therefore a large percentage of the mob has regressed a few decades. I see my lifetime quota of crimped hair, fingerless gloves, leg warmers, and day glow. On a positive note, if there is one for this whole shitty evening, it's that I recognize most of the songs.

Soon enough, the crowd swallows me down its gullet, and tipsy as I am, I don't even mind dancing with guys in zipper jackets and parachute pants. I focus my attention on the hottest one in my immediate vicinity. He happens to be wearing a Linkin Park shirt, which has overshot the eighties by twenty years, but he is really fun to dance with. As far as dispositions go, his is easy and playful, so he should do the trick of distracting me this evening.

We dance together so long and so hard that we have a sheen of sweat coating us, and I've burned off all my shots. I don't even care that he probably has the wrong impression of me and assumes I'm going home with him. I don't care about anything right now.

When he wipes his sweaty face with his t-shirt, I gesture to the Linkin Park graphic and say, "I think you missed the mark." I almost have to shout even though he is a mere two feet away, giving me his full and completely fixed attention.

"I know, but my acid washed jeans were in the dirty laundry. I had no choice. What's your excuse?" he asks, with a smile so big he reveals the sliver canine tooth that keeps flashing with his attentive grin.

"I don't need an excuse. I'm just here to get drunk and forget a few things."

"Is that right?" he asks, drawing out the question. "Maybe, I can give you a hand with that," he offers, his voice dripping with the possibilities. Then, he glances over my shoulder and puffs up his chest. I've seen this look on a guy's face before. It's possessive and clenched in a cautionary manner. His posture straightens in warning while emitting some preemptive declaration. His stance also carries the promise of thrown fists.

"That won't be necessary." The voice comes from behind me, confident and maybe *amused*. I spin around, not expecting Justin to be behind me in a million years, yet he is. He ignores my open-mouthed shock to parley with the refrigerated voice and nefarious glare now standing to my right.

"Nobody asked for your input, bro," this comes from my silver-eye-toothed suitor, who delivers it on a snarl.

"She won't be forgetting anything tonight, least of all her senses or her taste in men," Justin scoffs. His words have hidden amusement, but I know he would level this guy if given half a chance. Justin pays zero attention to the warning glare from the guy, all without breaking eye contact with him.

Justin's demeanor is unmarked by his anxiety, which is surprising in itself, but his steely resolve and utter confidence are admirable in light of the situation. If I were not crazy pissed off at him, I would find his unruffled, cocky disposition sexy—Alpha even, and his agoraphobic bravery commendable. Not today, though. Not that anyone is interested in my two cents at the moment anyway because the guys are squaring off.

"I'm only giving you one chance to back off," Linkin Park t-shirt says, with the hostility clouding his face getting thicker by the second.

"And if I don't?" Justin asks, with a self-indulgent smile that makes me think he *wants* to get in a fight. I've never had two guys get all scrappy over me before. Part of me feels critically relevant, and the other part is scared someone really will throw a punch.

"Then I'll knock you the fuck out." An hour of dancing with someone usually doesn't elicit this possessive of a response, but I think Justin's arrogance is what's poking this bear.

"Yeah, ok, buddy," Justin mocks. Then, taking a step closer to the guy and morphing into something deadly serious, he growls, "I'd like to see you try." Justin's dominant attitude is only stoking this guy's rage. I feel like it's my duty to jump in before someone gets hurt. I place a gentle hand on each of their chests.

"Guys, wait a sec—" Just as I'm trying to infuse some civility, Sophia bowls into the guy, wrapping her arms around his neck for an ambush hug and knocking him back a few steps.

"I'm so happy you're here! I've missed you so much!" Sophia gushes all over the guy as Davis backs Justin up, away from the skirmish. It's Sophia's sacrificial act of literally throwing herself on a live grenade to save the rest of us.

I'm so stunned by the whole thing, and, let's be honest, my response time has dulled significantly, so I get caught up in the current of Davis and Justin heading back to the bar. I'm not even aware of Justin holding my hand at first, but when realization dawns on me, I yank it back.

Chapter 37

JUSTIN

"Why are you even here?" Norah spits out. I could explain the fact that Sophia sent Davis a distress text full of red alerts and emergency emojis and that he jumped at the chance to see Sophia— or, maybe even, saw it as an opportunity to drag me out of the house, but I don't think that is what she means by her question.

"You think you can screw whoever you want and still keep me under your thumb?" she asks incredulously. Her eyes dart back and forth between my right eye and my left, and she has that haze around her that tends to accompany too much alcohol. I'm pretty fed up with this whole situation if you want to know the truth.

The third wheel is suddenly quite apparent, and he realizes it immediately. Davis slaps my chest and says, "I'm needed on recon. You have fun with this." Then, he disappears back into the fray to retrieve Sophia.

"Is that where I have you, under my thumb?" Then I lean in and murmur into her ear, "I much prefer you on the end of my dick."

She is not amused. Even though she's as plastered as the Sistine Chapel, she won't let me redirect her fury. She crosses her arms sharply across her chest, and her eyes spew pure venom. She hasn't even acknowledged that I am standing in a crowded bar for the first time in three years.

"And what if I refuse to share the end of your dick with anyone else?" She tries to sound vicious, but the crêpiness in her voice is unmistakable as her voice wavers. I think she was looking for the alcohol to take the edge off. However, if anything, it seems to have enhanced her emotional susceptibility.

I'm glad she's upset by this whole thing because when I first saw her, I thought the exact opposite. She doesn't realize how seeing her dancing and laughing with another man affected me. My barely contained panic attack vaporized the moment I laid eyes on her. The anxiety took a rapid and immediate back seat to the hurt and jealousy that was scratching and clawing inside of me, looking for a way out.

"Norah, do you really think I had sex with Kate?" I ask with a softness to my voice I don't recognize. Now, I'm serious; no more teasing pokes or attempts to make light of the purely ridiculous notion that I would have slept with someone else.

"I saw you," she says. Her chin quivers, and for some reason, her naked vulnerability sends a fiery spear straight through my heart. Her pain is as raw as my need to explain. I drag my thumb across her lipstick stained bottom lip, then take her chin between my finger and thumb and pull her in for a ghost of a kiss.

"You saw nothing," I say as I lightly graze her lips with mine again. It's not a kiss, but it's more intimate somehow. Here is the chink in her armor, she wants to believe me. The problem is, she has worked herself up into such a lather that she can't let go of her convictions.

"Norah, you saw nothing because there was *nothing* to see," my words are patient yet steadfast. She closes her eyes on a tear as it streaks down her cheek. People crowd the bar, and I am clearly out of my element, but right here and now, it feels like it's just the two of us.

"Look at me, Norah," I encourage her to open her eyes as I tip her head up to face me, "Look me in the eyes and tell me you sincerely believe I slept with someone else," I state as a challenge, but the truth is, if she can say it I will feel like less of a man for not ensuring that kind of security for her. If she truly believes I'm capable of such a thing, I have not done my job as her boyfriend. She should have zero doubt about my trustworthiness by now.

"I saw you get rid of her before I was supposed to arrive at your house," then her voice drops to a whisper, "She wasn't even all the way dressed." She closes her eyes again, giving up the fight against her tears as they stream down her beautiful face. She uncrosses her arms and tries to wipe the emotion away, but she can't stem the flow.

"Listen, I'm not happy about your lack of trust, but I can see why it might have looked like that. All I'm going to say is, you're wrong. I was ready to explain a couple of hours ago, but now I'm too chapped that you wouldn't even give me that courtesy before running straight into the arms of another man." I deliver my statement and then let it hang there for a while. She needs to understand the gravity of this—and the nonsense of it. If we can't have a tiny misunderstanding while still retaining our trust in one another, we have bigger problems than I initially thought.

"Did you kiss her?" she asks with a small voice. Her lingering doubt pricks on my skin like static. I answer her through clenched teeth and flaring nostrils because of that trust thing again. I hope her inability to see reason is due to her alcohol intake instead of deliberate stubbornness.

"Absolutely not. Are we done?" Before she can answer, Davis and Sophia stumble over. They are sweating profusely from dancing and clearly have dissolved any and all sobriety boundaries.

"See, Norah," Sophia trills as she teeters next to Davis, "He didn't sleep with someone else because he loves you!" I want to wire Sophia's mouth shut after her classless delivery of such a tender sentiment. I do love Norah, I recognized it a while ago, but I won't impart those words in a situation like this. The last thing I want to do is tell her I love her for the first time on the same night I had to track her down and about break some guy's jaw. Beyond that, how can I tell her I'm in love with her when I know she doesn't even trust me?

I'm relieved from having to address the whole thing when Norah steps closer to me and tucks herself into my chest. Any persisting frustration or cynicism on my part dissolves on contact, and I wrap my arms around her.

"I can't believe you are here," she says. It's hardly audible through the muffle of my shirt, but it speaks volumes. I am here. I've not left my house in three years except to walk increasingly long distances. Still, when Davis showed up at my door spinning his tale of Norah getting drunk and awfully cozy at the bar, it only took a few minutes to "sit with" and then overcome my anxiety. On the ride over, I used every weapon in my therapist's arsenal to calm my racing thoughts and still my mind.

The biggest mind fuck of all, was that a public panic attack or my feelings of losing control were not even my primary worries. At the forefront of my anxious thoughts were Davis's words: *get in the car; Norah thinks you cheated on her, and now she is drunk at The Casbah, cozying up to some random dude.*

"I needed to get my girl," I breathe into her ear. "Now, let's go." I worry about my state of mind once the adrenaline wears off, and I know I have to get out of here now.

***

Closing tabs and corralling Davis and Sophia into the waiting Uber had taken a preposterously long time. My mounting panic and basic frustration with the pace at which drunk people move had nearly unraveled me. I felt like clawing my skin open to free my clipped breaths and pounding heart. Davis sat in the front seat with the driver and regaled him with stories of increasing stupidity while I leaned my sweaty face against the cool window and tried to remember to breathe.

Norah lifted my limp arm over her shoulders and then cuddled against my unreceptive body. She spoke to me in a calming voice and prattled on about how brave I am and how I need to focus on the fact that everyone is safe and that everything will be fine. It wasn't until she said we were almost there that I started to feel the tightness in my bones begin to loosen.

Now, finally, inside my house, I feel safe but utterly exhausted and run down. I toe off each of my shoes and flop down on the couch, perfectly willing to lie here until next week. Physically and mentally, I feel empty and drained of substance. Norah stands at the foot of the couch, but heaven only knows what she's thinking. I have my forearm draped over my eyes, and I make no attempt to let Indy out of his kennel—even though he is going berserk with his continued confinement.

"Hi, big boy! Do you want to go outside and go potty?" Norah asks Indy before unlatching the door to his cell and laughing at his high energy exit. I don't need to look to see what's going on because I have seen it a hundred times, and Indy's freedom routine never deviates from his standard formula. Norah laughs as he darts around with uncontained glee and then hurls himself on top of me, narrowly avoiding crushing my balls with the clumsy paws that are way too big for his body.

"Indy, damn! Watch the jewels," I say, using my free hand to protect my greatest asset. He leaves the proximity of my nut sack, only to thump the breath out of my lungs as he topples over and then tries to curl up in the two-inch space between my armpit and the back of the couch. He is a needy little thing and has grown accustomed to balling up and sleeping against my body. I fought it at first, not wanting him on my bed, but it's so cute how he wants to be near me all the time, so I caved. It took all of three minutes.

"Come on, you little stinker, I don't want you to have an accident in the house," Norah says while trying to hold back the *awwwwww* that sits spring-loaded on her lips. She closes the distance and scratches his chin. Once she finally coaxes him down to the floor, the little asshole pees right where he is standing.

I make no move to get up and clean the urine, mainly because I've cleaned up the other seven hundred messes he made in his short tenure in this house.

"No, sir!" Norah scolds him. "Bad boy! You do not potty in the house!" She grabs him by the fluffy scruff of his neck and hauls him outside, admonishing him the whole way. I've never raised my voice to Indy, so I have to fight the urge to jump in like a mama bear to protect him. Even though he is huge for a puppy, he is very tender-hearted. His feelings are fragile, just like a kid's, so I'm never that harsh with him. I usually just call him a dickhead, clean up the mess, then go about my day. Wait. Maybe that's the problem?

I remove my forearm from its perch across my eyes and then lace my fingers behind my head, waiting for Norah to return. This day has rivaled an eternity in its laborious passing, and I'm ready to put it behind me. However, I don't think Norah shares my sentiment because when she returns, she stands by my reclining feet and peels off her dress in one smooth, over the head motion.

Her bra and panties are skimpy and evocative in a violet hue that heats my groin. The contrast of the erotic lace against her pale skin reminds me that I have a penis, and it's pulsing with the need to bow to her, pledge its devotion, and do anything she asks of it. However, my over-analyzing brain picks up on one tiny detail.

"Too bad you didn't put those on for me," I cock my head and meet her eyes. She can't flaunt her sexy body over me and expect me to forget her mission to seduce that meatball in the club. The thought of her impulsive pettiness re-chaps my ass.

"No?" she asks. "Well, how about when I bought them?" She puts her knee on the arm of the couch and proceeds to crawl over it and then up my prone body. My penis doesn't happen to care who she put these panties on for, only the way they fit her curves and hug her ass. She stops her advance near the top of my thighs and then drags a long, slow lick up the crotch of my jeans. *Fucking hell!*

"When I bought them, all I could think about was you." She continues stalking up my frame, her face pouty. "About how much you would appreciate the way they ride up my ass… and how good my tits look in lace. All I could think about was how you would reach between my legs and slide your hand inside these panties so you could graze your fingers against my tight, little—"

I've already lost the will to resist but I stay quiet anyway. I'd like to see how far she goes with this sensual cock tease. The drinks at the bar have taken away her inhibitions and turned her into quite a persuasive little vixen.

Regardless of her initial intentions this evening, I know her well enough to know she wouldn't have slept with someone else. It's more likely that she felt like she needed to remind herself that she is desirable to the opposite sex—a fact she is proving right now in spades.

She brings her lips to the shell of my ear for the pièce de résistance, "I couldn't stop thinking about how you would slide these panties down my legs before pressing into the naked depths of my body—the same body that's starving for you right now."

I haven't moved my hands from the arm of the couch where my head rests against them. My lack of physical engagement is torturing Norah. However, my mental engagement is another story entirely. She sits up, straddling my fierce, denim-clad erection, and then exquisitely slow, begins to grind against me.

I need her to know I don't appreciate her knee-jerk reaction of assuming my guilt and retaliating by flirting with another guy. Even though I've already let it go, I don't want her to think that sex erases my need to discuss it. Lack of trust is not something to gloss over.

"Take off your bra, Norah," I concede. She gives me a half smile, recognizing my slipping composure, and then reaches back to undo the clasp. I like how her breasts press forward with the motion, so when she drops the flimsy lace on my chest, I reach up to tease them.

Then, I undo two buttons on my shirt before tugging the whole thing over my head. When I lie back again, she presents herself to me as if she's a gift waiting to be played with and enjoyed.

"Come here," I say, softer but still gruff in tone. When she leans down, I place my hand on the side of her face, cupping her jaw and guiding her in for a kiss.

The way she hovers over me causes her nipples to brush against my chest. It makes me want to skip all the preliminaries, cram myself inside her, and root like a deranged animal. Instead, as I kiss her sweetly, I reach over her ass and ease the fabric between her thighs to the side, granting my fingers access.

As I lasciviously fondle the most eager, solicitous part of her body, I realize I need to address my feelings before this ramps up anymore. Admittedly, my timing is atrocious, but I need to say my peace.

I look into her eyes and murmur, "Norah, don't ever question my integrity again. If you don't know me well enough to be one hundred percent certain I would never fuck around, then you need to pay closer attention." I close the three-inch gap between our lips and kiss her with the intent of reminding her exactly how devoted I am.

"I'm sorry, you're right," she breathes against my mouth. "Even Sophia knows you well enough to realize that," she says after rising a fraction from our kiss. I use the margin of opportunity to disengage my fingers from her body and shove my jeans down.

She sits all the way up with her panties still shoved to the side, so I can see how the underside of my dick sits nestled against her skin. Then she arches her spine and rocks herself back and forth along my length.

I already know the lace of her panties will cause problems for me upon entry by chafing against the side of my penis, so I preempt this by saying, "Stand up so I can take off your panties." She does, and as I slide the delicate material down her thighs, I lean in and place a chaste kiss against her slit. She shivers and then lets out an airy sound. I hastily remove my jeans the rest of the way and then freeze for a second, automatically thinking about how far away the condoms are.

She reads my thoughts precisely and whispers, "I want you bare." Her breathy voice convinces me, so I respond by lying back on the couch. With my hands on her hips, I steady her unbalanced return to straddling me. I make no attempt to guide myself inside her, so she lolls her head back and resumes her painstaking crusade, up and back along the length of my shaft.

With her neck arched back like this, her hair reaches to her low back, and her tits thrust forward. They taunt me and fill me with covetous need. I reach up to slide my palms nimbly over them, rubbing her nipples and pulling a scratchy vocalization from somewhere deep inside of her.

She is beautiful. I hate to think about what will happen if I can't overcome this destructive phobia. Tonight was a perfect example of her ability to attract guys. I can't lose her by refusing to snatch my life back from the clutches of anxiety.

I roll and tug both of her nipples until she reads the cue and bends forward. She brings both hands to my face and then leans down to kiss me. Her lips are apologetic, delicate even. While my thumbs tend to her highly responsive nipples, she kisses her way down my jaw, where she fills me with a thousand shivers as she breathes into my ear.

"Justin, I'm sorry about tonight." She nibbles and then sucks my earlobe before continuing, "I am scared to lose you." Then she hovers her face above mine to look me directly in the eyes. The sincerity drips from her statement, and the furrow in her brow emphasizes every word. "I'm scared to lose you because this is the best thing that has ever happened to me, and I'm terrified I don't deserve you." My heart swells from her honesty; frankly, I share her fears. I'm afraid I don't deserve *her*, and she will come to her senses and leave me choking on her dust.

"I worry about those same things," I admit, a little surprised at myself for readily disclosing that insecurity. I slide my right hand through her loose, wavy hair to cup her head with gentle fingers.

"Is that why you put aside your agoraphobia and came to the bar?" she smiles, and it lights up my world. If I can ever *put aside* my agoraphobia, it will be for her, of that I am certain.

"I wasn't going to give up without a fight," I say as I pull her the rest of the way to my mouth, nipping her lower lip before claiming her kiss. I use my other hand to guide myself into her. She dissolves around me as I sink in. Our lovemaking is slow and reverent. It's unhurried in the way it is when you know your love story has just begun.

Chapter 38

Norah

Weeks later, sitting on the couch in my apartment, I announce, "I've never even heard of a divorce party." Then, after a pondering moment, "Who does stuff like that anyway?" I ask Sophia over our coffee table dinner of delivered sushi. In my mind, I'm wondering if it's too soon for Justin. He has made steady progress over the last six months. It's remarkable how far he has come since he committed to the journey, but I worry about the chaos of a party, even if it is at Davis' house.

"I don't know. Who orders sushi in Styrofoam? We're living in some crazy times, Norah," Sophia says right before she rips open her hundredth soy sauce packet with her teeth. "Would it kill them to put more than six drops of soy sauce in each packet?" Her question is rhetorical, so I don't answer it. I can't anyway because I just shoved a giant spider roll into my mouth.

It is getting progressively harder to eat because the purifying clay mask is starting to dry and tighten my face into that of a Terracotta Warrior. Sophia and I have gone full savage for our night in, and both have a head full of deep conditioner and clay masks on our faces. We both got the evite at the same time, so our phones notified us just as we sat down with our delivery containers and crusty faces. Hers with a quiet chime, and mine with a quick vibration from its spot on the table.

"It sounds like everyone dolls up in wedding dresses and tuxedos, and you trash the wedding attire throughout the night?" Sophia scrunches her face, but the only thing that moves is her hairline. "Am I interpreting that correctly?"

"Based on the invitation photo? Yes. Hopefully, the bonfire is an exaggeration, though." My phone vibrates with another notification, so I put my sushi on the coffee table and look at the new text.

SexyMotherFucker: *Did you see your invitation?*

Me: *Soph and I were just talking about that. Is Davis serious?*

SexyMotherFucker: *Actually, yes. Take off your shirt and Facetime me, I'll explain.*

I shoot Sophia a panicked look. There is no way I'm Facetiming him looking like this. My face has started to chip off, and dust my tank top with the fallout, and my hair looks like a duck caught in an oil spill.

Me: *No can do. I'm not looking very sexy right now.*

SexyMotherFucker: *I didn't say sexy. I said, topless.*

Me: *Give me ten minutes.*

SexyMotherFucker: *Must be a lot of buttons on your shirt.*

After putting the rest of my sushi in the fridge—where it will sit for three days and then get tossed out—and taking a turbo-fast shower, I sit down next to Sophia with my hair still wrapped in a towel and not a stitch of makeup on.

Justin answers and then smiles a rascally slow grin. "You said you didn't look sexy. You'll need to explain yourself because I've got nearly eight inches that vehemently disagrees with you." I scrunch my newly purified face, I should have warned him Sophia was here.

"Did you say, nearly eight inches?" Sophia pops her tight face and greasy head into view. All I can do is mouth *I'm sorry*, but he isn't even fazed by her presence.

"Sorry, Sophia. I shouldn't brag, not when you're stuck with Davis's micropenis," Justin snickers. I can tell he's in his kitchen because I hear him filling a glass with water from the refrigerator dispenser. He is shirtless and tousled, too. If I had to guess, I would say he just finished his weighted pull-ups.

"I'm not sleeping with Davis, you little gossipmonger," Sophia scolds. "Not until I'm certain I'm the only maraca in his band." Then she continues, huffing out a dramatic sigh, "He's fun, but he'll have to work harder to get me into his bed."

"Oh, good. Then there's still time to run away screaming," Justin says before taking a long chug of his water. "Wait until after the divorce party, though, because that will be a ton of fun. I'd probably wash that crap off your face first, though."

"Yeah, tell us about the whole divorce party," I say, as I take the towel off my head and then run my fingers through the damp clumps.

"Our friend Caroline from the fire station, aka Sunny, is getting divorced. The whole thing is really sad and cliché—husband cheated with the baby's nanny or some such shit. So, she is good and pissed, and we all want to show her our support."

"That's really sweet," I start before Sophia barges in again with her questions.

"Do we all dress up in wedding attire, or just her?"

"Yeah, everyone does. But the idea is not to look all hot in your dream wedding gown. Go to a thrift store and buy a wedding dress from twenty-five years ago, one that looks ridiculous or doesn't fit right. Everyone ends up destroying their wedding garb by the end of the night anyway."

"Will there be cake?" Sophia asks, and even I can't tell if she is being serious.

"That I don't know. Is that a deal breaker for you, Soph?" he asks as he sits down on his couch. Before she can answer, I stand up and walk into the kitchen to revisit my sushi from the fridge.

"Are you comfortable going to Davis' house?" I ask before putting a spicy tuna roll in my mouth—with my fingers, no less.

"I watched the fight over there last weekend, I think it will be ok. Don't you?"

"Justin, you amaze me daily with how much you can conquer. Of course, I think you will be ok," I lie. It's not an outright lie, though, because parts of my statement are true. He has progressed lightyears since our front yard picnic. He has even started driving short distances again, mainly to the grocery store and dog park, but still, those are tremendous accomplishments. His progress was initially slow but has picked up speed in the last few months. I even refer to his twice-weekly therapy appointments as his *bromance* with Dr. Edward.

Nonetheless, the part that worries me is him being around all his firefighter friends. He has no trouble hanging out with them in small groups or at his house, but this will be a lot of chaos in a different location. Not to mention, a fair amount of the party-goers are some of the same people who were there the day Jax died.

It's funny because now, I'm the one who worries. As Justin continues to get better and expand his 'safe zone,' I'm getting worse. He is learning how to overcome his anxiety, and all the while, I'm the one picking it up—I'm the one freaking out. I try to keep my new-found neurosis to myself and always play the role of supportive girlfriend, but the worry gnaws through my gut. I'm afraid all his fragile progress will come crashing down at my feet. Of course, *fragile* is only my anxious interpretation of his steady improvement. Everyone else believes that he made a breakthrough months ago and has only continued to blow everyone's expectations away.

Nowadays, it's nothing for him to walk Indy down to Starbucks for a coffee, or drive to his new gym, or come pick me up for an actual date. He still has to fight back his demons, but just like Dr. Edward told us it would happen, the amount of time he needs to 'sit with the anxiety' before he can calm himself is getting shorter and shorter.

I'm worried because his evolution is so fresh and because he still has regular bouts of panic when he's out. He may be getting better at managing them, but they still happen. I seem to be waiting for *the big one*, the one he can't talk himself down from and the one that will send him scurrying back to his confinement. I'm petrified of that one because now, after more than six months together, there is no question that I'm in love with him.

"Davis, Otto, and I are shopping for tuxes on Sunday, want to come with us and look for a dress?" Justin loosens the lump in my throat with his question. I open my mouth to answer, but Sophia beats me to it.

"No, you monster! She wants to go wedding dress shopping with her best friend," she admonishes from behind me. Justin chuckles. He views Sophia the same way I see Davis. The regard we hold them in is caught somewhere between cautious appreciation and amused fascination.

Davis and Sophia are great together, even though she dangles him from her fishing line longer than most. I think it's because their connection is so authentic and reliable. I also suspect she wants to establish her superiority over any other woman in his life. Justin swears Davis isn't seeing anyone else, so watching their relationship unfold is almost better than a season of Game of Thrones.

"Sorry, Sophia. I wouldn't dream of stepping on your toes," Justin laughs. "Anyway, Norah, you'll never guess where Indy and I went today."

I shove the Styrofoam container once again into the fridge, then give a backward wave to Sophia as I head to my room. I need to hear about his adventures today before I can settle down to watch a movie with my roommate. Justin's progress is the only thing I care about at this moment.

Chapter 39

JUSTIN

"Davis, you look like a butler," I laugh into the side of my fist, trying to temper the hilarity. "Are you sure a jacket with tails was the best idea?" My comment is the first of what will, no doubt, be legions of others throughout the night. He raises his middle finger in response, but it only makes me laugh harder.

In the spirit of Caroline's divorce, we tried to find the most ridiculous tuxedos we could get our hands on. In order of ridiculousness, Otto landed the green and navy plaid tux that is way too tight in the legs and fits like skinny jeans. Davis scored the tails, and the best I could do was navy blue. It turns out tuxes haven't evolved much over the years, and the second-hand pickings had been slim. I couldn't find a pastel or bright teal cummerbund to save my life. I had to, instead, opt for suspenders to go with my bow tie. But from what I can see of the other guys, no one but Otto had much luck with looking ridiculous—well, maybe the butler.

The women all seem to have had more luck than the guys, and I have seen everything from full hoop ballgowns to high necklines and puffy satin sleeves. The good news is that my normal social anxiety has taken a backseat to all the nonsense, and I can see Caroline's ear to ear divorce smile from across the room.

Norah and Sophia are almost forty-five minutes late, so I pull my phone from my pocket to call her and make sure everything is all right. I'm worried about her more than I am about having a panic attack, which is both good and bad, I suppose. I planned on picking her up when I went to get the keg, but she wanted to come with Sophia. I'm relieved to see I have a text from her, but it's from almost thirty minutes ago.

DirtyGirl: *Be there soon, we had a zipper mishap & I have to sew Sophia into her hilarious dress.*

I slide the phone back into my pocket just as Davis announces, "There's my girl, Sophia!" Before I even completely raise my head from putting the phone away, I see Norah. My mouth dries out, and the thump of my heart slows to a crawl. I can't take my eyes off of her. This is it for me. She's it.

She is wearing a wedding dress with enormous satin sleeves from her shoulders to her elbows, at which point they become fitted, sheer lace down to the V-point that hooks around the base of her middle fingers. The neck of the dress has a satin strip that looks like a choker, and then sheer white fabric covers her chest down to where the white lace begins. This, incidentally, is where her dress stops looking ridiculous and has me wishing she really was my bride. The rest is floor-length, hanging lace, and fits her body like it's the dress's only job.

When she sees me, she smiles brightly and takes a step towards the statue of my body, frozen to the floor. With her first step, the dress opens up the front, making room for her leg with the sexiest slit I've ever laid eyes on. There is another layer of lace from her knees down, so when she walks, the layers swirl around her ankles, and the longer back drags on the floor behind her. As gaudy as the sleeves are, I'm not too sure this dress shouldn't be walking down the runways in Paris. Thoroughly entranced, I find I have absolutely no words.

"Don't laugh," she says as she advances on me like a rare angel of mercy. I'm thunderstruck by her approaching me in a wedding gown, and I have to fight back the moisture that feels shockingly imminent behind my lids. I swallow her in my arms, disbelieving my good fortune and still unable to speak.

"Damn, baby! You look hot in a tux," she says against my neck, where she tucked her face. I can feel her soft breath against my throat and smell her faint perfume. She slides her arms inside my tuxedo jacket and wraps her arms around me. I have her pressed up against my body, and it's still not close enough.

"Norah, you are the most beautiful woman I have ever seen," I murmur into her ear, and then add, "I love you so much."

She eases her head back so she can look me in the eyes. It looks like she might be taking a second or two to collect herself, but in the instant before my lips find hers, she whispers, "I love you, too." Our kiss is so tender and compelling that neither of us is aware of our surroundings. That is until a grenade-sized balloon filled with blue cornstarch hits us right where my palm cups her face. My hand takes the brunt of it, but the blue powder scatters all over our necks and chests.

"Hey," Davis calls out with amusement in his voice. "Those are for outside." Norah licks a dusting of powder off her upper lip and then closes the gap to kiss me again. This time, she's laughing in the process.

Once I introduced Norah to some friends of mine she hadn't met, including Caroline, the guest of honor, we decided to head outside. It's a war zone out here, but also where the bar is set up, so it's a necessary evil. By now, most of the attendees have damage to their wedding garb in the form of colorful paint and/or a cloudy smear of dyed cornstarch. And most of the guys, myself included, have ditched our tuxedo jackets.

It's late June, and the temperature is blazing hot, so I have my sleeves rolled up, but all I can think about is going home to swim with my girl. I'm even looking forward to getting hit with a colorful water balloon, anything to cool off.

Davis and Sophia make their way over to us, and I can't help but snicker at her dress. It is a satin monstrosity, where fabric bunches up around her body and then flairs out at her knees in a satiny explosion of epic proportions. Davis has cut the legs of his pants down the outside seams but is still wearing a dress sock pulled up to mid-calf on his non-robotic leg. The seams are open and flowy, so he must feel like he's wearing a dress instead of simply cutting off the fabric like others have.

"I know you just sewed this dress onto my body, but now, will you help me cut it off?" Sophia asks. Norah takes the scissors from her and then squats down to cut off the satin explosion just above Sophia's knees. Then Norah stands and hands the scissors back to her.

"My turn," Norah says, but before anyone can get close enough to touch it, I stop them. The dress fits too perfectly to cut a single inch off. There is no chance of anyone cutting it—

"Well…maybe the sleeves," I concede, prompting Sophia to get to work. In compliance with Divorce Party rules, a few of the guys have cut their pants into shorts, and by now, almost all of the girls have chopped long sections of their heavy dresses off.

Once Norah's dress alterations are complete and there is a pile of discarded fabric at our feet, Davis and Sophia take off to ambush some clean wedding attire. The two of them together is like having impulsive teenagers underfoot, but there's never a dull moment.

While I'm admiring the look of her current dress, Norah asks, "How is your anxiety doing?" I haven't thought much about it tonight because Davis's house has been my second home for many years, so I'm comfortable here. But the pure and simple truth is that I've been so laser-focused on Norah that I can hardly string two intelligent thoughts together, let alone feel anxious. But that's not to say I'm not counting down the minutes until we can leave because I have all sorts of dirty things I want to do to her once I get her alone.

"I've had some, but I am pretty seasoned about getting it under control now, so it's been manageable," I answer, then add, "Do you think it's socially acceptable to leave yet?" She shrugs and looks around, assessing the feasibility of the maneuver. I see her eyes widen the second before we get pelted with purple and yellow cornstarch bombs. We stand in the dusty fog for a few seconds, stunned, and then we both take off after Davis and Sophia.

***

Once back at my place, I unlock the front door and then scoop Norah up like a proper bride and carry her over the threshold. This is just practice. The next time I do it, it will be for real. She giggles from her Prosecco buzz but says nothing as I walk straight through the dining room and out the French doors to the back patio.

I've wanted exactly two things this evening. One, to be alone with her. And two, to jump in my pool and finally douse the heat that has grown on me like damp moss. She sees me toe off my shoes and quickly does the same before I walk us right into the pool, clothes and all. She gasps against the chill of the water, but for me and my sweltering tuxedo pants, it's a blast of heaven.

She adjusts how I'm holding her and then leans into my body while I fuse my mouth to hers. I could give her everything, and it still wouldn't be enough. Because of her, a future is possible for me. She has given me back my life.

No, she led me to the precipice, but I jumped for myself. I have taken my life back. I'm amazed at my capabilities, and this is only the beginning.

Optimism:

noun

Hopefulness and confidence about the future.

Chapter 40

Norah

My buzz has all but worn off as I lie here on this bobbing raft, staring at the flickering stars. I pushed the bottom of my dress off the raft so the lace floats innocently in the water beside me. Justin lounges on the raft beside me, his tuxedo shirt now see-through and clinging to his chest and arms. The inflatable rafts are less than two feet apart, and our clasped hands keep us from drifting further apart. The air settles like peace all around us.

"This is exactly where I want to be for the Fourth of July," Justin says through a haze of serenity. "You can see the downtown fireworks from right here, in my pool." Then he quickly adds, "But first, I'm going to buy a double raft so you can lie here with me while the fireworks shimmer down on us."

"That sounds perfect. You know what else I can see from right here in your pool?" I ask as I tug his hand, pulling my raft closer to his. "The bravest man I've ever known." Then I snort out a laugh because even *I* recognize how cheesy that sounded.

"Don't laugh," he says, sounding genuinely wounded. "Come here," he murmurs, giving me a little tug. I slide off the raft into waist deep water. He eases into the water and closes the space between us. "Do you know what *else* I can see from right here in my pool?"

"What?" I ask, grinning because I'm expecting something corny in return.

"Your nipples." I drop my eyes to my chest, not because I doubt him, but because I wonder if they are as showy as they feel.

The dress is made of lace, with sheer spaces between the delicate patterns, so it looks mostly white when the fabric is dry. However, now that I'm wet, the sheer spaces are see-through. The fleshy, translucent areas display my skin the same way Justin's clingy shirt shows his. Now that it's wet, the lacy pattern does a better job of showcasing than it does of concealing.

He brings his hands up to cup the sides of my breasts as his mouth takes mine. Dragging his thumbs roughly over my showy nipples, he groans.

"Maybe it's time to get out of these wet clothes," he suggests, as his hands slide around to the zipper at my back. It releases its hold one tooth at a time, and the heavy, wet dress peels away from the top of my body.

Justin rips his shirt open, sending rogue buttons flying in various directions. I help him tug his arms out of the sleeves while navigating around his suspenders, which sounds easier than it is. My dress pools around my waist, floating like an innertube as if it belongs between us.

"I have to feel you against me," Justin pants as he takes hold of my face and hauls my lips to his. The heat of his chest feels nice pressed up against my pebbled skin. When he slides the tip of his tongue down my neck, tasting the beat of my pulse and nipping delicate skin, I gasp.

"Justin, take me to bed," I demand on a whisper. "I have to get out of this thousand-pound dress, and I can't wait any longer to be with you."

He disengages his mouth and then takes my hand, walking me to the steps. My dress still floats around me like the rings of Saturn, and I can't wait to get rid of its weighty bulk. I know he's watching me, so I turn my bare torso to watch his feral gaze as I take each step. The heaviness of the saturated fabric makes it easy to step out of as I ascend each stair.

"Damn, baby! Are you trying to kill me?" he exclaims once I step out of the dress enough to reveal my skimpy white panties, garter belt, and thigh-high stockings. "Jesus, I almost just came in my pants," he says with a fat grin.

Initially, I worried about wearing them because it seemed like too much of a wedding night thing to do, but now I'm glad Sophia talked me into it. I smirk at his emphatic reaction while I step the rest of the way out of my sodden dress.

"Stop," he whispers his demand. I have one foot on the top step and one on the pool deck. When I hesitate before taking the last step, my skin prickles to life, and a shiver runs through my body. Not only from the night air on my wet skin but from how Justin looks at me.

He brings his hands to rest on the outside of my thighs and then drops a featherlight kiss on the back of my leg, right above the lace of the thigh-highs. His mouth tickles its way along the strap of the garter belt all the way to the base of my ass. Then his tongue lightly drags to the inside of my thigh, where he bites and then sucks a small patch of skin into his mouth.

The section of skin that now bears his mark is right below where the edge of my panties meets the crease of my leg. The proximity of his mouth to my core causes me to gasp and then hold my breath.

I'm trembling now as water droplets make a final dash down my chilled skin. Justin is still waist deep in the pool and apparently immune to the cool night air. While he dusts kisses down the back of my other thigh, he unhooks and releases the thigh-high from the garter belt. He gently eases the stocking down my leg while caressing my responsive skin the whole way. When he does the same with the other one, he's just as tender and equally as deliberate.

Once both stockings lay in a soggy heap on the edge of the pool, he ascends the first step and then another until he presses up against my back, and hugs me against his body.

"I can't wait to get you inside," he whispers against my ticklish ear. "So I can show you how much I love you." He gently squeezes my nipple between the knuckles of two fingers as he kisses and nuzzles my neck. In response, I shimmy my butt against him. Quickly following his groan is a hasty pool exit and the subsequent hauling of me into the house.

Indy whimpers his indignance at being left in his kennel, but Justin calls over his shoulder, "Sorry, buddy," as he leads me up the stairs to his room. He shivers as he peels his soaking wet tuxedo pants off. It's a warm night, but the air conditioning inside does not mix well with wet clothes. I shiver for a different reason entirely.

After hanging his sodden clothing over the shower door and fiddling with his phone to stream some music, he makes his naked way back to the foot of the bed. I don't recognize the song, but it drips like sinful honey through the wireless speakers. The smoky vocals and the velvety guitar riffs are perfect for the look on his face.

"That image of you getting out of the pool, topless with those panties and garter belt on, will torment me forever. Every time I close my eyes, I will see you just like that on the backs of my eyelids. I'll never forget it as long as I live," Justin says in a low, uncolored voice. The rise and fall of my shoulders increase in tempo as my lungs expand at a double-time pace, fortifying me with his words.

"You're shivering. Come here, let me warm you up," I say, on my knees from the middle of his bed. The way I'm kneeling, with my legs spread and the straps from the garter belt skimming my bare thighs, compels his attention with the same magnetic force as a north pointing compass.

He prowls across the bed to me, then rises to his knees. When our bodies come together, I suck in a breath of air with a sharpness that speaks to how cold his skin feels on first contact.

He wraps one hand around the back of my neck and eases the other into my panties. The white lace is still damp from the pool, so when it pulls away from my skin, I feel the coolness of the air with a clarity that intensifies the sensation. Then he slides his fingers along newly awakened skin.

"Perhaps I should warm *you* up first," he says with a grin as he maintains steady pressure with his fingers. I slide my hands through his hair as he lowers his face to scrape over my nipple with the rasp of his emerging whiskers and then strums it with his teasing tongue. I can't respond, but I don't think he's looking for one. When he straightens back up, he has a burning twinkle in his eyes that both compels and inflames me.

"Turn around and put your hands on the bed," he says assertively. He speaks the words on a whisper, but he might as well deliver them through a trombone because they rattle the air around us.

I do as he says. Once he's behind me, he slides his fingers inside my panties and garter belt and then eases them down as far as he can before I have to lift one knee at a time awkwardly. Then he tugs them the rest of the way off my body.

This position feels incredibly vulnerable for me because he is still on his knees behind me, but he isn't moving—only looking. Before my raunchy display makes me feel more insecure, he brings his fingers between my legs to dawdle and tease.

"Norah," he says, his voice ragged and scratched apart. "I need you." I look back at him over my shoulder and see his all but blown pupils. It's as if his light eyes are not even blue anymore. They look darker, like deep ocean water or the sky right before dawn.

He adjusts our bodies until I'm straddling his abs, reverse cowgirl style, and his thick erection strains before me—bobbing like a ponderous ocean buoy.

"Scoot back, baby. Give me your body." Then Justin hooks my thighs and pulls me back so my legs spread above his face, and my stomach presses against his chest. The feel of his warm mouth is so sudden, and his tongue so determined, that I whimper with the contact.

After a few minutes, he adjusts his arms so my thighs drape over his shoulders. This positions my body tightly against his mouth, and I would worry about his breathing were it not for his periodic moans of pleasure.

After a few indulgent moments of his mastery with my body, I peel open my eyes and address the erection before me. He drops his head back to compose himself when I slide my mouth down.

I start slow and languidly, easing him further and further to the back of my throat. I show him nothing but reverence until his hands grip my ass cheeks, spreading me for his mouth and leaving me raw and utterly exposed while he flickers his tongue against tender skin.

Then, I rededicate myself to his prominent display. The naughtiness of riding his face while devoting myself to his orgasm only intensifies the erotic nature of the act.

He alternates between licks, flickers, and sucks, but when he presses the flat of his tongue against me and wiggles his face back and forth, I pull off of him and cry out as the orgasm takes me by the throat and squeezes. The rolling spasms cause me to grind against his tongue and shudder with complete abandon.

My raunchy orgasm and the inadvertent tightening of my fist trigger his release. When he lets go, it comes out in explosive surges all over my cheek and neck, then drips thickly back onto his belly.

Once my body stops pulsing, I crawl forward and roll onto my back between Justin's legs. I am panting heavily, and my mouth has utterly dried out. Justin sits up and then laughs lazily as he looks down at me.

"You have cum on your neck and in your hair."

With my breathing still labored, I pant, "I hear it's good for your skin." Justin laughs harder at that and then tugs me forward by my limp arms so that I'm facing him, and my legs drape over his thighs. I lean the rest of the way in, and our lips meet.

I wrap my legs around him as he lifts me from the bed to the cradle of his lap. I could stay in this position all night—it's disarming and sensual.

"I love you, Norah," he breathes into our kiss, infusing it with a level of intimacy that I never want to let go of.

I smile widely, breaking the seal of our mouths and disturbing the reverential air around us.

"And I love you."

My body is exhausted and completely wrung out, but with his arms hugging me tightly against him and the deference in his voice, I'm suddenly alive with adoration for him.

Leaving one hand on the back of his neck, I place the other behind me on the bed and lean back. It's an offering. As I present myself to him, he uses one hand to notch the head of his penis in place. Then he circles my waist with a forearm and pulls me against him while sinking illustriously into my body.

Each time he first bores into me, I always lose my breath. The stretch and the fullness are so all-encompassing that it diverts my entire focus to the melding of our bodies. For those few moments, I'm not even sure my heart beats. It's as if the rotation of the Earth grinds to a halt, and everything stops—everything except the sensation of his commanding advance.

The way he sits cross-legged with me wrapped succinctly around him and our chests pressed together is incredibly intimate. Our mouths kiss in a slow rhythm to accompany the methodical motion of my hips.

I've never had this before. I've had sex with a handful of men, but never, and I mean never, has there been this kind of an emotional connection before. It makes me realize this is the first time I've ever been in love. As if the times I thought I was, were just practice. Looking back, it seems laughable now because I love Justin so much, I *need* him in my life. That need feels like something inherent to my being. It's like a deep, resonating ache because the feeling is a part of me.

Neither one of us talks. We kiss and move together like a perfect kinematic pair. In this instance, our lives have blurred together into one. One intense fusion of two worlds, two people, two souls. Now one.

I come first, with my head straining back and Justin's lips at my throat. When he follows, I watch his eyes roll back into his head and the veins in his neck flair.

After a few lazy minutes still wound together, Justin grabs a fistful of my hair and presses his forehead against mine. He has not yet disengaged from my body, so I still feel part of him. He looks into my eyes with an earnestness that tells me he is about to say something truly profound.

"Maybe it's time to shampoo the cum out of your hair," he says, making me exhale a giggle due to the lack of profoundness in his declaration.

We make our way to his bathroom on shaky legs, or at least I do. I don't think my body was built to withstand a sexcapade of Justin proportions. In my past relationships, multiple orgasms were unheard of, and a single one was cause for extreme self-importance and puffed-up chests on behalf of my lovers. Then there is Justin. He would probably be insulted if I only got off once.

As I turn the shower faucet on, Justin calls over his shoulder, "Alexa, volume twenty," and then smacks my ass as I step into the shower. We just went from the sweetest, most intimate sex we have ever had to him leaving a pink handprint on my ass cheek. I suppose that further demonstrates the poles of his versatility.

As I'm rinsing out my hair and Justin indulges his genetic predisposition for a fascination with breasts, he starts singing along with the song. His voice is strong and confident, and I somehow doubt this is the first time he sang in the shower.

"We got all dolled up in wedding gear and didn't even have our first dance," he says, as he pulls me against him and takes one of my hands in his. I lay my cheek against his chest while we dance in the shower, and he sings along to Tom Petty softly in my ear.

I haven't heard this particular song before, but I can tell you right now it's my new favorite. In fact, although it's not a traditional first dance song for a bride and groom, it will be ours because of this exact moment. I nuzzle into the crook of his neck as we sway together, and he continues singing, "*I followed an angel…*"

Chapter 41

JUSTIN

After our shower, Norah announces, "You know this will be a disaster tomorrow, right?" as she winds her hair up into some sort of crazy submission hold and twists a hair tie around it. Now, most of her hair is contained, but there are still rogue pieces that fought against their confinement and won. This is my favorite look of Norah's—the clean-faced, messy hair, effortless beauty that shines through all the pomp and circumstance of makeup and hair products.

"I'm counting on it," I say. If I could keep her looking sexed-up all the time, I would. It's such a hot reminder of how she got rumpled in the first place. "Now, get in here," I command as I tap the sheet next to me.

She slides in, all warm and naked, as I hold her close to me. We are both exhausted, and sleep itches behind our eyes, but I still raise Norah's chin to kiss her goodnight. Just like I intend to every night for the rest of my life.

After a kiss and whispered *goodnights,* we both start to succumb to the nagging demands of sleep. After a few moments, I manage to crane my eyes open.

"I forgot to tell you, my therapist wants me to set a goal for my recovery. More importantly, he wants us to pick a reward for me to strive for." My statement hangs in the darkened room long enough that I start to wonder if she has already fallen asleep.

"What kind of reward?" she asks as her eyelashes flutter against my chest.

"Like a trip or something," I answer. I hope it doesn't scare her that I'm already making plans for us a year from now.

"I would love that," she says as she sits up on her elbow to look at me. Even in the shadows, I can tell she is smiling. Maybe she never thought I would recover enough to travel, but since I finally started to deal with my anxiety, I see a future for me—a future for us.

The last seven months of intense and concentrated therapy allowed me to experience what freedom from my mental confines feels like. I want to chase that feeling. The life that has felt out of reach for eons is suddenly within my grasp. I'm going to track it, stalk it, and claim it. I will never again be a prisoner of my own making.

"Based on my steady progress, Dr. Edward thought a year from now would be plenty of time for me to get my life back. He anticipates much sooner, but he wants to allow for some setbacks. So, let's pick a destination where we can celebrate my liberation from myself a year from now."

"Vineyards in Tuscany?" she offers. Or an African safari?" She is excited now because the prospect of an unencumbered trip is enough to knock the sleep from her eyes.

"What about fishing in Alaska? Or Carnival, in Brazil?" I throw out there. The truth is, I don't care where we go. We could head to the middle of nowhere, and I would be thrilled to be there with her.

"I don't care where we go," she says, mirroring my thoughts. "I just want to sip cocktails on a beach somewhere with you."

"Hawaii?" I suggest.

"No. What about Bali?" she asks, with enthusiasm in her voice and a sparkle in her eyes. What she doesn't know is that when Dr. Edward suggested the whole thing, the first two places I thought about were Capri....and Bali.

"Bali it is," I say, and then seal the decision with a kiss that has the potential to keep us from going to sleep anytime soon.

Epilogue

JUSTIN

One year later, in Bali.

When I thought of Bali or Indonesia in general, all the Hindu Temples and sacred shrines jumped to mind. But Norah plastered pictures of the beautiful beaches and crystal clear water all over my house and 4-Runner. Not that I needed the reminders, or *incentive benchmarks*, as she called them, but the last twelve months have been filled with them anyway.

I think Norah was worried that my recovery wouldn't stick. However, what she may not have realized is that from the moment I committed myself to getting better, I have not let my guard down once. I continued twice-weekly visits with my therapist—in his office, no less, and challenged myself at every conceivable opportunity.

I expected setbacks or maybe to regress here and there, but not once did my resolve ever waver. I approached these anticipated setbacks with outright aggression and almost dared them to surface. I wouldn't let them or anything else derail me because once I got a taste of freedom, I wasn't quite so happy to abstain from life any longer.

I think my thorny approach was actually therapeutic because I finally had power—and that was a very persuasive motivator. Yeah, I empowered myself. I liked the taste of strength and worthiness instead of fragility and complete vulnerability. Once I was no longer a victim of my own circumstance, my momentum continued to propel me. Now, the passive shell that used to encrust me is gone forever.

It sounds easy in hindsight, of course, but let me be clear, overcoming such powerful anxiety was one of the hardest things I've ever done—second only to losing my son. So, don't be disillusioned by how far I've come because there were times when the struggle choked me into unresponsiveness. Simply put, the last eighteen months haven't all been rosy.

The most debilitating roadblock I faced was once my exposure therapy started to include Jax. Speaking about him so much and allowing Norah to get to know him through my memories almost felt like I was conjuring him back from the dead. My stories breathed life back into his still body and gave him a vitality that would inevitably rip him away from me all over again.

All the reflection required me to remember how I had been robbed of him in the first place. It was agonizing. I was completely raw, as if someone had peeled the skin from my body. I had to re-realize Jaxson was gone so often that it required me to mourn him all over again, and again, and again.

Once the memories began forming a sort of scar tissue, I was happy that Norah could get to know him a little. But, I still cursed God every time I calculated what Jax *should* be doing instead of ashing into eternal dust.

He should be in Bali with us right now—demanding we watch him swim to the bottom of the pool to retrieve a coin for the thousandth time. He should be in kindergarten. He should be finger-painting walls and getting gum stuck in his hair. He should have been allowed to become a mouthy, entitled teenager getting in trouble for something he snapchatted at school. He should have been allowed to do absolutely *anything*, no matter how mundane or prolific it may have been.

But he wasn't, so I had to deal with all that anger, too. The truth is that anger is a glutton. It's a bottomless well that requires you to drink from it no matter how rancid it might be. Then, it infiltrates your system, and like any other contagion, it germinates until it can feed and sustain itself. It's a parasitic relationship of the highest order. Anger steals from you, all the while mocking your vain attempts to control it. And suppose, by some miracle, your immune system can beat the invader back into submission. In that case, you're still forced to acknowledge that the infectious organism will evolve, mutate, and materialize at any moment.

Except with anger, it's not your immune system you have to call into action. It's your brain. It's not so easy for the mind to release such powerful feelings and emotions. It requires something difficult to give. It requires a choice, and that choice always seems impossible—until it's not.

It may be impossible *not* to sustain the anger seven million times, but seven million and one might just be the time you manage to conquer it.

For me, letting go of my anger was the key to releasing the anxiety. I will always feel the loss of my son, but I *choose* to seal up the poisonous well—and never again drink from its brackish endowment. In reality, I have to make that choice every single day.

Once I was able to get a handle on my deep-rooted anger, everything progressed at a pretty decent clip. I became a master at experiencing and then conquering my anxiety, so much so that it almost became a well-rehearsed parlor trick.

Long story short, I have reclaimed my life, and I no longer struggle with agoraphobia. Actually, the one-year trip should have been the ten-month trip because by then, I was ninety-eight percent done with the process. Norah and I referred to these last two months as the adipose layer because they provided the insulation and cushion we needed to feel completely secure about this trip.

This vacation to Bali is a big step, but not as big as you might think. The first few months of my process were grueling, but once I got the hang of the treatment, the location didn't really matter because the steps were all the same. In the beginning, the park down the street might as well have been in Indonesia, but now everything is flipped. The other side of the world could just as easily be Davis's living room. It's remarkable.

You know what else is remarkable? The woman walking toward me right now with two very fruity-looking frozen cocktails. Her skin is kissed by the Balinese sun but far from tanned, and her purple bikini might just be the death of me.

I'm about to give her my mother's pearl necklace, but she will have no idea how significant the transaction is. She doesn't know I traded necklaces with my mother as I stood over her deathbed. How I wanted to keep a piece of her in exchange for a part of myself. A silver chain and crucifix were traded for a perfect strand of Akoya pearls.

"How is it that you already have a golden tan?" Norah asks as she hands me my drink and then sits back on her matching lounge chair to sip hers.

"Melanin, I think," I answer before moving the giant fruit bounty that adorns my cocktail and taking a tentative sip. I never imagined I would be this happy ever again. The feeling makes it a little hard to swallow with the tightness of my throat, but I can honestly say I am happy and looking forward to a bright future.

Norah gives me a dubious look over the top rim of her sunglasses and then takes a long pull from her straw. "Very funny, melanin-boy," she says with an unrestrained grin.

"Listen, no-melanin-girl, maybe this is a good time to reapply your sunscreen. You're looking a little pink from your long trek to the grass hut bar that's only forty feet away," I tease.

"Ok, hon, but if you want to rub me—all you have to do is ask," she says as she deposits her drink on the side table between us. I swing my legs over the side of my lounge chair to face her, then make room for her to sit between my legs.

After sitting down, she drags her long hair to the side so that it hangs in front of one shoulder. I place a light kiss near the back of her neck, and I can almost hear her eyes flutter closed. When I reach for the sunscreen with one hand, I also retrieve my mom's pearls from my pocket with the other.

She is a little confused when I fasten it around her neck, but right away, I tell her they were my mother's and I want her to have them. She pivots so she can hug me tightly around the neck. She's quiet for a while, so I know the sentiment is not lost on her. Then she finally clears her throat and leans slightly back so she can look into my eyes.

"Justin, this is the most precious gift you could ever give me. I will treasure it forever," her voice is tender, and her eyes glisten with the significance of the gift.

"You're welcome, sweetheart. It looks beautiful on you," I say, but the words damn near don't make it out of my mouth. Seeing my mother's pearls—the very symbol of Clara Abernathy—on Norah's neck stirs up so many emotions.

"Let me take a picture of you so you can see how it looks," I say after clearing my throat and gaining some traction. She adjusts her position while I reach for my phone.

I take a handful of pictures and then pull her back against my chest so we can both look at the images together. I like her nestled between my thighs like this because it allows me to look over her shoulder while she scrolls through the pictures.

She looks at the first one and then leans closer to the screen. She pauses, not quite sure what she sees, and then swipes to the next photo. This image is more of a close-up, and she can definitely see the diamond ring hanging from the strand of pearls.

Her hand goes immediately to her throat, and she whispers, "*Justin.*" Even through her whisper, I can tell her voice is ragged and *somehow* still a little bit confused.

"Is this…is this what I think it is?" she asks, apparently afraid to jump to conclusions.

"I certainly hope so," I smile. I hadn't planned out what I would say because I didn't want it to sound rehearsed when I asked her to marry me, but now I wish I had.

"Because if it's not, then I'm doing it all wrong," I tease, then take a steadying breath.

"Norah, I can't imagine my life without you. You loved me when I was nothing but a shell of a man. You believed I was worthy, and in return, I wanted to prove to both of us that you were right. In the meantime, you helped me get my life back, and for that, I will always love you. But Norah, I want to marry you, not because of what you've done for *me*—but because of what we can be *together*." My hands are shaking with unshed emotion, and she is crying, so I almost don't even ask the question.

"Norah, will you m—"

"YES!" she exclaims right before she crashes into me, smothering me with laughing kisses and unrestrained affection as we tumble back into a reclining position.

Somewhere in the middle of the rather head-turning PDA, I swear I hear my mom's voice as clear as day.

"I always believed in you, Darling."

Epilogue 2

Norah

I'd like to say nailing down a new teaching position was easy once I finally polished up my resume, but that would be a straight-up lie. I stayed on with Hand to Heart until right before we left for Bali and then slid relatively seamlessly into my new position in the fall. The new school year was refreshing, and the different district was even more so.

The kids warmed up to me pretty quickly, especially when Justin and his fellow firefighters came blazing up to the school playground with full lights and sirens. My students could check out the fire truck, then try on helmets and various other bunker gear. They also asked a billion questions—most of which placed the firefighters on the same level as the Avengers.

The other big change that fall was that my lease with Sophia was up. She downsized to a one-bedroom in the same complex, and I officially moved in with Justin—even though that transition had already been steadily happening.

I needn't have worried about Justin relapsing back into his old ways because he was able to conquer his demons and now only meets with Dr. Edward once a month. It also helps that his buddies from work know the drill and are tuned in to his anxiety. If Justin were ever to be triggered at work, they have a fail-safe system in place. In fact, the first five months he was back, they treated him as nothing more than a kid on a ride-along. The fire chief allowed him to return, but he had to earn his place in the department first. The Chief was not taking any chances, so Justin really had to convince him he wasn't a department liability.

We married over my Christmas break because I had three weeks off from teaching for the Holidays. We had the wedding in Aspen, Colorado, and it was the most magical day of my life. Of course, I wore Clara Abernathy's pearls, which made it all the more special to include her in our big day. I also had one of Jaxson's teddy bears worked into my bridal bouquet, and Justin wore a locket with his photo and first haircut trimmings tucked inside. Our first dance was to the Tom Petty song, Angel Dream. That was the song Justin sang to me in the shower after his friend's divorce party. It was perfect. *Everything* was perfect.

Now, today is the anniversary of Justin's pool party three years ago when we first became a couple, so it's the fourth annual "Sink or Swim Pool Party." Justin got off work at seven this morning and fell face first into bed the moment he got home. Poor guy just wrapped up a thirty-six-hour shift with very little time between calls to sleep.

Needless to say, the pool party prep has fallen squarely on my shoulders. Normally, that wouldn't pose a problem, but lately, I can't keep my head out of the toilet long enough to get much done. Mixing the vat of margaritas was an exercise in extreme breath-holding, as was making the hamburger patties. Basically, anything with a smell, no matter how benign, brings me to my knees in front of the toilet.

Justin has been spared from my dramatics because he has been picking up so much overtime for the down payment on our new house. So, he doesn't know I'm pregnant yet. I wanted to be absolutely sure because his reaction would be one of two extremes. Either he will be terrified to take that step again, or he will shit himself with excitement.

We've talked about having kids before, and Justin's overwhelming feeling on the matter is that he's petrified to ever love someone that much again. The fact that there are no guarantees in life, and your entire world could burn to the ground in the time it takes to strike a match, is almost enough to ignite the anxiety all over again.

I'm with him on that. I have my own fears about bringing children into this fickle world. Will I do it right? Can I keep them safe? Never mind the potential for car accidents, broken bones, life-threatening allergies, the possibility of drowning, and calls to Poison Control. And really, why stop there? Because if we are blessed enough to get our children through their childhood, then we have to worry about them experimenting with drugs, drinking and driving, or not getting into a good college. Will they be depressed and suicidal? Oppositional defiant thugs? Or happy, well-adjusted members of society?

Really, the pressure to raise good people with self-confidence, integrity, and an upstanding moral compass is oppressive when you actually start thinking about it. We all want kids who don't shoot up schools or stick needles in their arms, but what guarantees are there?

Yes, having kids is scary, but I choose to be optimistic even in the face of overwhelming obstacles. I choose love over fear. I choose to trust myself and my future offspring and proceed with caution instead of paralyzing anxiety. I've learned this from Justin, and together, we will choose love over fear.

To that end, I'm happier than I've ever been—present nausea notwithstanding. I already know what a fabulous father Justin is, and I can't wait to add to our perfect family. Some days, I hope for a daughter, though, just so the experience is new for him. Although, there are those times I hope for a son, not as a do-over for him, but because Justin deserves all the experiences he missed with Jax.

Plus, I can't get the image of Jaxson standing on the bathroom counter beside Justin, pretending to shave out of my head. That visual is seared in my mind, beckoning me like a whisper from beyond.

The part of that vision that captivates me entirely is that in my mind, I'm watching it happen…and then Jax looks at me from his reflection in the mirror,

And waves to me.

Also by KC Decker:

Standalone Books

Little Dove

My name is Etta Freeman.

There is something special about me.

Not special in a good way, though, more like special in a way that will get me killed one day.

It's not something I talk about with anyone, but that doesn't stop me from trying to snare my neighbor in my devious web.

He is angsty and brooding and completely sexy in a scrappy, bloody knuckle kind of way.

I should also mention that he's a scheming, felonious drug dealer and I'm drawn to him like flies on shit.

The problem is, he doesn't yet know his role in my narrative, but he will fall in line.

They always do.

Trigger Warning: Little Dove contains content that some readers may find distressing.

Of Ash and Angels

* *Silver Medal Winner of the* *International Reader's Favorite Book Awards*

Justin:

I've never had a therapist I didn't want to punch in the face. As a collective group, they all say there is no way around grief, only through it, but for me, grief has become who I am. The idea of shedding it is as ludicrous as stepping outside of my own skin.

The fact is, some things can break you. I mean, shatter your soul and cast it into the wind in a billion tiny pieces. To think you might one day be able to find all those infinite pieces of yourself, patch everything back together, and move on with life—well, I don't even need to dignify that with a response.

Norah:

A few months ago, I shaved off a hundred and eighty-five-pound parasite. Then, once I was rid of him, I wondered why I didn't stick it out because the dating world is treacherous these days. Turns out, so is unemployment.

I suppose, to offset all the swiping left and streaming marathons in my life, I should take this job. There is a massive problem with the position, though.

The problem's name is Justin Abernathy.

Gradation

Friends. Ride or die, right?
Always have your back.
Know all your dirty little secrets.
Love the shiny parts of you, and embrace the crappy ones.
Yeah? Well, I don't know about all that nonsense because my friends are a bunch of assholes.
They're taking over.
They're commandeering my love life.
They're constructing a dating profile for me, and it's bad...
Because I don't even have the *password* for it,

and I have to do *exactly* what they say.

Mercy

**INTERNATIONAL BOOK AWARDS FINALIST and
KIRKUS FEATURED REVIEW RECIPIENT!**

My parents abandoned me a decade ago to the walls of this institution. They believed my troubled childhood mind was something sinister instead of homegrown or explainable. The truth is that my condition is complicated. It's messy and often misunderstood.

I've worn all types of labels over the years: Non-believer, pariah, deranged, *orphan*... It's all in my file if you care to understand me better. However, the label that implanted the deepest and garnered the most attention is the one I wear, like a Scarlet Letter. It precedes me when I enter a room and gets whispered about like a schoolyard crush.

Paranoid Schizophrenic.

Dr. Sutton has some lofty ideas about my condition and claims mental illness is only one aspect of hundreds that make me who I am. Not one to shy away from a challenge, he thinks he can help me. His confidence is legendary, but I've carried this burden for a long time. Despite what he thinks, I can't be fixed.

He doesn't realize I'm falling for him or that I have some lofty ideas of my own. He should know better because people like me deserve a hero, too.

The Jessie Hayes 4 Book Series

(Must be Read in Order)

<u>1462 South Broadway (Book 1)</u>
**Winner of the National Excellence*
in Romance Fiction Award)

It's said that a bird never has to doubt the stability of her branch because her trust is in her own wings.

I myself, am trying to grow some wings of my own, but I'm kind of mired in place right now.

My roommate fondly calls my situation *a rut* and seems to think he knows how I can climb out of it.

The problem with his solution is that he's stone-cold crazy.

There is no way in hell I'm going to a *sex club*.

A scorching, witty, and unexpectedly tender story about finding courage in the unlikeliest places—and discovering the kind of freedom that doesn't come from a stable branch, but from daring to fly.

<u>720 Linden Street (Book 2)</u>

My kinky introduction to BDSM has been less about dipping my toe and more about being tossed into the deep end…bound.

That simple fact has required me to make some pretty hefty leaps outside of my comfort zone.

Turns out, there is a whole lot more to the BDSM scene than I initially thought.
There's a staggering array of possibilities, all wide open for me to see and experience.

You see, my boyfriend owns a sex club.

And I have a lot to learn.

Trigger Warning: 720 Linden Street contains content that some readers may find distressing.

1700 Grant Street (Book 3)

Have you ever found yourself at a crossroads on your journey, with your entire future depending on tiny little decisions here and there?

Do you resist temptation and stick with your current choice? Or will you always wonder how life *could have been*?

When you get to this branching of your life's path, it's not enough to merely choose one direction. You must distance yourself from the rejected road. Because dancing between the two will slowly unravel you.

And it will start with your fickle heart.

945 Cedar Avenue (Book 4, Salinger's Story)

A wedding engagement is a joyous occasion, right?

Well, I suppose that depends on your perspective.

If you happen to be on the side of the path that branches to the left, when the love of your life chooses to go right, you may have a different opinion.

So, what do you do when someone else's choice annihilates the future you counted on?

The answer to that may depend on your membership status at a certain sex club.

Namely, 1462 South Broadway.

COMING SOON!

<u>*The Space Between*</u>

<u>*Midnight Sun*</u>

JOIN KC DECKER:

Mailing List: www.KCDeckerBooks.com

Instagram: www.instagram.com/author_kc_decker

X: www.X.com/KCDeckerBooks

Facebook: www.facebook.com/kc.decker.79

Bookbub: www.bookbub.com/profile/kc-decker

www.KCDeckerBooks.com

Author's Note:

Although I would love to say that Jaxson Abernathy's story is completely fiction, tragically, it is not. The character was inspired by a sweet little boy named Daxton Borchardt, who was killed by his babysitter's dogs in 2013. I encourage you to visit www.DogsBite.org for an unbiased analysis of dog attack statistics.

Acknowledgments:

I would like to take a moment to thank all my readers! Your support allows me to chase this crazy dream of mine, and for that, there are simply not enough words of gratitude. I would also *seriously* like to thank my Literary Agent…except that none have responded favorably to my manuscripts, so I'm forced to self-publish and do everything wrong in the process. For now, I'll continue to swim upstream in the raging current of the literary world, but I certainly don't claim to be good at all the non-writing aspects of it. And finally, I would like to thank my amazing family, perhaps one day I will start acting like a wife and mother instead of that crazy woman who lives with you, demanding peace and quiet—Because seriously, someone really needs to tend to that laundry pile.

www.ingramcontent.com/pod-product-compliance
Lightning Source LLC
Chambersburg PA
CBHW020256200626
46816CB00001BA/324